SOME LAUGHTER, SOME TEARS

SHOLOM ALEICHEM

❦ ❦ ❦

Some Laughter, Some Tears

TALES FROM THE OLD WORLD AND THE NEW

SELECTED AND TRANSLATED,
WITH AN INTRODUCTION BY

Curt Leviant

A PARAGON BOOK

In memory of my beloved aunt and uncle,
Sonia Schneersohn Kahan, née Dusawicki,
and
Dr. Mark Glinert.

C. L.

Paragon Books
are published by
G. P. Putnam's Sons
200 Madison Avenue
New York, New York 10016

Library of Congress Cataloging in Publication Data

Rabinowitz, Shalom, 1859–1916.
  Some laughter, some tears.

  (A Paragon book)
  I. Leviant, Curt, 1932-   II. Title
[PZ3.R113So 1979]   [PJ5129.R2]
839'.09'33   79-13849
ISBN 0-399-50395-1

First Paragon Printing, 1979
Printed in the United States of America

ACKNOWLEDGMENTS

As in my previous volumes of Sholom Aleichem translations, *Stories and Satires* and *Old Country Tales,* I take pleasure in once more expressing my deepest gratitude to my parents, Jacques and Fenia Leviant, for their assistance in translating rare Yiddish words and idioms, especially those of Slavic origin, and for their reading and checking of the stories.

I am also happy to record my thanks to my uncle, Monia Dusawicki, for his kind assistance, and to Art Sirotkin, for his meticulous proofreading and valuable suggestions.

For their kind cooperation, thanks are also due to B. Z. Goldberg, and his wife, Marie Goldberg, of the Sholom Aleichem family; to Charles Dwoskin, of G. P. Putnam's Sons, whose association I have been fortunate in having for all my Sholom Aleichem collections; and to Mrs. Jacqueline Spivack for typing the manuscript.

I am also very grateful to my wife, Erika, whose help and keen critical faculty were invaluable in every stage of preparing this volume.

Finally, to complete the list of acknowledgments, a word of loving appreciation to Sholom Aleichem, the master of Yiddish humor.

C. L.

CONTENTS

Kasrilevke Characters

Satire

From America

Glossary

INTRODUCTION

The two decades since World War II have witnessed an interesting—and radical—transformation in American literary taste. From almost total neglect Yiddish literature in translation has become a presence in the literary marketplace. (The same has happened with literature by and about Jews, but that is another matter.) The evidence may be found in a bibliography of translations from the Yiddish,* which shows that more than 125 Yiddish books have been published in English translation since 1945. Not surprisingly, the author who heads the list with the most entries is Sholom Aleichem, one of the classic figures of Yiddish literature. The translated works of this beloved humorist are now available in numerous hard- and soft-covered editions, and he is included as a standard author in almost every library throughout the land.

Without analyzing the complex social, historical, and cultural reasons for this gradual acceptance, I would merely observe that this is a truly remarkable achievement for Yiddish literature in general and for Sholom Aleichem in particular. An example of his inrootedness in American culture is the fact that the most recent Sholom Aleichem collection, *Old Country Tales* (1966), was selected by the American Library Association as one of the Notable Books of 1966 (one of 60 works so cited, out of the nearly 22,000 new books published that year). Another indication of Sholom Aleichem's impact can be measured to a degree by the reviews that have appeared in states sparsely settled by Jews. Written by gentiles, the reviews show an understanding

---

* Dina Abramowicz, *Yiddish Literature in English Translation: Books Published 1945-1967* (New York, YIVO Institute for Jewish Research, 1967).

of East European Jewish life and its obviously unfamiliar cultural patterns. What once was considered exotic, remote, parochial is now thoroughly accepted literary fare in the byways of America—thanks to the humane vision and universal humor of Sholom Aleichem.*

Concomitantly, with the proliferation of Yiddish literature in translation, Yiddish literature itself, contrary to Cassandran prognostications, is thriving in many parts of the world. More than 100 Yiddish periodicals (dailies, weeklies, monthlies, etc.) are being published on every continent (except Asia), and about 150 Yiddish books appear every year. Were it not for the suppression of Yiddish writers and Jewish creativity in the Soviet Union, the total would undoubtedly be higher. (Russia's 3,000,-000 Jews have only one organ of cultural expression, the Yiddish monthly *Sovietish Heimland.*) Until the late 1940's, when Stalin initiated his infamous liquidation of Yiddish writers, cultural figures, and institutions, Yiddish as an expression of national culture in the Soviet Union was flourishing. And now, in the land where Sholom Aleichem created most of his works, where modern Hebrew and modern Yiddish literature was born, there is almost total silence. Despite the restrictions, the few Yiddish novels recently published in the Soviet Union show a mastery of form and an excellent command of Yiddish as a living literary language. In sum, then, the combination of Yiddish periodicals and books is a very respectable achievement for a language and literature which according to *fin-de-siècle* predictions was to have given up the ghost by the 1950's. In reply, Yiddish appropriates Mark Twain's classic assertion: "Reports of my death have been greatly exaggerated!"

Sholom Aleichem (pen name for Sholom Rabinowitz) was born in 1859 near Kiev, in the Ukraine, and died in New York City in 1916, after having lived there for almost two years. Interestingly enough, he began not as a Yiddish but as a Hebrew

---

* Sholom Aleichem is a pseudonym, a Hebrew expression which means "How d'ye do!" or, more formally translated, "Peace unto you!" Sholom Aleichem should be considered one name; an invisible dash binds Sholom to Aleichem. One should no more refer to him as Aleichem than to the Russian composer Rimsky-Korsakov as Korsakov.

writer. The classic *Jewish Encyclopedia* (1901–1906) cites Sholom Aleichem as a Hebrew novelist, an author whose works "rank with the highest of their kind in neo-Hebrew literature," and then goes on to describe his contributions to Yiddish letters. This bilingual tradition of Jewish literature has deep roots and still has its practitioners today. In fact, Mendele Mocher Seforim (1836–1917), Sholom Aleichem's literary mentor, is perhaps the only mortal to have been the founding father of two modern literatures, Hebrew and Yiddish. Although they stem from two different language groupings, both tongues are related expressions of one people and one common ideal, and have produced one literature that speaks with two voices but one soul. It is not surprising then that Sholom Aleichem began with Hebrew, switched to Yiddish, the language of the masses, yet always longed to translate his own works into Hebrew.

The 28 volumes that constitute the complete works of Sholom Aleichem contain a variety of genres: novels, plays, satires, romances, an autobiography, literary memoirs, and hundreds of shorter works of fiction. In these stories, monologues, and sketches, he describes Jewish holidays, Jewish children (always a favorite topic), and even Jewish love, in a lyrical story whose metaphors are based on the Biblical Song of Songs. (One chapter of this classic four-part romance, which Sholom Aleichem titled *The Song of Songs,* is included in this volume. Another chapter appears in *Old Country Tales.*) Sholom Aleichem also portrayed dozens of characters who reside in his mythical *shtetl* (village) of Kasrilevke, who travel in that *shtetl*-on-wheels, the railroad car, and who migrate to the largest *shtetl* of all, America. Whether his subjects are the memorable minor figures or his major creations, Tevye the dairyman, Mottel the cantor's son, or the ne'er-do-well Menakhem-Mendel, Sholom Aleichem always sees his people through lenses of love.

During his lifetime Sholom Aleichem became Jewry's most representative writer. He spoke to all the people, rich and poor, educated and semiliterate, religious and assimilated, and re-created for them—and for us—a complete civilization, a world that was vibrant when the author was alive, but which a generation after his death the Germans turned to ashes and smoke.

In his volume *Stories for Jewish Children* (*Mayses far yidishe kinder*), of which several stories are included in the present collection, Sholom Aleichem displays his versatility in portraying the child in the *shtetl*. It is a mark of his depth as an artist that his stories develop a spectrum of character types and situations. "The Penknife," Sholom Aleichem's first major Yiddish story (1886), one that immediately made him famous, accents guilt, while a twofold deception is the theme of another well-known tale, "The Dreydl." In contrast with these, we see innocence and kindliness in "Pity for Living Creatures," a story which may be considered a paradigm of all his stories about Jewish children.

With economy of means, "Pity for Living Creatures" evokes a sensitive child's soul and shows it in reaction to the adult world, a frequent leitmotiv in Sholom Aleichem's stories. On the eve of a holiday a little boy helps his mother by grating horseradish and watches a fish—the main course—spending its last few hours thrashing in a tub. The doomed fish, the death of a living creature, reminds the boy of a pogrom he once experienced. A host of memories flit through the child's mind: an incident with a mistreated dog, a fowl taken to the *shokhet* to be slaughtered, a bird that two peasant lads brutally beat to death, and—the crux of the story—the crippled baby, Perele, who was cruelly killed in a pogrom, no doubt by the fathers or uncles of the boys who killed the little bird. Sholom Aleichem here not only juxtaposes the values of the child's world with those of the adult, but, in so doing, also limns two cultures which existed side by side (the peasant's and the Jew's), yet which in values and attitudes were light-years apart. The story's final irony is the mother's statement that the boy's tears are caused by the horseradish—another penetrating metaphor for the gap between the adult's world and that of the child.

A completely different style is discernible in Sholom Aleichem's satires, a genre with which he began his literary career. The humorist tells a wonderful story about the time he visited Mendele Mocher Seforim to show him his first novel, a lengthy satire. While the young Sholom Aleichem's heart thumped in apprehension, Mendele read without saying a word. Then, when he had finished reading the manuscript, Mendele asked innocently, "Has the stove been lit for supper yet?" When he was told that it had been, Mendele told Sholom Aleichem, "In that case, take this novel and throw it into the flames. Satire is not your métier."

Mendele's statement, however, was only partially correct. What Mendele meant was that satire in imitation of Mendele (that is, rather harsh and didactic pieces) was not Sholom Aleichem's métier. As Sholom Aleichem matured as a writer, the humorist in him guided and disciplined his satiric bent. He particularly liked to excoriate puffery and pretension: Kasrilevke's feuding newspapers and theaters, bickering writers, vainglorious, self-proclaimed intellectuals, the newly rich at their spas.

In "The Little Redheaded Jews"—a literary code name for his *shtetl* brethren—Sholom Aleichem seeks to reform the sleepy denizens of Redville and make them aware of the saving graces of Zionism. (The inaccessible Little Redheaded Jews, popular in Jewish folklore for nearly 1,000 years, lived in Africa beyond the legendary Sambatyon River, which constantly cast stones except on the Sabbath.) Events in "The Little Redheaded Jews" accurately reflect the political attitudes of the Jewish masses in the late nineteenth century. With few exceptions the Jews mocked all attempts to induce them to consider Zion as a realistic alternative to their terrible plight in Czarist Russia. Historically rooted in the *shtetl* and religiously oriented to a belief that only the Messiah could take them to the Land of Israel, the Jews at first looked skeptically at Zionism and Theodor Herzl; in their minds arrogating the role of the Messiah was worse than heresy. A fervent supporter of Herzl, Sholom Aleichem wrote many nonfictional pamphlets advocating Zionism and believed (prophetically, as it turned out) that there was no future for Jews who lived under an antagonistic regime and among an antagonistic population.

Nevertheless, instead of choosing Palestine as a way out, the Jewish masses chose America (as Sholom Aleichem ultimately did in 1914). The prevalent myth that had penetrated the folk consciousness of the East European Jews was that America was a golden land where money could literally be scooped up in the streets. Always sensitive to folk attitudes, Sholom Aleichem

wrote about the New World even before he visited it. For the
most part, his approach is somewhat ironical, satiric, and tongue-
in-cheek. In the latter part of "The Little Redheaded Jews"
(written in 1900), he uses the Hebrew image of Egyptian slavery
as a symbol for America and vents his bitterness toward the
charlatans and exploiters of innocent immigrants. At first Sholom
Aleichem took the magic myth and deflated it for his readers.
Later, after his first visit to the United States (for several months
during 1906 and 1907), his view became tempered by personal
experience. For instance, *Mottel the Cantor's Son,* written in
1916, during the last months of Sholom Aleichem's life, shows
Mottel's love for America. "Try *not* to love such a country,"
Mottel says. In Part Two of the novel *In America,* we see a
subtle change in Sholom Aleichem's attitude to the New World.
Where America had previously been approached strictly from
a satiric and mocking viewpoint, here for the first time we see
the humorist prevailing. This is perhaps an indication of what
Sholom Aleichem could have accomplished with his experiences
in America had not tuberculosis cut short his career at the rela-
tively young age of fifty-seven, less than two years after his
migration to the United States.

The few stories taken from the New World, included here
in the section *From America,* show some immigrant types
and their reactions to the American experience. Sholom Aleichem depicts dishonest schemers, the hoodwinked greenhorns,
the ambitious immigrant. He particularly focuses on the newcomer who, while criticizing his children's speedy Americaniza-
tion, writes Yiddish letters filled with Americanisms that are
incomprehensible to the *shtetl* friend in the old country.

Although Sholom Aleichem chose America as his promised
land, he never quite felt at home here. For him, I suppose, it
was a spiritual comedown; he found himself removed from the
cohesiveness of an all-Jewish society, where if one chose to—
and many did—one could shut out the gentile civilization, even
in urban centers, and create in essence a self-contained Jewish
world. In America, however, this was not possible, at least not
in early twentieth-century America, and hence the spiritual
struggles and readjustments that plagued many sensitive immi-

grants. And yet, despite the fact that Sholom Aleichem lived in the United States slightly less than two years, he displayed insights into the American scene and created stories with American settings, a feat that contemporary Yiddish writers who have lived here for more than a generation have not yet been able to accomplish. Sholom Aleichem once wrote, "My muse does not wear a black veil on her face. My muse is poor, but cheerful." The muse and Sholom Aleichem's genius were always part of his portable spiritual baggage. And so, in America, too, his muse rejected that black veil and remained cheerful to the end.

Note: Whereas my previous Sholom Aleichem collections have celebrated some literary anniversary (*Stories and Satires* the Sholom Aleichem centennial and *Old Country Tales* the fiftieth anniversary of his death), this volume marks no special occasion, but merely seeks to make available a group of memorable stories, some of which have never before appeared in English translation and others which are newly translated. The older English version of many of these stories appeared in *Jewish Children,* the first Sholom Aleichem short story collection, published in England in 1918 and long out of print. In this old volume, some of Sholom Aleichem's finest stories have been frozen for half a century in an inaccessible text that was somewhat cumbersome and difficult to comprehend. And so it has been a pleasure to render these tales afresh and place them into the hands of a new generation of English readers.

CURT LEVIANT

Holiday Tales

ELIJAH THE PROPHET

1

It's no fun being an only child, fondled and fussed over, the sole surviving son of seven children. Don't stand here. Don't go there. Don't eat this. Don't drink that. Wear a hat. Button your collar. Keep your hands warm. Blow your nose.

Ah me, it's no good being an only son—and a rich man's son at that. My father, you see, was well off. A money changer. He went from store to store with a bagful of coins. Exchanged silver for coppers and coppers for silver. That's why his fingers were always black and his nails chipped. He worked very hard. Every day he came home tired and run-down.

"My legs are going," he complained to Mama. "They're failing me."

Failing him? Possibly. But on the other hand, he had a good business. That's what everyone said. And everyone was green with envy that we made a living, and such a good one, too. Mama was very pleased that we were well off. And so was I.

"What a Passover we're going to have! May all Jews have such a Passover, dear God!" Mama said. She thanked God for the fine festival we were going to have. And so did I, anxiously awaiting the arrival of this happy holiday.

2

Passover finally came. That dear lovable holiday. I was dressed like a king, as befits a rich man's son. But what good did it do me, if I couldn't race around outside—for I was prone to catch cold? If I couldn't run around with the gang of poor boys—for I was a rich man's son? I had such nice clothes. And no one to show them off to. A pocketful of nuts—and no one to play with.

It's no fun being an only child, fondled and fussed over, the sole surviving son of seven children. And a rich man's son at that.

3

After Father put on his best gaberdine and went to *shul* to pray, Mama suggested, "You know what? You ought to lie down and take a nap. Then you won't be sleepy at the Seder. And you'll be able to ask Father the Four Questions."

Was I out of my mind? Going to sleep before the Seder?

"But remember," Mama added, "you're not allowed to sleep during the Seder. Because if you fall asleep, God forbid, Elijah the Prophet will come with a sack on his shoulders. . . . For tonight he goes from house to house, and if he sees anyone napping at the Seder, he whisks him into his sack."

"Me fall asleep at the Seder? *Me?* I'll stay up all night with you. Even to the crack of dawn. . . . What happened last year, Mama?"

"Last year you fell asleep right after the Kiddush."

"So how come Elijah the Prophet didn't come with his sack then?"

"Because last year you were a little boy and now you're bigger. Tonight you have to ask Father the Four Questions and recite with him 'Slaves were we unto Pharaoh.' And you have to eat fish and soup and matza balls with us. . . . Oh, here's Father coming back from *shul*."

"*Gut yontev*. Happy holiday."

"*Gut yontev*. Happy holiday."

4

Thank God. Papa finished the Kiddush. So did I. Papa drank the first cup. So did I. Filled to the brim, too. Down to the last drop.

"Look at that!" Mama told Father. "To the last drop!" Then she turned to me. "A full cup of wine? You're going to doze off!"

Me fall asleep? *Me?* I'll stay up all night with you. Even to the crack of dawn. Go ahead, ask Father how I rattled off the Four Questions, how I recited the Hagada, and how along with him I rocked back and forth, saying, "Slaves were we."

Mama did not take her eyes off me. She smiled and said, "You're going to doze off. Fall asleep."

Oh, Mama, Mama! That alone could make a ten-headed man fall asleep. How would you like someone sitting opposite you, droning in your ear, "Fall asleep. Doze off. Fall asleep"?

So naturally, I fell asleep.

5

I dozed off and dreamed that Father was already reciting "Pour Out Thy Wrath." Mama was getting up to open the door and welcome Elijah the Prophet. How nice it would be if Elijah appeared with a sack on his back and told me to come with him! Just as Mama said.

The fault would be Mama's alone, with her constant "Don't fall asleep, don't fall asleep." Suddenly I heard the door squeak. Father rose and called out, "Welcome!"

I turned to the door—yes, it was him. He was coming. He was coming. Slowly. You could hardly hear him. Elijah the Prophet—he was a good-looking Jew. An old man. With a curly gray beard reaching to his knees. His face was yellow and wrinkled, but infinitely kind and beautiful. And his eyes—oh, what lovely, friendly eyes! Gentle, loving, faithful eyes. With a sack on his bent back, he leaned on a huge staff and silently walked toward me.

6

"Well, little boy, hop into my sack, and let's go," the old man said sweetly.

"Where?" I asked.

"You'll see later," he replied.

I didn't want to go, and he repeated his request.

"How can I go with you? I'm a rich man's boy," I pleaded.

"What sort of privilege does *that* entitle you to?"

"I'm their only son," I said.

"*I* don't consider you an only son," Elijah said.

"I'm fondled and fussed over. The sole surviving son of seven children. If they see that I've gone, they won't endure it. They'll die. Especially Mama."

The old man looked at me and said as sweetly as before, "If you don't come with me, then sleep well—but keep on sleeping. Forever."

"That means I'll die." I began to cry. "They won't endure it. . . . Especially Mama."

"If you don't want to die, then come with me. Say good-bye to your parents, and come along."

"What do you mean? How can I go if I'm an only child, the sole surviving son of seven children?"

"For the last time, little boy," Elijah said more severely now, "make your choice. One or the other. Either say good-bye to your parents forever and come with me, or remain here fast asleep forever. For all eternity."

7

Having said this, he stepped away from me, about to face the door. What to do? If I went with the old man to God-knows-where and disappeared, my parents would die. I'm an only child, the sole surviving son of seven children. . . . But to remain here fast asleep forever meant that I would die.

I stretched my hands out to him and said with tears in my eyes, "Elijah the Prophet. Dear, beloved, wonderful Elijah. Give me one minute to think it over."

He turned his fine, old, yellow, and wrinkled face to me.

"I will give you one minute to consider it, my child," he said, and his loving and faithful eyes smiled. "But no more than that."

And the old man with the knee-length, curly gray beard

leaned on his huge staff and waited. Now I ask you. What should I have done during that minute to avoid going with the old man and yet not remain asleep forever? Well, go ahead and guess!

THE ESROG

1

My real name is Arye-Leib, but everyone called me Leibl. In *kheder*, my classmates labeled me Leib Blubber Drubber. Everybody in class had a nickname: Motl-Kapotl, Meir-Brayer, Mendel-Fendel, Itzy-Shpritzy, Berl-Pigtail. Some rhymes, eh? At least the rhymed names made sense. But what link was there between Berl and Pigtail? And what was the point of Leib Blubber Drubber?

Since I couldn't stand my nickname, I was always getting into fights. Punches, pinches, and blows rained on me from all sides. And I ended up black and blue. For I was the smallest boy in *kheder*. And the weakest and poorest as well. Absolutely no one stuck up for me.

In fact, when two rich boys would lace into me—one riding on my back like a horse, the other tweaking my ear—a third boy, whose father was an absolute pauper, would just stand idly by and rhythmically egg them on:

> That's the way
> To beat him up.
> That's the way
> To beat him up.
> Tweak his ear,
> Pinch his cheek.
> That's the way
> To beat him up.

When this happened, I would lie still as a cat. And when they let me go, I would move to a corner, cry my eyes out quietly,

26

dry my tears, then rejoin the gang and become pals with them again.

So if you see the name Leibl in this story—that's me!

I was short and stocky-looking. Packed like a pillow. Not because I was fat. I happened to be quite thin. But I wore thick cotton-padded trousers, a thick padded shirt, and a thick padded jacket. My mother, you see, wanted me to be warm. So I shouldn't catch cold, God forbid. That's why she wadded me and padded me with cotton from top to toe. But Mama didn't realize how handy that cotton was. I distributed the cotton to the kids, and with it we made an endless supply of balls. I kept pulling it out of my pants and jacket until I finally got caught. Then slaps and pinches, whacks and cuffs rained down on me. But I went on my merry way distributing cotton to anyone who wanted it. And everyone under the sun drubbed me and beat me black and blue.

"Serves you right, Leib Blubber Drubber."

Actually, dear children, I was going to tell you something else. I wanted to tell you a story about an *esrog**—but got sidetracked to goodness-knows-where. So let's return to the main story.

2

My father, Moshe-Yenkel, had been a cashier in the tax farmer's office for many years. He earned four and a half rubles a week and was expecting a raise. He declared if he got a raise, he would buy an *esrog* this year, God willing. But my mother, Basye-Beile, didn't put any stock in this. "There's more of a chance that the barracks will collapse and kill all the soldiers than for the tax farmer to give you a raise."

The following conversation took place before Rosh Hashana:

Father: "I don't care if the world turns upside down, this Sukkos I'm going to have an *esrog*."

Mother: "The world won't turn upside down, and you won't have an *esrog*."

---

* A citron, used for the Sukkos festival—Tr.

Father: "That's what you say. But what will you say if they promised me something toward my *esrog?*"

Mother: "Unbelievable! Inscribe it in the Book of Bugs, the chapter on bookworms! But you know what? Don't think of me as a great heretic if I don't believe you."

Father: "You can believe me or not, as you like. I tell you that this year we will have our own *esrog.*"

Mother: "Amen. So be it. From your mouth into God's ears."

Amen, amen, amen! I thought. I imagined my father coming to *shul*, like a respectable householder with his own *esrog* and *lulav*. Although Father only had a rear seat in *shul*, when the congregation paraded around the pulpit holding their *lulavs* and *esrogs*, he also joined the most respected villagers who sat at the east wall next to the Holy Ark. I beamed. I was overjoyed. Reb Melekh the cantor was at the head of the line, stepping smartly like a field marshal, his head proudly held high. In his quavering voice he sang, "Save-us, the afflicted, sa-ave-us!" Right behind him came the rabbi, a small, emaciated man, his prayer shawl over his face. Behind the rabbi marched the rabbinic judge. He had a yellow, parchmentlike face, broad shoulders and a potbelly that shook beneath his shiny satin gaberdine. Behind him walked the cream of the town's society, those who had seats next to the Holy Ark. Next came the men of average means, followed by all the kids. The rich men and the householders marched according to status and wealth, just like (forgive the comparison) an army in battle formation: first the field marshal, then the generals, the officers, the noncommissioned officers, and only then the ordinary soldiers.

I imagined my father slipping in among the rich men, ahead of Reb Yisroel the tailor, a workingman and a first-degree pauper, who nevertheless marched along with all the other respected villagers. I imagined him clutching the *esrog* that a newly rich merchant had presented to him, as a reward for his decency and honesty. . . .

When I heard my parents talking about buying an *esrog*, I could no longer restrain myself. I spread the news in *kheder* that this Sukkos we would have our very own *esrog*. But all my oaths were of no avail. Not a soul believed me.

"Look who's getting his own *esrog!*" some of my pals snickered. "That pauper is going to buy himself his own *esrog!* He probably thinks it's a cheap lemon or a penny apple!"

And they all began to chant: "Leibl-Blubber's lying, Drubber Blubber's fibbing."

What's more, they honored me with an assortment of slaps, cuffs, punches, and whacks. This upset me, naturally, and I was almost convinced that my father was indeed a pauper, who, like any poverty-stricken wretch, should not aspire for things beyond his reach.

Imagine my surprise when I came home and found Henzl the *shokhet* sitting at the table, wearing his famous Napoleonic cap, and displaying a box of *esrogs* whose heavenly aroma wafted all over the room.

3

The Napoleonic cap that Henzl wore was a hand-me-down from the time of Napoleon I. In France this cap had gone out of fashion ages ago. But in Kasrilevke it apparently survived (the only one of its kind) in the possession of Henzl the *shokhet*. The long, narrow cap, split in the front, had a button and two tassels that always enchanted me. Had that cap fallen into my hands for only a minute, those tassels would have been mine forever.

Those were *my* plans. But Henzl never removed his cap. His cap, tassels, head, and earlocks seemed to have grown together. When he talked and gesticulated, his earlocks bobbed and his tassels trembled. Reb Henzl the *shokhet* displayed his entire stock, chose an *esrog*, held it up with two fingers, and suggested that my father buy it.

"Here's the *esrog* for you, Reb Moshe-Yenkel. One you'll enjoy. I tell you it's exquisite. A gem from gemland."

"But is it from the isle of Corfu?" Father asked, his hands quivering with joy. He examined the *esrog* from all sides, as though inspecting a diamond.

"What a question!" Henzl laughed, and his tassels trembled. "Of course, it's from Corfu."

Father was delighted with the *esrog* and could not take his eyes off it. He called Mama and smilingly pointed to it, as though pointing out an expensive necklace, a rare gem, or an unusually beautiful child. Mama approached silently and slowly stretched her hand to take hold of the *esrog*.

"Oh, no," Henzl said. "Look, but don't touch."

"But if you want to sniff it, you may," Father said.

So Mama had to be content with a sniff, but *I* wasn't even offered *that* much. I wasn't even allowed to get too close to it. Not even to have a peek at it. For it was too risky.

"Uh-oh! Look who's here," said Mama. "If you let him come close he'll bite off the stem."

"God forbid," said Father, wary of the evil eye.

"Heaven forfend," Henzl added, his tassels trembling. He gave Father some flax in which to nestle the *esrog*, whose heavenly fragrance spread to every corner of the room.

Father handled the aromatic *esrog* like a priceless object given to him for safekeeping, and which upon pain of death he dare not lose or damage. Wrapped in flax like a newly swaddled only child, the *esrog* was comfortably bedded down in a finely lathed, round, and painted wooden box. Before the lid was closed, the *esrog* was padded with some more flax. The box was then placed in the cupboard, the glass door closed, and the *esrog* was bid good-bye. Mama took me by the hand and dragged me away from the cupboard.

"I'm worried," she said. "The little rascal's likely to make a move for the cupboard, God forbid, and bite off the stem."

But, alas, I hovered around that cupboard like a cat that had got a whiff of butter and restlessly paced back and forth, plotting what to do next. I looked through the glass door and kept ogling the *esrog* box until Mama spotted me. "The little devil's got an urge to make a move on the *esrog*," she told my father.

"Back to *kheder*, you rascal," Father yelled. "May goodness-knows-what not happen to you."

In other words, they were telling me to pick up my feet and beat it. I bowed my head, lowered my eyes, and went back to *kheder*.

4

Mama's remark (that I might bite off the *esrog's* stem) was sheer poison for me, a venomous potion that seeped into my bones. From that moment on, the stem of the *esrog* invaded my consciousness and didn't leave my thoughts for a minute. At night I dreamed of the stem. It teased me; it urged me on.

"Don't you recognize me, silly? It's me. The *esrog* stem!"

Moaning, I awoke, turned over on the other side, and fell asleep again. Then the torment began once more.

"Get up, silly. Open the cupboard. Take out the *esrog* and bite me off. What ecstasy that'll be!"

I rose in the morning, washed my hands, and, rushing to go to prayers, took some breakfast with me. Passing the glass doors of the cupboard, I quickly glanced at the *esrog* box. It seemed to wink and blink and call to me. "Come here . . . come over here, little boy."

But I turned on my heels and took off for *kheder*.

When I awoke one bright morning, the house was still. Father was at work, Mama was at the market, and the baby lay in the cradle, his hands by his head, smiling in his sleep.

Angels are playing with him, I thought. I washed my hands, then peeked through the cupboard's glass door at the *esrog* box. It winked and blinked and called to me, "Come here . . . come over here, little boy."

I slowly approached the cupboard, opened the glass door, removed the box—the beautiful, finely lathed, round, and painted wooden box—and lifted the cover. Before I even unwrapped the flax, the *esrog's* pungent and heavenly fragrance pierced my nostrils. A split second later the *esrog* was in my hands, and the stem leaped toward my face.

"Want a thrill? A taste of paradise? Here. Bite me off. Don't be afraid, silly. No one will know. Not a living soul will see. No little bird will tell on you."

Would you like to know what happened? Did I bite off the stem, or did I control myself? What would *you* have done if people had warned you a dozen times not to dare bite off the *esrog's* stem? Wouldn't you have wanted to know what it tasted like?

5

Father was unable to build a *sukka* by himself. But his neighbor, Zalman the carpenter, could build one easily enough. He provided the boards, and we contributed two pillowcases and sheets and blankets to nail onto the walls. Since Zalman's wife had recently died, leaving eight orphaned children, Mama baked the holiday *khalle* for them and helped the eldest daughter, Tsviya, make gefilte fish—for Mama made the best gefilte fish in Kasrilevke. .And of course, Zalman would also have use of our *esrog*.

"You're an equal partner in the *esrog*," Mama told him.

"Only for the blessing," Father quickly corrected her.

"Well, naturally not for eating it," Zalman responded.

Not only did Zalman yearn to recite the blessing over the *esrog* in the *sukka,* but all his children, too, looked forward to it, as though to the Messiah. What joy to hold the *esrog* in one hand, the *lulav* in the other, to say the blessing, and then shake the *lulav* and hear the palm fronds rattle!

"How many more days to Sukkos?" everyone asked, eagerly counting the days.

On the eve of Sukkos, Father gathered branches of myrtle and willow and bound them to the *lulav* in the finest possible manner. He placed the neatly decorated *lulav* in a corner on top of the cupboard, and there it slumped, as if taking a nap. Father didn't even warn me not to dare approach the *lulav,* for even had I wanted to reach it, I couldn't. Not even with a chair. For the chair would tip over and I would crash to the floor and break all my bones. And then I'd be punished so severely I'd remember it the rest of my life.

There was also another reason why I didn't bother with the *lulav*. In fact, I didn't even think of it. For another thought kept pecking at me. What would happen if, God forbid, they'd inspect the *esrog* and discover that the poor thing's stem was bitten off?

It's true that I immediately stuck it back on with spit. But who knows if spit would make the stem stick? Oh, God, what would happen? What excuse would I make? How could I look my parents in the eye and swear that I didn't know a thing about it? Who would believe me? Why had I done this? What had I gained by it? What sort of taste did the stem have? To tell the truth, it was—phoo—bitter as gall, terribly nauseating. I had spoiled such a lovely *esrog* for no reason, rendered it unfit for ritual use. (I had learned from my *kheder* friends that a damaged stem permanently ruined the *esrog*.) What purpose was there to my act? Why had I done such a thing? I thought of myself as a murderer. I had taken a living thing, bitten its head off, and taken its life. Why? What for? What good had it done me? The bitten-off stem swam before my eyes—yellow as wax, lifeless, a dead *esrog*, a corpse.

At night, I dreamed about the *esrog*. It annoyed me, tugged at my sleeve, and woke me up.

"Did you have anything against me? Why did you bite off my stem? Now I'm not kosher anymore, completely unfit for use."

I turned over on the other side, groaned, and dozed off until I was disturbed once more.

"Murderer! What did you have against my stem? My stem? My stem?"

6

The first day of Sukkos came. After a night of frost the sun rose in a clear blue sky and covered the earth with a lovely light that filled every heart with an odd sensation, an inexplicable yearning for the summer gone by. The sun gave light, but no warmth. Like a stepmother, as they say in Kasrilevke. Gone was the summer heat. Gone were the birdcalls and everything green. In fact, everything had disappeared with the first winds of Elul.

That day Father rose early to review the holiday Torah portion, chanting the beautifully familiar festival melody. Mama, too, rose early to prepare the holiday fish, the *farfel* and the carrot *tsimess*. That day Zalman the carpenter also rose at the crack of dawn. He wanted to be the first to make the blessing over the *esrog*, after which he would be able to relax with a glass of tea and milk and enjoy the festive atmosphere.

"Reb Zalman wants the *esrog* and *lulav*," Mama told Father.

"Open the cupboard, and remove the box gently," Father replied. He stood on a bench, brought the *lulav* down from the top of the cupboard, then took both the *esrog* and *lulav* to the *sukka* and offered them to Reb Zalman the carpenter.

"Here, say the blessing," he told Zalman. "Be careful with the *esrog*. For God's sake, hold it gently."

Zalman the carpenter, God bless him, was a solidly built man with a healthy pair of paws. With one thick finger he could have laid out three like me. His fingernails were filled with glue and stained red by varnish, and when he drew a line across a plank, they scratched an indentation in the wood. In honor of the holiday, Zalman had put on a white shirt and a new gaberdine. He had spent much time cleaning his hands at the baths with soap, ashes, and sand. But to no avail. His fingers were still sticky, and his nails were still red with varnish.

Into these hands fell the fragrant and delicate *esrog*. So Father had good reason to tremble when Zalman grabbed the *esrog*, squeezed it right well, recited the first benediction, and mercilessly shook the *lulav*.

"Gently, gently," said Father, concerned for the *esrog*. "Now turn the *esrog* upside down, stem downward, and say the second blessing, 'Blessed art thou . . . who has permitted us to live and sustained us to this day.' . . . But gently! For God's sake, easy!"

Suddenly Father lunged forward and emitted an unearthly shriek:

"Oy!"

Hearing his yell, Mama came dashing into the *sukka*.

"What's the matter, Moshe-Yenkel; what is it?"

"You savage! You boor!" Father yelled at the carpenter, ready to kill him with a glance. "How can you be such a rough-neck? Such a clout? Is an *esrog* an ax? Or a chisel? Or a gimlet? It's none of these. You've just cut my throat without a knife. You've mangled my *esrog*. Look! There's the stem, you savage! You clunk!"

We were all thunderstruck. Poor Zalman the carpenter stood motionless, unable to comprehend how such misfortune had befallen him. What could possibly have caused the stem to sail off that way? He was certain he had held the *esrog* gingerly, with the tips of his fingers. What a tragedy! A terrible calamity!

Father, too, was stunned; he turned white as a corpse. He hadn't yet gone to *shul* with the *esrog*, hadn't even said the first blessing. And here it was already ruined. Why had he put such an expensive and delicate fruit into such rough hands? Couldn't Zalman just as well have made the blessing over the congregation's *esrog* in *shul*?

"You brute! You lout!"

Mama, wringing her hands, was also stupefied.

"A ne'er-do-well," she said with tears in her eyes, "ought to bury himself alive. Sink into the earth while he's hale and hearty."

I, too, stood there petrified and trembling. I was pained by my father's sorrow, my mother's tears, and Zalman's humiliation. I didn't know whether to leap for joy because God had performed a miracle for me and saved me from such trouble and catastrophe; to weep over my father's sorrow, my mother's tears, and Zalman's humiliation; or to embrace Zalman the carpenter and rain kisses on his coarse hands, sticky fingers, and red nails for being my good angel, my deliverer, my redeemer.

My glance went from Father's white face to Mama's tears to Zalman's hands. Zalman gaped at the *esrog* on the table, lying there as dead as a doornail, yellow as wax. Stemless, lifeless, a corpse.

"A dead *esrog*," Father said, and his voice broke.

"A dead *esrog*," Mama repeated with tears in her eyes.

"A dead *esrog*," Zalman said and looked at his hands, as if to say: "What a pair of paws—may they wither away!"

THE GUEST

1

"Reb Yonah, I have a guest for you for Passover. I guarantee you've never seen anyone like him."

"What's he like?"

"He's no run-of-the-mill visitor, but a diamond, a peach of a man."

"What do you mean a peach?"

"I mean he's topnotch. All class. A man of distinction. But he's got only one fault. He doesn't understand Yiddish."

"Then what language *does* he understand?"

"The holy tongue, Hebrew."

"Is he from Jerusalem?"

"I don't know where he's from. But he speaks with a Sephardic accent—whatever he says is full of 'aahs.' "

Such was the conversation that my father had with Azriel the *shamesh* a few days before Passover. I was curious to see this peach of a man who spoke no Yiddish but only Hebrew with lots of "aahs." In *shul* I had noticed an odd-looking creature in a fur cap, wearing a Turkish cloak with yellow, blue, and red stripes. All the kids surrounded him and gaped. For this Azriel the *shamesh* raked us over the coals: It's a terrible habit for kids to go poking into a stranger's face.

After prayers the entire congregation greeted the newcomer with *Sholom* and wished him a happy holiday.

A sweet smile spread over his gray-whiskered red cheeks, and instead of our *Sholom*, he replied, "*Shalom, shalom.*"

His *Shalom* caused us youngsters to double over with laughter. Which annoyed Azriel the *shamesh*. He ran after us ready to dole out smacks. But we dodged him and sneaked up to the newcomer again to hear him say, "*Shalom, shalom.*" Once more we burst into hysterics and ducked away from Azriel's raised hand.

Proud as a peacock, I followed my father and the odd-looking character, sensing that all my friends envied me for having a guest of his caliber for the holiday. Their glances followed us from afar, and I turned around and stuck my tongue out at them. All three of us were silent on our way home. When we entered the house, Father called out to Mama, "*Gut yontev!* Happy holiday!"

The guest nodded, and his fur cap shook.

"*Shalom, shalom.*"

I thought of my friends and hid my face under the table, trying hard to keep a straight face. I kept glancing at our guest. I liked him. I liked his Turkish cloak with its stripes of yellow, blue, and red; his apple-red cheeks edged with a round gray beard; his beautiful black eyes that twinkled beneath his bushy gray eyebrows. I sensed that my father liked him, too. Father was delighted by his presence. He himself prepared the cushioned chair for our guest, and Mama considered him a holy man. Yet no one said a word to him. Mama, assisted by Rikl the maid, was in a dither preparing for the Seder. Conversation first began when we were ready to recite the Kiddush over the wine. Then Father spoke to our guest in Hebrew. I brimmed with pride since I understood almost every word. Here is what they said in Hebrew, word for word:

Father: "Nu?" (*Meaning in Yiddish: Please recite the Kiddush!*)

The Guest: "Nu, nu!" (*Translated, this means: You recite it.*)

Father: "Nu-aw?" (*Why not you?*)

Guest: "Aw-nu?" (*And why don't you?*)

Father: "Ee-aw?" (*You first!*)

The Guest: "Aw-ee!" (*First you!*)

Father: "Eh-aw-ee!" (*Please, you say it!*)

The Guest: "Ee-aw-eh! (*You say it, please!*)

Father: "Ee-eh-aw-nu?" (*Does it really matter to you if you say it first?*)

The Guest: "Eeeh-aw? Nu, nu!" (*Well, if you insist, then I'll say it!*)

The guest took the Kiddush cup from Father's hand and recited a Kiddush the likes of which we had never heard before and will never hear again. First of all, his Sephardic Hebrew pronunciation, full of "aahs." Second, his voice, which came not from his throat but from his striped Turkish cloak. Thinking of my friends, I imagined the giggles that would have broken out and the blows and smacks that would have flown had they been here for the Kiddush. But since they were not with me, I controlled myself, asked Father the Four Questions, and we all recited the Hagada together. I was proud as could be that this man was our guest and no one else's.

2

May he forgive me for saying this, but the sage who suggested silence during mealtime had no knowledge of Jewish life. When else does a Jew have time to talk, if not during mealtime? And especially at the Passover Seder, when we talk so much about the Exodus from Egypt? Rikl handed us the water for the ritual washing of hands, and we recited the benedictions. After Mama had distributed the fish, Father rolled up his sleeves and got into a lengthy Hebrew conversation with our guest. Naturally, Father began with the first question that one Jew always asks another:

"What's your name?'"

The guest's reply was one full of "aahs," rattled off in one breath, as quickly as Haman's sons' names are dashed off during the reading of the Purim Megillah.

"ZYXW VUTS RQPON MLKJIHG FED CBA," he said.

Father stopped chewing and looked with openmouthed amazement at the guest who bore such a long name. I fell into a fit of coughing and stared down at the floor.

"Careful with the fish," said Mama. "You might choke on a bone, God forbid."

She looked at our guest with awe, obviously impressed by his name, even though she didn't know what it meant. And since Father did know, he explained:

"His name, you see, contains all the letters of the alphabet backward. Evidently it's one of their customs to name their children in some alphabetical fashion."

"Alphabet! Alphabet!" The guest nodded. A sweet smile played on his apple-red cheeks, and his beautiful black eyes gazed at everyone so amiably, even at Rikl the maid.

Having learned his name, Father was curious about the land he had come from. This I gathered from the names of towns and countries which I heard mentioned. Father then translated for Mama, explaining almost every word. Each word impressed Mama. Rikl, too. And with good cause. It was no small thing for a person to travel ten thousand miles from one's homeland. To reach it one had to cross seven seas, trek forty days and forty nights through a desert, and climb an enormous ice-capped mountain whose peak touched the clouds. But once one safely passed this wind-whipped mountain and entered the land, one saw before him the terrestrial Garden of Eden filled with spices and condiments, apples and pears, oranges and grapes, olives and dates, and nuts and figs. The houses, built only of pine-wood, were covered with pure silver. The dishes were of gold (while saying this, our guest glanced at our silver goblets, spoons, forks and knives), and gems, pearls, and diamonds lay scattered on the streets. No one even bothered to bend and pick them up because they had no value there. (The guest now peered at Mama's diamond earrings and her pearl necklace.)

"Do you hear that?" Father said to Mama, beaming.

"Yes," said Mama and asked, "Why don't they bring all that treasure here? They would make a fortune. Ask him about that, Yonah."

Father asked and translated the reply into Yiddish for Mama's benefit.

"You see, if you travel there, you can take as much as you like. Fill up your pockets. But when you leave, you must return everything. If they shake anything out of your pockets, they execute you."

"What does that mean?" Mama asked, frightened.

"That means they either hang you from the nearest tree or stone you to death."

3

The more our guest spoke, the more interesting his stories became. Once we had eaten the matza balls and were sipping some wine, Father asked him:

"Who is the master of all that wealth? Is there a king there?"

He immediately got a precise answer, which he joyfully translated for Mama.

"He says that it all belongs to the Jews who live there. They are called Sephardim. They have a king, he says, a very religious Jew with a fur cap named Joseph ben Joseph. He is the Sephardim's high priest and rides about in a golden chariot drawn by six fiery steeds. And when he comes to *shul,* singing Levites come to greet him.

"Do Levites sing in your *shul?*" Father asked him wonderingly. He immediately got an answer, which he translated into Yiddish for Mama.

"Imagine!" he said, his face shining like the sun. "He says that they have a holy temple with priests and Levites and an organ—

"How about an altar?" Father asked, then translated our guest's reply for Mama.

"He says they have an altar, sacrifices, and golden vessels. Everything as it once used to be in ancient Jerusalem."

Father sighed deeply. Mama looked at him and sighed, too. I didn't understand why they sighed. On the contrary, we should be proud and happy that we had a land like this where a Jewish king reigned, where there was a high priest and a holy temple with priests and Levites and an organ and an altar with sacrifices. . . .

Beautiful and bright thoughts snatched me up and carried me away to that happy Jewish land, where all the houses were made of pinewood and covered with silver, where the dishes were of gold, and where gems, pearls, and diamonds were

scattered on the streets. Suddenly I had a thought. If I were
there, I would have known what to do and how to hide what I
had found. They wouldn't have shaken a thing out of my
pockets. I would have brought Mama a fine present—diamond
earrings and several strands of pearls. I looked at the diamond
earrings and the pearl necklace on Mama's white throat and
had a strong desire to be in that land. I had an idea. After Passover I would travel there with our guest. Naturally, in absolute
secrecy. No one would know a thing. I would reveal the secret
only to our guest, pour out my heart to him, tell him the whole
truth, and ask him to take me with him, if only for a little
while. He'd surely do that for me. He was an extremely kind
and pleasant man. He looked at everyone so amiably, even at
Rikl the maid.

So ran my thoughts as I looked at our guest. I fancied that he
read my mind, for he looked at me with his beautiful black
eyes, and I imagined that he winked and said to me in his own
language:

"Not a word, you little rascal. Wait till after Passover, and
everything will be all right."

4

All night long I was beset by dreams. I dreamed of a desert,
a holy temple, a high priest, and a lofty mountain. I climbed
the mountain. Gems, pearls, and diamonds grew there. My
friends clambered up the trees and shook the branches, bringing down an endless supply of precious stones. I stood there,
gathered up the jewels and stuffed them into my pockets. And,
amazingly enough, no matter how many I stuffed there was always more. I put my hand into my pocket, and instead of gems,
I took out all kinds of fruit—apples, pears and oranges, olives
and dates, nuts and figs. . . . This terrified me, and I tossed
from side to side. I dreamed of the holy temple. I heard the
priests chanting their blessing, the Levites singing, and the organ playing. I wanted to go into the holy temple but could not.
Rikl the maid held my hand fast and didn't let me go. I begged

her; I yelled; I wept. I was scared to death and tossed from side to side.

Then I awoke—

Before me were my parents, half-dressed, both as pale as death. Father's head was bowed. Mother wrung her hands, and tears brimmed in her beautiful eyes. My heart sensed that something awful had happened, something terribly dreadful, but yet I was unable to comprehend the extent of the disaster.

Our guest, the stranger from that faraway land, from that blissful land where houses were made of pinewood, covered with pure silver, and so on—that guest had vanished. And along with him a host of other things as well. All our silver goblets, all our silverware, all of Mama's meager jewelry, as well as all the cash in our drawers. And Rikl the maid had taken off with him, too.

I was heartbroken, but not because of the stolen silver, or Mama's jewelry, or the cash, or Rikl the maid—the devil take her. I was heartbroken over that blissful land where precious stones lay scattered about, and over the holy temple with the priests and Levites, the organ, altar, and sacrifices, and over the other good things that had been taken from me—brutally, brutally stolen.

And I turned to the wall and wept softly to myself.

Romance

PAGES FROM *THE SONG OF SONGS*:
THIS NIGHT

1

To my dear son,

Am herewith enclosing the rubles you requested. I beg you, my son, to do me a favor and come home for Passover. For in my old age I am ashamed to face people. We have only one son, yet we do not have the privilege of seeing him. Mama is also asking you to have some pity and come home without fail. Moreover, congratulations are in order for Buzie. Luck be with her, she has become engaged. God willing, she will be married the Sabbath after Shevuos.

Your father

This was the first time my father had written to me so crisply. The first time since our separation. We had parted amicably. Without quarreling. I had disobeyed him and gone my own way to seek a secular education. At first he was angry. He said he would never forgive me. Perhaps only on his deathbed. But later he forgave me. Then he began to send money, accompanied by short, dispassionate letters.

To my dear son,

Am herewith enclosing the rubles. Mother sends her best regards.

Your father

My letters to him were no different.

My dear, honored father:
    I have received your letter with the enclosed rubles. Give my best regards to Mama.

Your son

Our letters were cold. Terribly cold. But I had no time to notice this, for I was so deeply immersed in my world of dreams. Father's last letter, however, sobered me. I must admit it was not Father's shame or Mama's request for pity—but rather the few words: "Congratulations are in order for Buzie."

Buzie—Buzie who had no equal anywhere, except perhaps in the Song of Songs. Buzie, eternally bound up with my youth; always the enchanted princess of all my wonderful fairy tales, the loveliest princess of all my golden dreams—was she now engaged? Was Buzie someone else's now and not mine?

2

Who was Buzie? Don't you know? If you have forgotten, then I'll present once more a thumbnail sketch of her, repeating the description I used years ago.

I once had an older brother named Benny. He drowned. He left behind a water mill, a young widow, two horses, and one child. The mill was neglected, the horses sold. The widow remarried and went far away. The child was taken into our house.

This child was Buzie.

Buzie was as beautiful as the lovely Shulamite of the Song of Songs. Each time I saw Buzie I was reminded of the Shulamite of the Song of Songs. And each time I studied the Song of Songs in *kheder*, Buzie appeared before me.

Her name was short for Esther-Libe: Libuzie—Buzie. We grew up together. She called my father Papa, my mother Mama. Everyone thought we were brother and sister. And we loved each other like brother and sister.

Like brother and sister, we would hide in a corner where I would tell her fairy tales that my friend Shikeh had told me in *kheder*. He knew everything, even Kabala. I told Buzie that by means of Kabala I could do tricks: draw wine from a stone and gold from a wall. By means of Kabala I could make both of us soar to the clouds and even beyond. Oh, how she loved to hear me tell stories! There was only one story which Buzie could not bear to hear: the one about an enchanted princess, snatched away from under the bridal canopy and imprisoned in a crystal palace for seven years, to whose rescue I flew. Buzie loved to hear about everything, except this enchanted princess.

"Please don't fly so far," said Buzie, gazing at me with her beautiful blue Song of Songs eyes. "Listen to me and don't do it."

This was Buzie.

Now I had been informed that congratulations were in order for Buzie. She had become engaged. Buzie was to become a bride. Someone's bride. Someone else's, not mine. I sat down and replied to my father's letter.

> My dear, honored father:
>   I have received your letter with the enclosed rubles. I'll come home in a few days as soon as I complete my work. I don't know if I'll be home for the first days of Passover or the last ones, but I'll be there without fail. Best regards to Mama, and *mazel tov* to Buzie. I wish her all the luck.
>
> Your son

I had lied. I had no work to complete. I didn't have to wait several days. The day I received my father's letter and mailed my reply, I took a train and rushed home. I arrived on the eve of the holiday—a bright, warm, pre-Passover spring day.

I found my village exactly the same as I had left it years before. It had not changed at all. The same old village. The same people. The same seasonal weather and the usual eve of Passover bustle and tumult.

Only one thing was lacking. The Song of Songs. The lyrical, Song of Songs mood no longer prevailed as it did years before.

Our courtyard was no longer King Solomon's vineyard of the Song of Songs. The wood, logs, and planks which lay scattered near the house were no longer the fir and carob trees. The cat sunning itself by the door was no longer one of the Song of Songs gazelles. The hill behind the *shul* was no longer Mount Lebanon. . . . No longer one of the mountains of spices. . . . The women and girls who stood outside, washing, pressing, cleaning, and making things kosher for Passover, were no longer the daughters of Jerusalem mentioned in the Song of Songs. . . . What had become of my bright, young, and cheerful world, my spice-scented Song of Songs world of long ago?

4

I found my home exactly the same as I had left it years before. It had not changed at all. Father was the same as ever. Except that his silvery beard had become whiter, and worries, apparently, had set more wrinkles in his broad white brow. Mama, too, was exactly the same. Except that her ruddy face had become somewhat yellowish. I fancied that she had become smaller. But perhaps it only seemed so because she was stooped over now. And her eyes were red, puffy, and swollen. Was it from weeping?

Why had Mama been crying? Was it because of me, her only son? Was it because I had not obeyed Father, disregarded his wishes, gone my own way to seek a secular education, and not been home in years? Or was Mama crying because Buzie would be getting married the Sabbath after Shevuos?

And Buzie! She too had not changed at all. Except that she had grown up. Become taller and more beautiful. Even lovelier than before. Tall and slender, ripe and full of charm. Her eyes were the same beautiful Song of Songs eyes. But more pensive than ever were her deep, sad eyes, her beautiful blue Song of Songs eyes. A smile brightened her face. Buzie was friendly and delightful, charming and unpretentious. Buzie was quiet as a dove, silent and demure.

Looking at Buzie now, I was reminded of the Buzie of long

ago. I remembered the new Passover outfits that Mama had ordered sewn for her. I remembered the new small shoes that Father had bought. Thinking of the Buzie of old, once again I unwittingly recalled verses from the long-forgotten Song of Songs.

Your eyes are dovelike behind your veil . . . your hair is like a flock of goats, trailing down from Mount Gilead. Your teeth are like a flock of sheep all shaped alike, which have come up from the washing. Like a thread of scarlet are your lips; your mouth is comely. . . . And your voice is sugarsweet.

I looked at Buzie now, and once again the Song of Songs mood touched everything, as it did long ago, years back.

5

"Buzie, are congratulations in order?"

She did not hear me. Why did she lower her eyes? Why did her cheeks turn red? Nevertheless, I had to congratulate her.

"*Mazel tov,* Buzie."

"The same to you."

And not a word more. I could not ask her any questions. There was no place to talk. Because my parents and relatives were present, because the family and neighbors had come to greet me. One after another. Everyone crowded around me. All of them stared at me as if I were a bear, a creature from another world. Everyone wanted to see me and talk to me and ask what I was doing. After all, they hadn't seen me in years.

"Well, what's new in the world? What have you seen, what have you heard?"

While telling them what I had seen and heard, I gazed constantly at Buzie. I sought her eyes and met them. Her blue Song of Songs eyes, so big and deep and sad. But her eyes were as silent as her lips. Her eyes told me nothing. Absolutely nothing. And as in days gone by, the verse from the Song of Songs came back to me: *A garden inclosed is my sister, my bride, a garden inclosed, a fountain sealed.*

6

A tempest stormed in my head, and in my heart a fire directed at no one but myself alone. At myself and at those young and foolish golden dreams of mine, for the sake of which I had left my parents and forgotten about Buzie. Dreams for which I had sacrificed a part of my life and lost my chance for happiness forever.

Lost? Impossible. It could not be. I had come. In time. I wanted only to speak to Buzie alone. To say a few words to her. But how could I if everyone was here? If everyone surrounded me? All of them stared at me as if I were a bear, a creature from another world. Everyone wanted to see me and talk to me and ask what I was doing. After all, they hadn't seen me in years.

None of the others listened as attentively to me as Father. As usual, he sat with a sacred text before him, his broad forehead wrinkled. He peered at me over his silver-rimmed glasses and, as usual, stroked his silvery beard. But there was something different in his glance. I sensed that it was not the same. Father felt insulted. I had disobeyed him, refused to follow his ways but pursued my own instead. . . .

Mama cast aside her Passover preparations and stood in the doorway, listening to me with tears in her eyes. Though she was smiling, she secretly wiped away a tear with a corner of her apron. She gazed intently at me, devouring everything I said.

Buzie sat opposite me, listening, her hands folded on her chest. She, too, gazed intently at me, devouring everything I said. I looked at Buzie. I tried to read her eyes but could discover nothing. Absolutely nothing.

"Well, let's hear some more," Father said. "Why are you so quiet?"

"Leave him alone. Did you ever see such a thing?" Mama quickly intervened. "The child is tired. The child is hungry. And you keep saying: Let's hear some more. Let's hear some more."

7

The crowd of visitors gradually began to disperse, and we remained alone. Father and Mama, and Buzie and I. Mama went to the kitchen and returned quickly with a beautiful Passover plate—a familiar dish painted with large green fig leaves.

"Want to have a bite, Shimek? The Seder's a long way off," Mama said with abundant love and devotion. Buzie rose silently and brought me a knife and fork—familiar Passover silverware. Everything was familiar. Nothing had changed. Here was the same plate with its large green fig leaves. The same silverware with its white bone handles. The same aroma of the Passover goose fat. The same heavenly fragrance of freshly baked Passover matza. Nothing had changed. Nothing at all.

Long ago, on the eves of Passover we even ate together, Buzie and I. Out of one plate, I remember. Indeed, out of this very same Passover plate, painted so beautifully with green fig leaves. And Mama, I recall, gave us nuts. Pocketfuls of nuts. And we took each other by the hand, Buzie and I, and began to fly like eagles. I ran—she ran after me. I jumped over the logs —she jumped after me. I leaped—so did she. I descended—so did she.

"Shimek? How far are we going to run, Shimek?" Buzie asked me.

I replied with the words of the Song of Songs. *"Until the day grows cool—when the daylight blows away—and the shadows flee."*

8

This happened long ago, years back. Now Buzie had grown up and become tall. I, too, had grown up and become tall. Buzie was to become a bride. Someone's bride. Someone else's, not mine. . . . I wanted to remain alone with Buzie. To say a few words to her, to hear her voice, to tell her in the language of the Song of Songs, *"Let me see your face, let me hear your voice."* And I fancied that her eyes replied in the language of the Song of Songs, "*Come, my beloved, let us go out to the field.* Not here, outside. Outside. There I'll tell you. There I'll talk to you. That's where we'll talk. Outside."

I looked out the window. How beautiful it was, the eve of Passover springtime! Right out of the Song of Songs. The only drawback was that soon the day would end. The slowly setting sun painted the sky gold. The gold shone in Buzie's eyes, which were bathed in gold. Soon the day would die. I would not even have time to say a word to Buzie. The entire day was wasted in idle chatter with my parents and the family about what I had heard and seen. . . . I jumped up, looked out the window, and, in passing, said to Buzie: ·

"Want to take a walk? I haven't been home for so long. I'd like to look at the courtyard and see the village. . . ."

9

What could possibly be the matter with Buzie? Her face flamed with a hellish fire. She became as red as the sinking sun. She looked at Father, apparently to see his reaction. Father peered over his silver-rimmed glasses at Mama. He stroked his silvery beard and said to no one in particular:

"The sun is setting. Time to get dressed and go to *shul.* Time to light candles. What do you say?"

Apparently I would not be able to say a word to Buzie today. We went to get dressed. Mama was almost ready for Passover. She had already donned her silken holiday dress. Her white hands glistened. No one had such beautiful white hands as my mother. Soon she would kindle the holiday candles. With her white hands she would cover her eyes and cry softly, as always. The last rays of the setting sun would play on her clear beautiful white hands. No one had such beautiful clear white hands as my mother.

But what was the matter with Buzie? Her face was as lightless as the setting sun. As darkened as the waning day. Yet she was never more beautiful and charming. Her lovely blue Song of Songs eyes were very sad. Her lovely eyes were pensive.

What was Buzie thinking about now? Was she thinking of

me, the beloved guest for whom she had waited so long and who had rushed home so unexpectedly, after such a lengthy absence? Or was she thinking of her mother who had remarried, gone far away, and had forgotten about her daughter Buzie? Or was Buzie now thinking of her fiancé, whom my parents had surely forced on her against her will? Or of her marriage the Sabbath after Shevuos to a perfect stranger? On the other hand, perhaps I was mistaken. Perhaps she was counting the days from Passover to Shevuos and to the Sabbath after Shevuos. For *he* was her chosen one, *he* the one she loved, *he* the one she cherished. *He* would lead her to the bridal canopy, and to *him* she would give her heart and love. And *me?* For me—alas—she was no more than a sister. . . . She had been a sister and had remained a sister. . . . And I fancied that she looked at me with pity and vexation and said to me, as she once had, in the language of the Song of Songs:

"Oh, if only you were my brother—oh, why aren't you my brother?"

What should my answer be? I know what it will be. That all I wanted was the opportunity of saying a few words to her. Just a few words.

But no. Today I wouldn't be able to say a single word to Buzie, not even half a word. She rose, went softly to the cupboard, and inserted candles into Mama's tall old silver candlesticks. These familiar, hollow, hand-chased candlesticks had played an honored role in my golden dreams of the enchanted princess in the crystal palace. These golden dreams, these silver candlesticks, the gleaming candles, Mama's beautiful clear white hands, Buzie's lovely blue Song of Songs eyes, and the last golden rays of the setting sun—were they all not linked and intertwined?

"Well." Father looked out the window, then motioned to me that it was time to get dressed and go to *shul.*

10

Our *shul,* our ancient *shul* had not changed at all. Except that the walls had become blacker. The prayer stand smaller. The pulpit older. And gone was the Holy Ark's sheen of newness.

Our *shul* had always seemed to me to be a miniature holy temple. Now the holy temple stood somewhat atilt. Oh, what had become of the sacred beauty and sheen of our old *shul*? Where were the angels that hovered above us when we welcomed the Sabbath, and where were the angels when a festival evening service began?

Even the congregants had not changed much. Just grown a bit older. Black beards were now white. Straight shoulders stooped. Satin gaberdines frayed. White threads and yellow underlining discernible. Even now Melekh the cantor sang as beautifully as he did years ago. But his voice had grown a bit musty. A new tone had crept into his chanting. It was plaintive rather than prayerful. He wept more than he sang.

And our rabbi. Our old rabbi? He had not changed at all. He had always looked like fallen snow and still looked like fallen snow. Except for one slight change. His hands shook now. His entire body, too. Apparently from old age.

Azriel the *shamesh*—on whose face no hair had ever grown— would have been the only one who hadn't changed. Except that he had lost every one of his teeth. Now with his sunken jaw and hairless face he looked more like a woman than a man. But no matter. When the Silent Devotion began, he still slammed the table for silence with his wooden board. True, the blow was not as forceful as it used to be. Years ago it could have deafened one. Not today. Apparently the old strength was gone.

Years ago, I remember, I was happy here, infinitely blissful. Years ago, in this miniature holy temple, my childish soul had once hovered with the angels beneath the painted ceiling. Here, years ago, I had prayed in zestful devotion with Father and all the other Jews.

11

Now I once again sat in my old *shul*, praying with the old congregants. I listened to the old cantor singing the melodies of long ago. The congregation prayed with zest and warmth, using its age-old ritual. I prayed with the congregation, but my thoughts strayed far. I turned page after page in my Siddur and chanced upon the fourth chapter of the Song of Songs. *You are beautiful, my love*—how lovely you are, my friend. *You are beautiful. Your eyes are dovelike.* I wanted to pray with everyone, as I used to long ago. But I could not pray. I turned page after page in my Siddur and chanced upon the fifth chapter of the Song of Songs. *I have come into my garden, my sister, my bride. I have gathered my myrrh and my spice. I have eaten my honeycomb with my honey; I have drunk my wine.*

But what was I talking about? What was I saying? The garden was not mine. I would gather no myrrh nor sniff any spices. I would eat no honey nor drink any wine. The garden was not mine. And Buzie was not my bride. Buzie was someone's bride. Someone else's, not mine. A hellish anger seethed within me. Not directed at Buzie. Or at anyone. No, it was directed at myself alone. After all, how could I have remained away from Buzie so long? How could I have let her be taken away from me and given to someone else? Hadn't she always written letters to me, hinting that she hoped to see me soon? Hadn't I postponed returning home from one holiday to the next, until she finally stopped writing to me?

12

"*Gut yontev!* This is my son."

My father introduced me after prayers to the people in *shul*. They stared at me from all sides, greeted me, accepted my greeting as though it were an old debt.

"This is my son."

"Your son? Well, then, here's a hearty how-do-you-do!"

My father's words, "This is my son," contained a host of nuances. Joy, pride, and disappointment. His words could have been interpreted in many ways. "What do you say to him? That's my son!" Or: "Can you imagine, *this* is my son!"

I understood him. He felt insulted. I had disobeyed him, refused to follow his ways but pursued my own path instead. I had made him old before his time. No, he had not yet forgiven me. He did not tell me this. There was no need to tell me. I felt it. His eyes gazing through the silver-rimmed glasses into my heart told me. The silent sigh which tore itself out of his weak old chest told me. We both walked home from *shul* in silence, the last to leave. The night had spread its wings over the sky and cast its shadow on the earth. Silence and holiness pervaded this warm Passover night. A night full of secrets and mysteries, a night full of wonder. The holiness of the night was palpable in the air. It descended from the dark blue sky. The stars silently declared it. The night was suffused with the Exodus from Egypt.

I walked home quickly. Father could hardly keep up with me. He followed me like a shadow.

"What's the rush?" he asked, barely catching his breath.

Oh, Father, Father. Can't you see that I'm like a gazelle or a young deer upon the mountains of spices? . . . Time drags on for me, Father, much too slowly. The road is long, Father, much too long, since Buzie has become engaged. She will be someone's bride. Someone else's, not mine. I am like a gazelle or a deer upon the mountains of spices.

That's how I wanted to answer my father, in the language of the Song of Songs. I did not feel the ground beneath me. I walked home quickly that night. Father could barely keep up with me. He followed me like a shadow that night.

13

Father and I greeted everyone with the old, familiar *"Gut yontev"*—our usual greeting upon coming home from *shul*.

Everyone responded with the old, familiar *"Gut yontev, gut yohr"*—the usual greeting upon our return from *shul* on the night of Passover.

Mama, the queen, was dressed in her royal silken outfit, and the princess, Buzie, in her snow-white dress. The picture was exactly the same as it was years ago. Nothing had changed. Nothing at all.

Our house was full of charm now, as it was years ago. A special loveliness, a holy, festive, and majestic beauty, settled on our house that night, bathing it with radiance. The tablecloth was as white as fallen snow. Mama's candles gleamed in their silver candlesticks. The bouquet of the Kiddush wine wafted toward us. Oh, how modestly the matzas peeped out from under their napkins. And on the table stood the grated horse-radish, the *kharoses* (a mixture of apples, nuts, and wine), and the dish of salt water. The king's chair was cushioned and pillowed in festive fashion. Heavenly grace glowed on the queen's face, as it always did this night. And the princess, Buzie, was the quintessence of the Song of Songs. No, what am I saying? She was the Song of Songs itself.

The only trouble was that the prince sat so far from the princess. As I recall, our seating order at the Seder had always been different. We would always sit next to each other. The prince would ask Father the Four Questions, and the princess would snatch the *afikomen* matza from under his majesty's pillow. And how we used to laugh! I remember that long ago, after the Seder, when the king had already removed his white linen robe and the queen her royal silken outfit, the two of us, just Buzie and I, would sit in a corner. Either we would play with the nuts that Mama had given us, or I would tell her one of the fairy tales I had heard in *kheder* from my all-knowing friend Shikeh. A story about an enchanted princess imprisoned seven years in a crystal palace who was waiting for someone to utter the divine name and fly over mountains and valleys, rivers and deserts, to rescue her and set her free.

14

But all this happened long ago, in years gone by. Now the princess had grown up, become a young woman. The prince, too, had grown up and become a young man. But the seating plan that night was very inconsiderate. As was only proper, the engaged Buzie and I could not even see each other. Imagine! On the right side of his majesty, the prince, and on the left side of her majesty, the princess. My father and I melodiously chanted page after page of the Hagada, loud and clear, just as we did in years gone by. Mama and Buzie repeated the words softly, page after page, until we came to the Song of Songs. Father and I sang the Song of Songs with the traditional melody, just as we did in years gone by. One verse after another. Mama and Buzie softly repeated the verses after us. Finally, the king, exhausted by the Exodus from Egypt and slightly groggy from the wine, slowly began to doze. He snoozed awhile, then awoke and continued chanting loudly the Song of Songs: *"Floods cannot quench love."* And I accompanied him: *"Rivers cannot drown it."* Our chanting gradually grew softer until his majesty was finally fast asleep. With loving tenderness Mama touched the sleeve of Father's white robe. She gently woke him and told him to go to bed. Meanwhile, Buzie and I were able to exchange a few words. I rose from the table and drew near her. We stood next to each other. So close for the first time that night. I remarked how beautiful the night was.

"On a night like this it's good to take a walk."

She understood and replied with a half smile: "On a night like this?"

I fancied she was making fun of me. This disturbed me, for that was how she used to laugh at me in years gone by.

"Buzie, we have to talk," I said. "There is so much to talk about."

"So much to talk about?" she repeated, and I fancied she was making fun of me.

"But perhaps I'm mistaken," I said softly. "Perhaps now I have nothing to talk to you about."

I said this with such bitterness that Buzie stopped smiling. Her face grew solemn.

"Tomorrow," she said. "Tomorrow we'll talk."

My eyes brightened. Everything suddenly became bright and wonderful.

Tomorrow. We would talk tomorrow. Tomorrow . . . Tomorrow. I drew closer to her and breathed the familiar fragrance of her hair and her clothing. The words of the Song of Songs came back to me: *Your lips, my bride, drop honey, honey and milk are under your tongue; the fragrance of your garments is like the fragrance of Lebanon.*

The rest was said without benefit of words. We said much more with our eyes. With our eyes.

15

"Good night, Buzie," I said softly. God alone knew how hard it was for me to leave her.

"Good night," Buzie answered, not moving. Deeply troubled, she gazed at me with her beautiful Song of Songs eyes.

I bade her good night again, and she replied, "Good night," once more.

Then Mama came in and led me into a separate bedroom, where with her lovely white hands she had smoothed out the white cover of my bed.

"Sleep well, my child," she whispered. "Sleep well."

The ocean of love stored up in Mama's heart ever since I had left home was poured out in those few words. I was ready to fall at her feet and kiss her beautiful white hands. But I wasn't worthy of this. No, I was not worthy. That much I knew. . . . I softly wished her good night and remained alone, all alone that night.

16

All alone that night. On that soft and silent warm spring night.

I opened the window and looked outside at the dark blue sky, at the twinkling, gemlike stars. Is it possible? I asked myself. Is it really so? Have I really lost my happiness? Have I lost it forever?

Is it possible that I had burned my wonderful palace and set free with my own hands the beautiful, divine princess whom I had once enchanted? . . . Was it really so? Perhaps not. Perhaps I had still returned in time. *I have come into my garden, my sister, my bride.*

I sat for a long time by the open window that night, and whispered secrets to the soft and silent warm spring night, so strangely full of secrets and mysteries.

That night I discovered something: I loved Buzie.

I loved her with that holy flaming passion described so beautifully in our Song of Songs. Huge fiery letters hovered before me. Where they came from I do not know. One letter after another appeared from the Song of Songs that we had just finished chanting.

Strong as death is love, severe as the grave is jealousy, its flashes are flashes of fire, a flame of the Lord.

I sat by the open window on that night of secrets and mysteries, asking it to solve an enigma for me: Was it possible? Was it really so?

But that night of secrets and mysteries held its peace. The enigma would have to remain unsolved until tomorrow. . . .

Tomorrow. That's when Buzie had promised me that we would talk. Yes, tomorrow we would talk. Just let the night pass. Let this night cease to be.

This night. This night. . . .

Jewish Children

THE DREYDL

1

Benny Polkovoy was my best pal. I liked him more than any of my friends in *kheder* or in town. I liked him more than anyone else in the world. This affection was the result of an odd combination of adoration and fear. I adored Benny because he was the best-looking, smartest, and cleverest of the boys. He was loyal and generous to me and always took my part. Benny was also the oldest boy in our group. If anyone picked on me, he beat him up and, as a bonus, tweaked his nose and ears. Yet I was afraid of Benny because he liked to fight. He could pick a fight any time, since he was the tallest, as well as the richest, boy in *kheder*.

Although his father, Meir Polkovoy, was only the regimental tailor, he was well off and assumed the role of an upstanding burgher in our town. Meir owned a fine house and had a seat by the east wall of the synagogue—the third seat from the Holy Ark. On Passover he had the choicest extra-special-kosher matzas; on Sukkos, the finest *esrog*. For the Sabbath he always had a guest. He gave the biggest donations, extended free loans willingly, and hired the best teachers for his children. In short, Meir wanted to move up the social ladder, become a pillar of society, and join the inner circle. But all in vain.

In Kasrilevke, no man could readily buy his way into the inner circle. Kasrilevke does not forget so quickly one's familial pedigree and background. Although a tailor may thoroughly refine, improve, and better himself for twenty years in a row, in Kasrilevke he is still considered a tailor. There isn't a soap in the world that can wash *that* stain away.

2

But let's return to my pal Benny. Benny was a chubby, freckle-faced fellow with yellow prickly hair, bulging white cheeks, gap teeth, popping fisheyes where a shrewd smile always lurked, and, to top it off, a pug nose which made him look like an impudent young brat. Nevertheless, his face appealed to me, and the minute we met—during my first day in *kheder*—we became fast friends. In fact, that's where my friendship with Benny was sealed—under the table, while studying the Torah.

I got my first glimpse of the rebbi when my mother brought me to his *kheder*. The rebbi, a man with thick brows and a pointy skullcap, was studying Genesis with all his pupils. Without the slightest hesitation—there was no need to take an exam or prepare for matriculation—the rebbi told me: "Move to that bench over there—between those two boys."

I squeezed in between the boys and was immediately accepted. The rebbi and my mother did not spend much time chatting, for everything had already been arranged during the holidays.

"Remember now, study diligently," Mama said, standing by the door. She turned and looked at me with a feeling of mingled joy, love, and compassion. I understood Mama's look quite well. She was happy that I was studying in the company of respectable children, but her heart ached that she had to part with me.

Sitting there among so many new friends, I must admit that I felt happier than my mother. I sized them up; they sized me up. But the rebbi wouldn't let us sit idle for long. He rocked back and forth and yelled in a loud singsong voice, while we all repeated after him, one outshouting the other:

"*Now the serpent*—that's the snake . . ." said the rebbi.

"*The serpent*—that's the snake . . ." said we.

"*Was more subtle*—which means smarter . . ."

"*Was more subtle*—which means smarter . . ."

"*Than any beast of the field*—that is, all other animals . . ." the rebbi sang.

"*Than any beast of the field*—that is, all other animals . . ." we repeated.

"*Which the Lord God had made*—which the Almighty created."

"*Which the Lord God had made*—which the Almighty created."

If boys sit so close together—despite their shouting at the top of their lungs and their rocking back and forth—they have no choice but to get acquainted and exchange a few words. This is precisely what happened.

Benny Polkovoy, who was pressed right next to me, first tested me with a pinch on the leg and then inspected me from top to toe. Then he swayed fervently and bellowed along with the rebbi. Meanwhile, we occasionally interpolated some of our own remarks:

"*And the man*—that is, Adam . . ." the rebbi chanted.

"*And the man*—that is, Adam . . ." he repeated.

"*Knew*—he got to know her . . ."

"*Knew*—he got to know her . . . Here, take these buttons . . ."

"Eve—that's her name . . ."

"Eve—that's her name . . ."

"*His wife*—the one he married . . ." the rebbi sang.

"*His wife*—the one he married . . . Gimme carob, and I'll give you a puff of my cigarette . . ."

Then I felt a warm hand giving me a few small slippery-smooth pants buttons. I must confess that I didn't need buttons, had no licorice, and didn't smoke. But I liked the idea, and I replied, keeping the same tune and rocking back and forth along with all the boys:

"*And she conceived*—that is, she became pregnant . . ." the rebbi chanted.

"*And she conceived*—that is, she became pregnant . . . Who told you . . ."

"*And bore*—she gave birth . . ." sang the rebbi.

"*And bore*—she gave birth . . . that I have carob?" I said.

We kept this up until the rebbi noticed that despite my pious swaying, my attention was not focused on Genesis. He caught me by surprise and began to question me.

"Say, you there, whatever your name is! Do you know whose son Cain was? And what Cain's brother was called?"

These questions struck me as nonsensical as: "When is the next express to heaven?" or, "How does one make cottage cheese out of freshly fallen snow?" Actually, my thoughts were goodness-knows-where—down by the buttons.

"Why are you gaping at me like that?" the rebbi asked. "Didn't you hear me? I'm simply asking you to name Cain ben Adam's father and to describe the relationship between Cain and his brother, Abel, the sons of Eve."

All the boys were smiling and choking with laughter. I couldn't understand why

"You silly goose," Benny whispered to me, poking me with his elbow. "Tell him you don't know because we haven't learned it yet."

I obeyed and repeated each word like a parrot. Once again the class exploded with mirth. What are they laughing at? I thought While watching my classmates and the rebbi rolling with laughter, I counted the buttons in my hand. Exactly half a dozen.

"Come now, lad, let's see what your hands are so busy with?" said the rebbi, bending under the table.

Since you all are smart children, there's no need to describe how I was punished for my first transaction in buttons.

3

Blows heal; humiliation is forgotten. Benny and I became good friends. "Good friends" isn't even the term for it. A single soul is more like it. Bosom pals. This is how it happened. I came to school the next day, with the Pentateuch in one hand and my breakfast in the other, and found the gang happily strutting about, intoxicated with joy. What had happened? The rebbi wasn't coming. Where was he? He and his wife had gone to a circumcision feast. Not together, God forbid. As was the custom, the rebbi went first, and his wife followed at his heels.

"Let's make bets," said blue-nosed Yehoshua-Heshel.

"For how much?" said Kopel-Bunim, whose dirty elbow protruded from his sleeve.

"A quarter pound of carob."

"Fine. What're you betting?"

"I bet he can't take more than twenty-five."

"I say thirty-six."

"Thirty-six? We'll see in a minute. . . . Fellas, grab him!" ordered blue-nosed Yehoshua-Heshel. With demonic speed several boys suddenly grabbed me and stretched me out faceup on the bench. Two boys sat on my legs, two on my hands, one held my head to prevent me from squirming around, and another (he was a lefty, apparently) held two fingers in front of my nose. He curled his fingers into the shape of a bagel, took aim with one eye slightly closed, and with mouth half open began to fillip my nose. You can't even begin to imagine the pain! Each blow made me see my father in the other world. Those murderers! Those assassins!

What had they against my nose? What harm had it done them? Whom had it annoyed? What ill had they seen in it? It was just a nose like any other!

"Fellas, keep count!" Yehoshua-Heshel ordered. "One . . . two . . . three. . . ."

But suddenly—

I don't exactly remember if it was the fifth or the sixth fillip, but suddenly the door opened and in walked Benny. The boys immediately released me and stood there petrified. Like statues. Then Benny began to work them over, one by one. He took each one by the ear and gave it a right good twist, chanting with a Torah melody, "Now you know what you'll get for picking on an orphan, a widow's son."

After that the boys never pestered me again. They touched neither me nor my nose. They were afraid to start up with the widow's son, for Benny was his friend, redeemer, and protector.

4

In *kheder* I was known as the Widow's Son. Why the Widow's Son? Because my mother was a widow. She supported herself by the sweat of her brow, running her own little grocery. If memory serves me, she carried mostly chalk and carob—two items with a big turnover in Kasrilevke. Chalk was needed for whitewashing the houses, and carob provided sweet snacks that were cheap and plentiful. The *kheder* boys spent all their breakfast and lunch money on carob, and the groceries did a thriving business. I couldn't understand why Mama always complained that she barely made enough to pay for the store rent and for *kheder* tuition. Why did she single out tuition? What about food, clothing, shoes, etc.? All she thought about was tuition.

"Since God took my wonderful husband from me and left me a lonely young widow, the least I want for you, my son, is to be well versed in holy lore."

What do you say to that? She always went to my *kheder* to find out how I was progressing. As for prayers, she made sure that I said them daily. She tried to talk me into becoming at least half the man my father was, may he rest in peace. Whenever she looked at me, she would declare, "You're the image of him, may you live and be well." Then her eyes would fill with tears, and a curtain of gloom would cover her face.

May my dear father in the other world forgive me for saying this, but I simply couldn't understand what sort of person he was. According to Mama, he spent all his time either studying or praying. Didn't he ever have a desire, as I did, to step outdoors and see a summer sunrise? When the sun rose on a gloriously divine morning, how could one savor a plain weekday morning service? What pleasure was there sitting and studying in the small, desolate *kheder*, when the golden sun was making the earth aglow with light? At such times the world of nature lured you outdoors—to the foot of the hill, to the beautiful river covered with a green film. A strange odor, like that of a steam bath, hovered in the distance. You felt like undressing and quickly jumping waist-deep into the warm water. Down by the slippery mud bottom it felt cooler. Swarms of tadpoles gathered there, flitting in and out of view. Strange flies and long-legged gnats glided on the water's surface. You felt like swimming to the other side, where water lilies, sunflowers, and daisies shimmered under the young branches of a green willow tree. You dived and fell into the mud hands first, feet in the air. You kept splashing to give the impression that you were swimming. So I repeat, what pleasure was there staying at home or in *kheder* on a summer evening when the red setting sun glittered on the church spire, flared on the red shingles of the bathhouse, and (forgive the proximity) glinted off the big old windows of the cold synagogue? From the other side of town the flock was coming. Goats ran, lambs bleated, and the dust rose to the sky. Frogs croaked and jabbered. The noise was deafening—a hullabaloo, a tumult, pandemonium. Who could even think of praying or studying then? But had you spoken to Mama, she would have told you that her husband, may he rest in peace, was not like that. He was a different sort of person.

May he forgive me for saying this, but I don't know what sort of person he was. I only know that Mama constantly badgered and reminded me that I had had a father, threw up to me a dozen times a day the fact that she was paying *kheder* tuition for me, and asked only two things of me: to put my mind to studies and my heart to prayers.

5

No one could say that the Widow's Son was a poor student. I did not even trail my friends by a hair. However, I wasn't as good when it came to praying. All children are alike, and the Widow's Son was no less a scalawag then the others. Like them, I loved to fool around and pull tricks. We took the rebbi's wife's kerchief, tied it on the head of the congregation's goat, and let him run loose over town; gave the cat a nervous fit by hanging a paper snake on its tail; hung a lock on the door of the women's *shul* on Friday evening, necessitating the rescue of the fainting women; hammered nails into the rebbi's slippers or put sealing wax in his beard while he snoozed at the table to see what happened when he tried to get up; and so on and so forth. Don't ask how many whacks we got once they discovered the perpetrators!

Obviously every movement has to have its leader, headman,

trailblazer. Ours was Benny. Although everything originated with him, trouble always ended up with us. Moonfaced, big-bellied, popeyed Benny always managed to get out of trouble scot-free—he emerged unscathed, clean as a whistle, innocent as a lamb, pure as a dove. Our entire repertoire of tricks, grimaces, gestures, and practical jokes was inherited from Benny. Who taught us to smoke on the sly and exhale through our nostrils? Benny. Who took us skating in the winter with all the peasant lads? Benny. Who taught us to gamble with buttons? Benny. Who taught us all sorts of games of chance like odd or even, in which we lost our breakfast and lunch money? Benny. At gambling Benny was a master, and he outwitted us all. He beat us down to our last kopeck, then wiped his lips, and pulled a disappearing act.

Gambling was one of our favorite pastimes. But the rebbi was determined to extirpate and eradicate this evil habit, and he punished us severely for it.

"So you're going to gamble, huh? May the Angel of Death gamble with you!" the rebbi used to say, shaking our pockets empty and liberally dispensing smacks left and right.

There was only one week during the year when we were permitted to gamble. What am I saying, permitted? It was a moral obligation, a pious duty to gamble.

That week came during Hanuka, when we played, gambled, and made bets with the *dreydl,* the Hanuka top.

6

Frankly, modern card games like rummy, sixty-six, and poker are more sensible than our ancient *dreydl.* But when it comes to playing for money, nothing matters. I once saw two peasant lads banging their heads against a stone wall. I asked them why they were doing this. "Are you crazy or just plain dumb?"

"Get lost," they replied. "It's a money bet. Whoever quits first loses."

So go argue with them. The *dreydl* game is fierce, dreadful, dangerous. It can drive you out of your mind. You can play

away your very soul. Of the four letters on the top's four sides,
N stands for nothing, *G* for gather money, *H* for half the pot,
and *S* for settle accounts.* It wasn't so much the money as the
aggravation. Why should the next fellow win? Why does the
dreydl fall on the winning *G* for your opponent, while for you
it lands on *N*. The *dreydl* is like a lottery. The lucky one wins.
For example, take Benny. No matter how often he spun the
dreydl it always landed on *G*.

"That Benny is really something," the boys said, putting
more money into the pot. But Benny didn't care. He was a rich
man's son and took them all on.

"Again *G!* What luck!" all the boys said, continually staking
more money.

Benny's reply was another spin of the *dreydl,* upside down
this time. It spun, tottered like a drunkard, and stopped.

"*G,*" said Benny.

"Again *G?* This chap's amazing," the gang yelled, scratching
their heads and diving into their change purses again.

The game became more and more furious. The players grew
excited, staked their money on the table, crowded one another,
fought, poked one another in the ribs, and paid one another
compliments like "You snot-nosed dunderhead. You sloppy
ragpicker," and other such epithets, oblivious to the rebbi, who
stood there in his warm jacket. He wore a cotton hat over his
skullcap and held his *tfillin* and prayer shawl under his arm.
He was on his way to morning prayers, but seeing the children
so excited, he stopped for a while to watch us playing *dreydl*
from afar. So help me, he wasn't a bad chap after all. Since today was Hanuka, he did not interfere. We had an eight-day
vacation from *kheder* and were allowed to play *dreydl* as long
as we liked, on condition that we didn't fight or fly at each
other's throats. The rebbi's wife took her sick infant, Ruvele,
silenced his cries by nursing him, and stood behind the rebbi,
watching the boys putting money in the pot. And as usual,

---

* The Hebrew letters "Nun," "Gimel," "Hey," and "Shin" stand for "Nes
gadol haya sham"—a great miracle occurred there, referring to the Hanuka
events in Palestine in 165 B.C.E.—Tr.

Benny took on all their bets. Red-hot, sizzling, on fire, Benny spun the *dreydl.*

"*G* again! What a winning streak!"

Benny kept displaying his artistry and skill until he had taken away every last kopeck from us. Then he shoved his hands into his pockets, as though to say, "Well, who's next?"

We all went home, distressed and ashamed. There each of us had to concoct a different lie. One confessed that all his Hanuka money had been spent on sweets. Another's routine was that all the money had been stolen from his pocket the night before. A third went home and began to bawl.

"What are you crying for? What happened?"

"What do you mean? I bought a little knife for the Hanuka money."

"Then why the tears?"

"What do you mean, why the tears? Because I just lost my brand-new knife."

I, too, had my own cock-and-bull story. I told Mama some fairy tale and got another round of Hanuka money. With these seven kopecks I went straight to Benny, who relieved me of my money in five minutes flat. Then I dreamed up another tall tale. In short, minds were working; brains were busy inventing trumped-up yarns. Lies flew left and right like wood chips. All our Hanuka money was lost via the *dreydl.* It went into Benny's pocket and was gone forever!

There was only one person who sank tooth and nail into the *dreydl* game. Hanuka money alone did not suffice him, and he continuously played with Benny. Practically every day until the very last day of Hanuka. This person was yours truly, the Widow's Son.

7

Where did the Widow's Son get money to bet with? Don't ask me! Ask the world's biggest gamblers who have won and lost huge fortunes and kings' ransoms—they'll know how I managed. There is nothing more difficult in the world then subduing the evil urge to gamble. Ah, me, may that hour of temptation never come! It smashes brick houses and iron walls. It does unbelievable things. A formidable force, that evil urge to gamble!

First of all, I started to make money—to my everlasting shame —by liquidating my assets. I sold everything I had: first my knife, then my purse, and then all my buttons. I also had a box that opened and closed, a few wheels of an old clock, fine brass wheels which when polished shone almost like gold. I sold everything for next to nothing, slashed prices left and right. Each time I ran to Benny's house, I lost every last kopeck, and I left his house depressed, heartbroken, vexed to the quick, and terribly upset. But not at Benny, God forbid! I had nothing against him! Was it Benny's fault that he was lucky at *dreydl?* Had the *dreydl* landed on G at *my* turn, then *I* would have been the winner, but since it landed on G for *him, he* was the winner. That's what Benny said, and, alas, he was right.

Actually, I was angry at myself for having squandered so much money—Mama's hard-earned money—and all my possessions besides. I remained, as the saying goes, naked as the day I was born. I even sold my little Siddur.

Oh, that Siddur! What a prayer book it was! When I thought of the Siddur, my heart ached, my face burned with shame. It wasn't just a plain run-of-the-mill Siddur; it was a rare gem. My mother had bought it for me on the occasion of Father's *yohrzeit* from Pesakhya the porter, a man with a cataract and a trimmed mustache that made his sad face smile. What a Siddur it was! Among prayer books it was something extraordinary. A veritable encyclopedia. It had everything. It was full and thick. You name it, it had it. As far as I was concerned, it even had the proverbial bird's milk. In addition to all the prayers, it contained the Song of Songs, the entire Ethics of the Fathers, the Hagada, a complete list of laws, customs, and traditions for the entire year, and the entire Book of Psalms in the back. And let's not forget the binding, the golden lettering, the tinted edging to the pages, and the spine. This was no mere Siddur, but a devilishly tempting item to possess. Whenever

Pesakhya exhibited his merchandise by the *shul* door, I couldn't take my eyes off that honest-to-goodness, all-inclusive, encyclopedic, everything-in-it little Siddur.

"Well, what do you say, little boy?" Pesakhya asked. He pretended not to notice that I had often thumbed through the Siddur and asked him how much it cost.

"Nothing, I'm just looking," I said and went away so as to avoid temptation

"Oh, Mama, you should see the Siddur that Pesakhya has!"

"What kind of Siddur?" Mama asked.

"The sort of Siddur that—if I only had such a Siddur—I could—I don't even know what. . . ."

"Don't you have a Siddur? What about your father's Siddur?"

"How can you compare them, Mama? Papa's is just a plain Siddur, and the one I want has everything in it. Like an encyclopedia."

"An encyclopedia?" Mama asked. "Are there more prayers in that kind of Siddur, or does one pray with more devotion from it?"

Go explain to a mother the meaning of an honest-to-goodness, all-inclusive, encyclopedic, everything-in-it little Siddur with red binding, blue-tinted edging to the pages, and a green spine.

"Come," said Mama, taking my hand one afternoon. "Let's go to the *shul*. Tomorrow, God willing, is Papa's *yohrzeit,* and we'll light a candle for him. And while we're there, we'll see what kind of special Siddur Pesakhya has."

I knew in advance that on Father's *yohrzeit* I'd be able to get anything I wanted from Mama, even pie in the sky. And my heart already began to thump for joy.

When we came to the *shul,* we met Pesakhya. His bag of merchandise was still unpacked. Pesakhya, you see, was in no rush. He knew quite well that he had absolutely no competitors. No one would take his business away from him. It took him a year and a day to display his wares. I shivered; I trembled; I could hardly stand on my feet. But he went on his own merry way as if it were no concern of his

"Will you show me already what kind of extraordinary Siddur you have?" Mama said.

But Pesakhya took his own sweet time. After all, the sky wasn't falling. He slowly opened his bag and displayed his merchandise: Bibles big and small, prayer books for men and women, books of psalms of every size, books of laws and customs, holiday prayer books, collections of penitential hymns, an infinite supply of women's Yiddish prayer books, as well as stories and tales about the Baal Shem Tov. It seemed to me that the flow of books would never end. It was like a bottomless well. Finally, I saw his selection of smaller books, among them my little Siddur.

"Is this it?" Mama called out. "Such a tiny little thing?"

"This tiny little thing has a great big price," Pesakhya said.

"Just how much is this—God forgive my words—pipsqueak of a chipmunk?" Mama asked.

"Are you calling a Siddur a chipmunk?" said Pesakhya, gingerly removing the book from Mama's hand. My heart was torn to pieces.

"Well, can I hear a price on it?" Mama pleaded.

But Pesakhya had plenty of time. "You want to know the price?" he chanted melodiously. "Boy, does it have a price! What a price tag it has! I'm afraid it's priced beyond your means."

Mama wished her enemies a host of oppressive nightmares and told him to quote a price. Pesakhya quoted one. Mama remained silent. She took me by the hand and turned to the door.

"Come, let's go. There's nothing for us to do here. Can't you see that Reb Pesakhya's wares are very expensive?"

With bitter heart I followed Mama to the door, still hoping that perhaps God would have pity and Pesakhya would call us back. But Pesakhya was not that sort of person. He knew that we would return of our own accord. And indeed we did. Mama now asked him to quote a more reasonable price. Pesakhya was not moved. He gazed up at the ceiling. The cataract of his left eye glistened. We left but returned once more.

"Pesakhya is an awful person," Mama told me later. "I'd rather have seen the plague beset my enemies than have bought the Siddur from him. It was so expensive. So help me, it isn't right. The money could have been put to better use paying for tuition. But never mind. Since tomorrow, God willing, is Papa's *yohrzeit*, may he rest in peace, and you have to say Kaddish for him, I thought I'd do you a favor. So now *you* do *me* a favor, my son, and promise me that at least you'll pray faithfully every day."

Whether or not I kept my promise of praying daily is irrelevant. But my love for my honest-to-goodness, all-inclusive, encyclopedic, everything-in-it little Siddur was boundless. How great my love was could be seen by the fact that I slept with it, although, as you know, this was neither proper nor permissible. The entire *kheder* envied me. I cherished the little Siddur like the apple of my eye. But now, during Hanuka, of my own free will—ah, woe is me—I brought it to Moshe (the carpenter's son), who had had his eye on it for a long time. Finally, after begging him on bended knee, he agreed to buy it. I literally gave that little Siddur of mine away. When I think of it, my heart aches and my face burns with shame. I sold it, traded it. For what? On account of whom? On account of Benny. So that Benny could win a few more kopecks from me. But was it really his fault that he was lucky with the *dreydl?*

"That's why it's a *dreydl*." Benny tried to console me, pocketing my last few kopecks. "If you were as lucky as I, *you'd* win. But since I'm the lucky one, *I* win."

Benny's face was flushed. His house was warm and bright. The silver Hanuka candelabrum, with its handsome kindling candle, was filled with the finest oil. From the kitchen wafted the delicious aroma of recently rendered goose fat.

"We're making pancakes today," Benny declared, imparting the good news while I stood at the door, my stomach rumbling with hunger.

I ran home in my torn coat and met Mama coming from her little store, her nose red and her hands swollen with cold. Frozen through and through, she stood warming her hands by the stove.

"Coming from *shul?*" Mama asked, her face shining as she saw me.

"Yes, from *shul*," I lied.

"Have you said the evening prayer?"

"Of course," I lied once more.

"As soon as you're warmed up, my child, please make the blessing over the Hanuka candles. Praise God, today we light the last candle."

8

A man who lives a life of constant grief, devoid of pleasure and joy, would have no choice but to commit suicide. I mention this in reference to my widowed mother. Poor woman, she slaved away day and night. She froze, went hungry, never had sufficient sleep or enough to eat. She suffered all this only for my sake. Only for me. Why? Didn't she deserve to have a little pleasure, too? Everyone has his own criterion for joy. For my mother there was no greater pleasure in the world than my chanting the Sabbath and holiday Kiddush over the wine for her, or my conducting the Passover Seder, or lighting the Hanuka candles for her. Did it matter whether the Kiddush was made over wine or mead, or whether the Seder was graced with sugar pancakes or just matzas and water? Did it make any difference to her whether the Hanuka lights were kindled in a silver candelabrum or in scooped-out-potatoes filled with oil? Believe me, the importance lay neither in the wine, the sugar pancakes, nor in the silver candelabrum. The important thing was the chanting of the Kiddush, the rendition of the Seder, the blessings over the candles.

Looking at Mama's face while I recited the blessings and seeing her smiling and beaming face made mere comments superfluous. One saw that this was her greatest joy; here was authentic happiness. I bent over the scooped-out potatoes filled with oil and chanted the Hanuka blessing. I sang, and she softly repeated, word for word, using the same melody. I chanted, and she looked into my eyes and moved her lips. I knew her precise thoughts that moment. *He is just like my husband. He's the image of him, may he live and be well.* But I felt that I deserved to be cut up, like these potatoes. After all, I had fooled my mother, and fooled her so miserably. I had sold my beautiful

Siddur and lost the money playing *dreydl.* I had sold myself from top to toe.

The wicks of my Hanuka lights smoked in the potatoes; they flickered until they were extinguished.

"Go wash your hands, and we'll eat some potatoes with goosefat," Mama said. "In honor of Hanuka I bought a jar of fresh, delicious goosefat."

Overjoyed, I washed myself, and we sat down at the table.

"It's a custom to make pancakes the last day of Hanuka," Mama sighed.

I thought of Benny's pancakes and of his *dreydl,* which cost me a fortune. I felt a stab in my heart, as though a needle had pierced me. But most of all, my heart ached over my Siddur and I regretted what I had done

Even in my sleep my thoughts gave me no peace. I constantly heard my mother sighing and wringing her hands. I heard her bed creaking, but I fancied it was groaning. Outside, the wind blew; it rattled the windows, tore at the roof, whistled in the chimney, and expired with a lengthy moan.

A cricket that had long nested in the wall chirped away. Mama did not stop sighing, groaning, and wringing her hands. Her every sigh and groan pained my heart. I could scarcely control myself. I wanted to jump out of bed, go up to her, fall at her feet, kiss her hand, and confess all my great sins. But instead, I covered myself with all my clothing so as not to hear Mama sighing and moaning and her bed creaking. I shut my eyes. The wind whistled and wailed. The cricket chirped. Something that looked like a *dreydl* whirled before me, in the guise of a person, someone I knew. I could have sworn it was the rebbi with his pointed skullcap. Pentateuch in hand, he stood spinning on one leg like a *dreydl.* The pointed skullcap glinted and shimmered before my eyes, and his earlocks twirled in the air. No, it wasn't the rebbi. It was the *dreydl.* How odd! A live *dreydl* with a pointed skullcap and earlocks. Little by little, the rebbi-*dreydl* stopped spinning. In his stead appeared the Pharaoh of Egypt, about whom we had just been studying the week before Hanuka. Pharaoh stood naked before me, as though he had just emerged from the Nile, and held my Siddur in his hand. My honest-to-goodness, all-inclusive, encyclopedic, everything-in-it little Siddur. I couldn't understand how this evil, wicked man who bathed in Jewish blood had got hold of my little Siddur. I saw seven emaciated cows—bundles of skin and bones with long horns and big ears. They all marched toward me. One after another they opened their mouths, ready to swallow me. Suddenly Benny appeared, my best pal Benny. He gave their ears a good, long tweak. Someone cried quietly, sighed and wept, groaned, whistled, and chirped. Then someone stood next to me and said softly:

"Tell me, son, when is my *yohrzeit?* When will you say Kaddish for me?"

I assumed it was my father from the other world, about whom Mama had told me so many good things. I wanted to tell him when his *yohrzeit* was and when I would say Kaddish for him. But I forgot. At that very moment I forgot. I racked my brains, rubbed my forehead, wanted to remember but could not. Did you ever hear such a thing? I forgot the date of my father's *yohrzeit.* Help, Jewish children! Do you know when is my father's *yohrzeit?* Why don't you answer me? Help! Help! Help!

"What's the matter? What are you yelling for? What's the tumult about? Is something hurting you, God forbid?"

Naturally, this was my mother speaking. She stood over me, holding my hand. I felt her tremble and shiver. The dim lamp smoked and gave off little light. I saw Mama's shadow fluttering on the wall. The edges of her kerchief looked like two horns. Her eyes glittered in the dark.

"When is Papa's *yohrzeit?* Tell me, Mama."

"What's the matter with you? You just celebrated it. Did you have a nightmare? Spit three times, *tfu, tfu, tfu.* May it not harm you! Amen, amen, amen!"

Dear children! I grew up and became a young man. Benny, too, grew up and became a young man with a yellow beard. He developed a huge paunch, which he draped with a golden chain. Benny was apparently a rich man. Once he had been a rich man's son; now he was a rich man himself.

We met in the train. I recognized him on account of his fish-like popeyes and his gap teeth. We had not seen each other in ages. We grabbed each other, embraced and kissed, and began recalling good old times. We recounted the sweet and pleasant years of childhood and all the foolishness of the past.

"Benny, do you remember that Hanuka when you had so much luck with the *dreydl?* It always landed on G."

I looked at Benny and saw him turning colors, exploding with laughter. He held his sides. He was in stitches. He practically choked with laughter.

"What's the matter, Benny? Why the sudden laughter?"

"Oh"—he waved his hands—"don't mention that *dreydl!* That was some *dreydl!* Oh, what an amazing *dreydl* it was! A gem, a beauty, a divine little thing. With a *dreydl* like that it was hard to lose. Whichever way it landed, it had to land—ha, ha, ha—on G."

"What kind of *dreydl* was it, Benny?"

"It was a *dreydl*—ha, ha, ha—with no . . . other . . . letters . . . only G's. . . ."

ROBBERS!

1

"Is he still snoring away?"

"Like a saw."

"Blast him!"

"Let's wake him up!"

"Hey, Leib Blubber Drubber!"

"Rise and shine, my little sweetie pie."

"And open up your sleepy eye."

I tore open my lids, raised my head, and looked all around. The first rays of the bright morning sun streamed into the room. Beneath the open window I saw a pack of mischief-makers, my pals from *kheder*, their eyes agleam. I blinked, looking from side to side.

"Just look at him staring."

"Like a sinner."

"Don't you recognize us?"

"Forgot today's Lag B'Omer?"

Aha! Lag B'Omer. . . . The word shot through me like a bolt of lightning. Burned, I leaped out of bed. In a flash I was on my feet and, a minute later, was dressed, washed, and ready. I approached my mother, who was busy with breakfast and with the smaller children.

"Mama, today's Lag B'Omer!"

"*Gut yontev!* What do you want?"

"Give me something for the party."

"What should I give you," said Mama, "my troubles or my pains?" Nevertheless, she was willing to give me something. We even bargained. I wanted more. She offered less. I wanted two eggs.

"A headache is what you'll get," she replied.

So I got angry.

So she slapped me. Twice.

I began to cry.

She wanted to make up and gave me an apple.

I wanted an orange, too.

"You greedy guts! What will you think of next?"

My pals, standing outside, pestered the life out of me.

"Coming or not?"

"Hey, Leib Blubber Drubber."

"Hurry up."

"Make it snappy."

After a lengthy struggle with Mama I finally prevailed. I grabbed a bit of breakfast and the party snacks and ran out into the bright, warm outdoors. In high spirits, my friends and I ran gleefully down the hill to the *kheder*.

2

Pandemonium had broken loose in *kheder*. The kids were raising the roof. Twenty of them were all jabbering at once. The table was loaded with a variety of goodies. Our Lag B'Omer party had never before been such a success. We even had whiskey and wine. Thanks to our pal Berl, whose father was Yosl the wine maker. Berl contributed a bottle of aged whiskey and also brought two bottles of vintage wine made by Yosl himself. The whiskey his father had given him. The wine Berl had swiped.

"What do you mean, swiped?"

"Is it so hard to understand, you dunderhead?" Berl said. "I quietly lifted it from the shelf when no one was looking."

"What do you mean? In other words, you stole it!"

"Wise guy! So what of it?"

"What do you mean, what of it? What about the commandment 'Thou shalt not steal'?"

"I did it in honor of our holiday feast, you ass!"

"Then it's a pious duty to steal?"

"Sure!" Berl said. "Hey, give a look at this two-bit preacher."

"Which text allows it?"

"He wants me to quote book, chapter, and verse."

"Tell him it's written in the Book of Trigonometry."

"In the Chapter on Sharp Angles."

"Published by Hook and Crook."

Everyone roared with laughter.

"Pipe down, fellas. Here comes Mazeppa."

Suddenly everyone fell silent, as though reciting the silent devotion. We all sat around the table like mummies, good as gold, suddenly mute, and innocent as lambs.

3

Our teacher was called Mazeppa. Actually, his real name was Borukh-Moshe. But since he had recently come to us from the village of Mazepevka, our townspeople labeled him the Mazepevker. We *kheder* boys shortened it to Mazeppa. And if *kheder* boys crown a man with such a dandy nickname, he no doubt well deserves it.

Mazeppa was short, thin, and wrinkled. An ugly monster. There wasn't even a trace of a beard, mustache, or eyebrows on his face. Not that he shaved them off, God forbid. The hairs were stubborn; they simply refused to grow. But his lips and nose more than made up for this lack of hair. Boy, what a nose he had! It was a banana, a *shofar*. And his voice—a foghorn. He roared like a lion, bellowed like an ox. Why was such a puny creature blessed with so fearsome a voice box? And where did he get such strength? When he took hold of you with his thin, icy fingers, you got a glimpse of the world to come. When he smacked you, you felt it for three days running. He hated lengthy chitchats. Even for the slightest incident—whether you were guilty or not—he ordered you to lie down for a whipping.

"Rebbi, Yosl-Yakov hit me."

"Lie down."

"Rebbi, that's a lie. He kicked me first."

"Lie down."

"Rebbi, Khaim-Berl stuck his tongue out at me."

"Lie down."

"Rebbi, that's a downright lie. It was *he* who thumbed his nose at *me*."

"Lie down. . . ."

And you had to lie down. There was no way out. Don't you think that even Eli the Redhead, already Bar Mizvah, engaged, and owner of a silver pocket watch, got the taste of the strap? And how he did!

Eli declared that the beatings Mazeppa dished out would come back to haunt him. Someday he'd settle accounts with Mazeppa so that he'd never forget it to his dying day.

That's what Eli said after each beating. To which we added, "Amen. So be it. From your mouth to God's ears."

4

After prayers with Mazeppa (he didn't let us pray by ourselves—he knew that without him we'd skip more than half the pages), he roared in his lion's voice:

"Well, children, let's wash up now and sit down to the festive meal. And after grace I'll let you go for a hike."

Actually, we usually had the Lag B'Omer party on the other side of town. We sat on the ground in the fresh air, under God's open sky, and threw bread crumbs to the birds so that they too might enjoy the spirit of Lag B'Omer. But one didn't dillydally too long with Mazeppa. When he said, "Sit down," we sat down. Otherwise, he might tell us to *lie* down.

We said the blessing over the bread, and Mazeppa wished us a hearty appetite.

"Come join us," we mumbled, for courtesy's sake.

"Eat hearty," he told us. "I won't eat anything, but I think I'll say the blessing over a drop or two. What have you got in the bottle, whiskey?" He stretched his wrinkled hand and with his thin fingers took hold of the whiskey bottle. After pouring himself a tumbler, he tasted it, then screwed up his face and lips. We had to be made out of steel to keep a straight face.

"Mighty good stuff. Whose is it?" he asked and poured himself some more. "So help me, not a bad bit of brew." He took a third glass and drank to our health.

"*L'khayim,* children. God grant us long life and . . . What've you got for a chaser? . . . Have you got something that I can sink my teeth into? Well, never mind. I'll wash my hands and in honor of Lag B'Omer join you for the festive meal. . . ."

What had happened to our rebbi? He wasn't the same old Mazeppa. He was talkative, in good humor. His cheeks were flushed, his nose red, and his eyes shining. He chewed and spoke and pointed to the bottles of wine.

"What sort of wine is that? Seems to be Passover wine. [He tasted some, grimaced.] Wow! Strong as anything. [He drank.] So help me, I haven't had wine like this in ages. [He turned to the winemaker's son with a laugh.] The devil take your father's cellar, ha, ha. I see that he has plenty of barrels, an infinite supply, the finest vintage wines, and from pure raisins, too. Here's to you! *L'khayim,* children. . . . God grant that you become pious, upright Jews and that you . . . that you . . . open up the second bottle. . . . Take a drink. Each of you. Why don't you? God grant that [he licked his mouth and his eyes became drowsy] that . . . that . . . all Israel be blessed with everything. . . ."

5

"So we, um, have now fulfilled our pious obligation by eating the festive meal for Lag B'Omer. What's next, huh?" Mazeppa said after we had eaten and said grace. His voice was thick and hesitant.

"Next is the hike."

"Huh? The hike? Excellent. Where to?"

"To the Black Woods."

"Huh? The Black Woods? Excellent. I'll join you. Going for a walk in the woods is very good, very healthy. Because a forest— Listen and I'll tell you all about the forest. . . ."

We passed the town limits. First, we felt a bit strange that our rebbi was with us. But shh! Mazeppa walked in our midst, gesticulating and explaining the concept of a forest.

"The nature of a forest, you see—that is, the Almighty has created a forest to be full of trees, and on them—I mean the trees—there are supposed to be branches, which sprout leaves —green ones, that is—that smell good and give off a fine, pungent aroma."

Mazeppa inhaled deeply the delicious, pungent aroma, even though we were still far from the forest and its sweet smells.

"Well? Why the silence?" the rebbi said. "Say something nice. Sing a song. Come on! I too was a little rascal once, just like you, ha-ha! I also had a rebbi like you, ha-ha!"

The fact that Mazeppa had once been a rascal like us and had had a rebbi like us struck us as very odd. Almost unbelievable. Mazeppa a rascal? We exchanged glances and snickered quietly. We imagined our rebbi Mazeppa as a little rascal who had a rebbi who used to. . . . But we were afraid to imagine such a thing. . . . Only Eli stood up and asked him:

"Rebbi? Did your teacher whip you, too, as you whip us?"

"Whipping isn't even the word for it." Mazeppa laughed.

We looked at the rebbi, then at one another, and came to a silent understanding. We laughed along with him until we were beyond the village, in the wide-open meadow, not far from the Black Woods.

6

What a pleasure to be in the meadow! A veritable paradise. Sweet-smelling green grass. White flowers. Yellow blossoms. Green sprouts. The blue sky cap stretched infinitely above us. Before us was the forest, garbed in its holiday best. Chirping birds hopped from one branch to another. Thus, they welcomed us and greeted us in honor of our lovely holiday, Lag

B'Omer. As protection from the burning sun, we sought shade under a thick tree. We all sat down, with the rebbi in our midst.

The hike had exhausted Mazeppa. He plopped down on the ground and stretched out on his back. His eyes fluttered. His voice was thick and blurry.

"You're dear, lovely children. Pure gold . . . Jewish children . . . saints . . . I love you. And you love me. . . . Isn't it true that you love me?"

"Like a headache," Eli answered.

"What? I know you love me," the rebbi said.

"May God love you as much," Eli said.

Frightened, we asked Eli, "What are you doing?"

"Dunderheads." Eli laughed. "What are you scared of? Don't you see he's in his cups?"

"Huh?" the rebbi said, one eye open (the other was already asleep). "What's that you say? . . . Saints. . . . All of you. Saints. . . . On the contrary . . . a pleasure. . . . The protector of Israel . . . srr . . . srrr. . . ."

And so our teacher fell into a sweet doze, snoring with gusto, sounding like a ram's horn deep in the forest. We all sat around him, feeling melancholy.

"Is this our rebbi? Is this the creature whose look scares us so? Is this Mazeppa?"

7

"Fellows," Eli said. "What are we sitting here for like a bunch of clunks? Let's think up some punishment for Mazeppa!"

A fear fell over us.

"What are you afraid of, you dumb blockheads?" said Eli again. "Right now he's like a dead man. A corpse."

We became even more frightened.

"Now we can do what we like with him," Eli continued. "All winter long he beat us like a bunch of sheep. At least this once let's take our revenge."

"What do you want to do to him?"

"Nothing. Just scare him a bit."

"How are you going to scare him?"

"You'll soon see," said Eli. He rose, went to the teacher, removed his belt, and announced, "You see! We'll tie him to the tree with his belt so that he won't be able to free himself. Then one of us will go up to him and shout right in his ear, 'Rebbi, robbers!'"

"So what'll happen?"

"Nothing. We'll run away, and he'll yell for help."

"How long will he yell?"

"Till he gets used to it."

Without pondering too long, Eli took the belt and tied both of Mazeppa's hands to the tree. We stood by and watched, shivering with fright.

"Is that our rebbi? Is this the creature whose look scares us so? Is this Mazeppa?"

"Why are you standing there like a bunch of scarecrows?" Eli said. "If God has performed a miracle for us and put Mazeppa in our hands, let's break into a jig."

Joining hands, we all sang and danced and capered in a circle around our rebbi.

"And thus concludes this portion of our prayer service," said Eli, parodying a chant. We stopped dancing. Eli went right up to the rebbi, bent down, and shouted so loudly into his ear it could have waked a dead man.

"Help, rebbi! Robbers. . . . Robbers. . . . Robbers!"

8

Swift as an arrow we all ran away, afraid of even stopping for a moment or turning for a backward glance. A pall fell over us all, even Eli, although he didn't stop yelling at us:

"Idiots! Lame-brains! Animals! Why are you running?"

"Why are *you* running?"

"Because *you* are."

We burst into the village with the cry: "Robbers!"

Seeing us running, the villagers ran along, too.

"Why the running?" they were asked.

"How should we know? Everyone's running, so we're running, too."

Finally, one of us managed to stop. Then we all stopped, still shouting, "Robbers! Robbers!"

"Where? Where?"

"There. In the Black Woods. Robbers attacked us. Tied the rebbi to the tree. God knows if he's still alive."

9

If you're jealous that we're on vacation and released from *kheder* (for the rebbi is sick), your envy is all in vain. Absolutely in vain. No one can feel the pinch in another man's shoe. No one, absolutely no one, knows who the real robbers were. We boys hardly saw one another. When we met, the first thing we asked was: "How's the rebbi?" (we no longer call him Mazeppa). And when we prayed, we prayed to God for the rebbi and cried softly, "Lord of the Universe, God Almighty. . . ."

And Eli? Don't ask about Eli, blast him—may his name be blotted out.

Epilogue

When the rebbi recovered (he had been delirious for six weeks and had babbled about robbers), we returned to *kheder*. But he had changed so radically we hardly recognized him. His lion's roar was gone. His leather strap—lost. He no longer told us to lie down. He was no longer the old Mazeppa. A gentle melancholy had come over his face. A feeling of regret stole into us. Mazeppa suddenly became very dear to us, rooted into our hearts. Ah, if only he would scold us! If only he would say a nasty word to us as if nothing had happened!

Suddenly, in the middle of the lesson, he stopped and asked us to tell him once more the whole story of the Lag B'Omer robbers. We weren't lazy and told him the whole story by heart—how robbers had suddenly come out of the forest, attacked him, tied him up and intended to kill him with a knife, and how we had rushed back to the village and saved him with our cries for help.

With closed eyes the rebbi listened till we had finished our story. Then he sighed and asked again:

"Are you sure they were robbers?"

"What else could they have been?"

"Perhaps a pack of pranksters?"

The rebbi stared out into the distance, and we fancied we saw a sly smile hovering on his strangely thick lips.

ESTHER

1

If the Biblical Queen Esther was as beautiful as the Esther of my story, it's no wonder that King Ahasuerus fell in love with her. Everyone adored Esther. She was the rebbi's daughter, and everyone loved her. Everyone. Including me. Including my older brother, Mottel.* Despite the fact that he was already past Bar Mizvah, wore a pocket watch with a chain, had long been fair game for the matchmakers, and even had the first hint of a beard.

Want to know all about Mottel's love for Esther? Ask me for the details. Every Sabbath afternoon Mottel went to the rebbi's *kheder*, supposedly to study the Ethics of the Fathers with him. But Mottel wasn't aware that I suspected anything. While the rebbi snored away to the beat of the band; while the rebbi's wife gossiped outside with the women; and while we *kheder* boys played all kinds of games, Mottel and Esther were busy gazing at each other. He at her and she at him.

Sometimes we used to play blindman's buff. Do you know what that is? I'll tell you exactly. It's a game. A person is blindfolded and then led to the middle of the room, whereupon everyone walks around him, shouting, "Hey, hey—catch me!"

Mottel and Esther also played with us. They adored blindman's buff. I know why, too. They liked the game because it gave them a chance to chase and catch each other. He her, she him.

---

* Mottel: a common diminutive for Modecai—Tr.

And I have other evidence of their affection which I could talk to you about for hours. But I'm not that sort of chap.

Once I caught them holding hands. He hers, she his. Mind you, not on the Sabbath. On a plain weekday. At twilight. Between the afternoon and the evening service. Mottel was supposedly going to *shul*. But happened to stray into our *kheder*.

"Where's the rebbi?" Mottel asked.

"He's not here," we replied.

Then Mottel walked over and wanted to hold her hand. Esther's, that is. I stood there and watched. She took her hand away. He gave me a kopeck not to breathe a word of it.

"Two," I said.

He gave me two.

So I said, "Three.'

He gave me three. Don't you think he would have given me four if I had asked for four? And five? And six? But I'm not that sort of chap.

2

My big brother Mottel no longer studied in *kheder*. Nevertheless, he didn't want to study at home either. That's why the only name Father had for him was wild savage. But Mama could not stand that kind of talk.

"What sort of business is this, calling a grown youth about to be engaged a wild savage?"

"Makes no difference. He's still a wild savage," said Father.

Soon they were quarreling. I don't know about other parents, but mine were always fighting. Day and night. Bickering all the time. If I were to tell you about my parents' fighting, you'd be in stitches. But I'm not that sort of chap.

In short, my brother Mottel no longer attended *kheder*. Yet he never forgot to send the rebbi a Purim gift. After all, Mottel had once been his pupil. So he sent him a beautiful Hebrew poem, decorated with the Star of David, along with a gift of two rubles. And whom did he choose to deliver such a Purim gift? Me, naturally.

"Here, take this to the rebbi," my brother told me, "and when you come back, I'll give you ten kopecks."

Since ten kopecks was a small fortune, I had no complaints. So what was the snag?

"I want cash in advance."

"You're a rascal," my brother said.

"You may be right," I replied. "I won't dispute the point. But I want to see cash on the line."

Guess who won?

After paying me, he gave me a sealed envelope containing the rebbi's present. As I was about to leave, he slipped another envelope into my hand and whispered quickly:

"Give this to Esther."

"Esther?"

"Yes, Esther."

Anyone else in my shoes would have doubled the price then and there. But I'm not that sort of chap.

3

While on my way, I thought: Good Lord, what can my brother possibly be writing to the rebbi's daughter? Come what may, I must have a look. No more than a quick peek. It won't harm them a bit.

I opened the envelope addressed to Esther and read a lengthy epistle, based on the Megillah.* Listen, here it is, word for word:

> *There was a certain Jew in the capital city of Shushan*—that is, there was an unmarried lad in our village . . . *whose name was Mordecai*—called Mottel . . . *and he brought up*—he loved . . . *Hadassah, that is, Esther*—a girl named Esther. . . . *And the maiden*—the girl . . . *was of beautiful form*—was very pretty . . . *and fair to look on*—and lovely to behold. . . .

---

* Megillah, a scroll; often used in reference to the Book of Esther which is written on a scroll—Tr.

And the maiden pleased him—he was attracted to her. . . .
Esther did not make known—Esther didn't tell a soul . . . *for*
Mordecai—that is, Mottel . . . *had charged her*—ordered her
. . . *not to tell it*—not to breathe a word. . . . *And daily*—
every single day . . . *Mordecai walked*—Mottel passed by . . .
to know how Esther was faring—to take a peek at Esther. . . .
Now when the turn of Esther had come—when the time for
Esther would come to marry . . . *Esther was taken*—he will
take Esther. . . . *And he made her Queen instead of Vashti*—
and he will take her under the bridal canopy.

Well, how do you like the way my brother Mottel interpreted the Megillah? I was dying to know how the rebbi would
react to Mottel's commentary. But how could this be done?
Wait! I had a brilliant idea. I'd pull a switch. I'd give Esther
the Hebrew poem addressed to the rebbi; and the rebbi, the
epistle for Esther. Let the rebbi have some fun. Of course,
there'd be a big to-do later. But no fault of mine, right? Don't
mistakes happen? In fact, doesn't the mailman occasionally fail
to deliver a letter altogether? But that sort of thing I'd never
do. Not me. I'm not that sort of chap.

4

"*Gut yontev*, rebbi." I burst into the *kheder*, startling the
rebbi. "My brother sends you this Purim gift and wishes
you good health and long life."

I handed him the Megillah, which he opened, looked at,
and inspected from all sides. He was obviously expecting
something else.

Keep on looking, I thought, and you'll surely find something.

My rebbi put on his silver-rimmed spectacles, read the Megillah, but didn't even bat an eyelash. His only reaction was a
slight sigh.

"Wait," he said. "I'm going to write a little note."

Meanwhile, I wandered around the *kheder*. The rebbi's
wife gave me a piece of honeycake and some strudel, and while
no one was looking, I quickly slipped the envelope contain-

ing the rebbi's poem and the two-ruble gift into Esther's hand. She blushed, hid in a corner, and gently opened the letter. At once her face flamed, and her eyes burned with fury. Seems like she's not too pleased with the Purim gift, I thought, and went up to the rebbi to take the little note he had composed.

"*Gut yontev,* rebbi. Good health and long life," I blurted out, just as I did upon entering—and took off for home.

No sooner had I closed the door than Esther ran after me, her eyes red and full of tears.

"Here," she said angrily, "give this to your brother."

On my way home I opened the rebbi's letter first, for his was more interesting. Here's what it said:

My dear and faithful pupil, Mordecai, may your light shine forth!

I thank you very much for the Purim gift you have just sent me. Last year and two years ago you sent me tangible gifts. This year you sent me a new exegesis to the Megillah. I thank you for this Megillah. But I must inform you, Mottel, that your interpretation doesn't please me at all. First of all, Shushan is the capital city of Persia, and not our village. Secondly, where is it written that Mordecai was unmarried? And why do you call him Mottel? How does Mottel fit in here? And how can you interpret "Brought up" as "loved"? "Brought up" means that he raised her. And your interpretation "he will take her under the bridal canopy" for *"and he made her Queen instead of Vashti"* is absolutely mad, without rhyme or reason.

First of all, the phrase *"and he made her Queen"* refers to Ahasuerus, not Mordecai. Second, there is no mention in the Megillah that Ahasuerus actually brought Esther under the bridal canopy. It's easy, isn't it, to take a Biblical verse and pervert it like a lunatic? Every interpretation should be sensible. Last year and two years ago I received more than just a letter from you. This year the spirit moved you to send me an exegesis on the Megillah, and a strange one at that. Well, so be it—perhaps that's the way it should be. I am therefore returning your Megillah. May God grant you a good year.

Best wishes,
From your rebbi

That's what I call a first-class rebuff. And it served Mottel right. I had a feeling he wouldn't write such Megillahs anymore.

After finishing the rebbi's letter, I also had an urge to read Esther's letter. So I opened it—and guess what? Two rubles fluttered out. What sort of plague was this? I read the letter—a mere four lines.

> Mottel, I thank you for the two rubles. You can have them back. I didn't expect this kind of Purim present from you. I didn't ask for any presents, and I certainly don't want any donations. . . .

What do you say to that? She didn't want donations. I swear, what a beautiful story! Well, what next? Anyone else in my shoes would have taken both letters, ripped them up, and pocketed the money. He would have brought home two horse-laughs instead of two rubles. But not me. I'm not that sort of chap. I pulled off a neater trick. Listen to this. I decided that since I'd already been paid for my trouble, I didn't need my brother Mottel anymore. So I handed over both letters to my father. Out of sheer curiosity. Just to hear what he'd say. He'd appreciate the Megillah much more than the rebbi, despite the fact that Father was only a layman and not a learned man like the rebbi.

5

What happened when Father read the two letters and the Megillah, and began to cross-examine Mottel and ask him for an explanation? Don't ask! To properly imitate Mottel, I'd have to quote the Megillah:

"And the city of the Shushan was perplexed. . . ."

But that's not the main part of the story. You probably want to hear what the upshot was. What happened to the rebbi's daughter, Esther, and to my brother Mottel? What should have happened? Nothing. Esther got married. To a widower.

Oh, how she wept. I attended her wedding. Come to think of it, I don't know why she cried so much. Apparently her heart told her that with him she would not live to a ripe old age. And that's precisely what happened. Six months later she died. From what, I can't say. I don't know. In fact, no one knew. The rebbi and his wife didn't know either. Some said she poisoned herself. Simply took poison and killed herself. But that's a lie.

"A tale concocted by our enemies," I heard the rebbi's wife say.

What about my brother Mottel? He married and moved to his father-in-law's house even before Esther had become engaged. But he quickly returned. And alone, too. What happened? He wanted a divorce.

"You're a wild savage!" Father told Mottel.

Mama couldn't stand that kind of talk. So they had a fight. What fun! But it didn't do any good. Mottel divorced his wife and married someone else. He even has two kids now. A boy and a girl.

The boy was named Herzl, after Dr. Theodor Herzl. The girl was called Esther. Father had insisted that the girl be named Gitl, after his mother, Grandma Gitl. And Mama was dying to have her named Leah, after *her* mother, Grandma Leah. So Mama and Father had another fight. They fought all night and all day. Then they finally decided to name the girl Leah-Gitl. After both grandmas. Period! At which Father decided he didn't approve of Leah-Gitl.

"How come?"

"Just like that," Father said. "Why should her mother's name go first?"

Then my brother Mottel came from *shul* and announced that he had named the baby Esther.

"You wild savage!" Father cried. "Where did you dig that name up from?"

"Have you forgotten that Purim is around the corner?" Mottel replied.

Well, how does one respond to that? So that finished it.

Henceforth, Father no longer used the term "wild savage." But both my parents exchanged odd glances and suddenly fell silent.

I haven't the faintest idea what those glances and the sudden silence meant. Perhaps *you* have.

PITY FOR LIVING CREATURES

[Recollections of a Foolish Boy]

1

"Be a good boy," Mama told me on the eve of Shevuos, "and help us grate the horseradish." It was noontime, and Mama was preparing the dairy meal and helping the cook scrape fish scales.

The fish thrashed about in a big, water-filled tub. Most energetic was a red-eyed, potbellied little carp. The poor thing desperately wanted to return to the river. He leaped out of the glazed, earthen tub, opened his round mouth, slapped his tail, and splashed water at me. "Help me, little boy. . . . Save me!"

I wiped my face and began grating horseradish for the holiday. Poor little carp, I thought. I can't do a thing for you. Soon they'll set to work on *you*. They'll scrape your scales off, slit your belly, and clean your guts out. Then they'll cut you to pieces, season you and cook you till you're done.

"It's a pity," I told Mama. "A pity for living creatures."

"A pity for which living creatures?"

"The fish."

"Who told you this?"

"My teacher, the rebbi."

"The rebbi?" she said and exchanged glances with the cook. They both burst out laughing.

"You're a fool, but your rebbi is a bigger one." She laughed. "Just keep grating the horseradish."

That I was a fool I knew quite well. Mama was always tell-

ing me this. Father, too. My brother also. And my sisters as
well. But the fact that my rebbi was a bigger fool than I—*that*
was news to me.

2

Once, when I was visiting my friend Pinele the *shokhet*'s son,
a young girl brought in a huge purebred rooster with his feet
tied. Since my friend's father was sleeping, the girl sat waiting
by the door. The rooster, a cocky, spunky young thing, was
straining to escape. He pressed her stomach with his powerful
legs, pecked at her hand, gave out a throaty cock-a-doodle-doo,
and protested with all his might. But the girl was no dumbbell.
She tucked the rooster's head under her arm, poked him continually with her elbow, and muttered:

"Sit there and choke."

The rooster obeyed and sat there, choking.

Later, when the *shokhet* awoke, he washed his hands, took
his knife, and with a silent gesture asked for the bird. I saw the
rooster get a new lease on life. He apparently thought they intended to unbind his feet and let him return to his hens, millet,
and water trough. Instead, the *shokhet* put him between his
legs, pulled back his head with one motion, and with another
plucked out a few feathers. He graced the bird with a blessing
and—*swishhh*—passed the knife across his throat. The *shokhet*
poured a bit of blood into the ashes on the ground and flung
the rooster away so forcefully I thought he'd be smashed to
pieces.

"Pini, your father's a *goy*," I said.

"Why is he a *goy?*"

"Because he doesn't have pity for living creatures."

"I never knew you were such a sage," Pini said, thumbing
his nose right in my face.

3

Our cook was blind in one eye. Everyone called her Frume
One-eyes. The lass was absolutely heartless. She once beat the

cat with nettles because she thought it had nabbed a chicken liver from the salting board. But when Frume took inventory, she realized her mistake. She had assumed there were seven chickens. Which meant *seven* livers. But since she had only *six* chickens to begin with, there could be only *six* livers. It was a miracle! She had suspected the cat in vain.

You'd think that Frume would have taken it to heart and begged the cat's pardon. Rubbish! She forgot about it immediately. So did the cat. For a couple of hours later it sat quite unconcernedly on the stove, licking itself clean, as though nothing at all had happened. No wonder folks say sarcastically —so and so's got the brains of a cat.

But *I* didn't forget. Not at all.

"You beat the cat for nothing," I told Frume One-eyes. "You sinned for no good reason. You ought to have pity for living creatures. God will punish you."

"Get out of here, or I'll smack your face with this dish towel," said Frume. "God Almighty! Where do such foolish children come from?"

4

The following incident concerns a dog that Frume One-eyes had scalded with boiling water. Oh, was that dog in pain! He screeched, yelped, and barked something awful, complaining to beat the band. The entire village came running to gaze at this strange sight and promptly went into stitches. All the other dogs in town responded from their trash heaps, each according to his means, as if asked to give an opinion. Later, when the scalded dog had had his fill of shrieking, he howled, barked, licked his burned hide, and whimpered softly. It touched me to the quick. I approached and wanted to pat him.

"There, there, Sirko."

Seeing my raised hand, the dog scrambled up as though scalded again, flicked up his tail, and scampered away.

"Stop, Sirko." I tried to calm him with tender words. "Why are you running away, you silly goose? I won't hurt you."

But a dog's a dog. Has no sense. Knows nothing about the precept of pity for living creatures.

When Father saw me fooling around with the dog, he really gave it to me.

"Get to *kheder*, you dog whipper."

All of a sudden *I* was the dog whipper!

5

This story is about two little birds. A pair of birds stoned by two peasant boys. When the birds fell to the ground, they were still alive. Their feathers were in disarray, and they shook and trembled all over.

"Move, you idiot," said the bigger one to his smaller friend, and they picked up the wounded birds. Then, the same way we beat the willow twigs against the prayer stand on Hoshana Rabba, the two boys smashed the birds' heads against a tree until they died.

I couldn't bear it any longer and ran over to them. "What are you doing?" I said.

"What do you care?" They shrugged. "They're only birds, plain old birds."

"So what if they're only birds? Don't you have any pity for them? Don't you have any pity for living creatures?"

Both boys exchanged odd glances. And as though they'd planned it in advance, they began to work me over.

When I came home, my tattered coat told the entire story, and I got my just reward.

"You crazy fool," Father yelled.

That epithet didn't bother me. But why the smacks?

6

Why did I get smacked? Didn't the rebbi himself tell me that God loves all His creatures? One shouldn't even annoy a fly on the wall, he declared, because of the precept of pity for living creatures. One shouldn't kill even a harmful spider. For when the hour of death comes, the rebbi explained, God

Himself will take its life. Well and good. But the problem remained: Why were oxen, calves, sheep, and fowl killed every day? And not only animals, beasts, and birds—didn't human beings kill one another? During the pogrom weren't children and infants thrown from the roofs? Wasn't our neighbor's daughter Perele killed in a most cruel manner? Ah, how I loved that child! And how she loved me! She used to call me Uncle Beh-beh-beh—my name is Velvele—and pull my nose with her tiny fingers.

Since then everyone calls me Uncle Beh-beh-beh.

"There goes Uncle Beh-beh-beh," the people used to say to her. "He'll pick you up, Perele."

7

Perele was a sickly child. I mean, there was nothing really wrong with her. Except that she couldn't walk. Or stand or sit. She had to be carried out of the house. They would place her in the sand to sit in the sun. She adored the sun. Loved it. When I'd carry her, she'd put her sweet, thin, little fingers around my throat, press her little body to mine, lean her little head against me and say:

"Love Uncle Beh-beh-beh."

Our neighbor Kreni declared that she never could forget her daughter's phrase, "Uncle Beh-beh-beh." Each time she looked at me, Kreni said, she was reminded of Perele.

Mama scolded Kreni for crying. "One shouldn't cry," said Mama. "It's a sin to cry. One ought to forget . . . forget. . . ." Mama tried to console her.

Then Mama chased me away. "If you wouldn't be underfoot and go where you're not supposed to go," she said, "then people wouldn't remember things they ought not to remember."

Oh, my! How could one possibly forget? Sitting there in the kitchen, I thought of Perele. My eyes filled with tears, and I began to cry.

"Look at him, he's crying again, the little sage," Frume One-eyes called to Mama.

Mama cast a quick glance at me and burst out laughing.

"Did the horseradish get in your eyes? Ah, me, what strong horseradish! Forgot to tell him to close his eyes, woe is me! . . . Here's my apron. . . . Wipe your eyes, you foolish boy, and while you're at it, your nose . . . wipe your nose, too. . . ."

A LOST LAG B'OMER

1

Our rebbi, Nissel the Short (he was called that, you see, on account of his small stature), was led by the nose by his assistants, who did absolutely as they pleased. If the first assistant came along and declared that the children should be dismissed early, Nissel prepared to dismiss them early. If the other assistant came along and stated that the kids would run wild unless they were kept in *kheder*, Nissel kept them in school. He never thought of anything himself. That's why the assistants and not the rebbi prevailed over us. In other *kheders* the assistants washed the kids' hands, recited the blessing over bread with them, carried them over mud puddles on their backs, and brought their lunch pails to *kheder*. *Our* assistants were too lazy to wash our hands, recite the blessing, and carry us on their backs. But to offset all this, they loved to bring us our lunch pails—and gobble up the contents themselves. We couldn't complain to the rebbi, for the assistants scared us to death. They warned us that if anyone dared to say even boo to the rebbi, he'd be whipped and scalped. In fact, when one of the boys once snitched on an assistant, they thrashed him so mercilessly he was sick for an entire term. This gave fair warning to the others not to tattle on an assistant.

That era could well be called the Tyranny of the Assistants.

2

It happened during the period of tyranny. That year Lag B'Omer in Kasrilevke was wet and cold, one of those dreary

days that occasionally come at the beginning of May. The sun
made a halfhearted appearance, giving light but little warmth.
A cold wind, not at all springlike, blew clouds in from afar;
the wind snapped at your coattails and swirled underfoot.
Just then it struck our assistants' fancy to take us on a hike beyond the town limits and, as was the custom of Jewish children
on Lag B'Omer, pack a bagful of delicacies and have a field
war.

Another age-old tradition was that on Lag B'Omer Jewish
children became warlike. They packed food for the journey
and armed themselves from head to toe with wooden swords,
popguns, and bows and arrows and then went out into the open
field for mock battle. All year long the poor Jewish children
were cooped up in a dark, cramped *kheder*, bearing the yoke
of Torah studies, standing in dread of the rebbi and in awe of
the assistants' whips. But on Lag B'Omer they left for the field
of battle, fully armed. They imagined that they were heroes
who could take on the most ferocious foe and conquer the
world. Suddenly infused with courage, they took giant strides
and sang rhymes like:

> One, two, three, four,
> We study Torah more.
> Hear O Israel, have no fear,
> Because our God the Lord is near.

We maintained our old custom. We brought down last
year's wooden swords from the attic. We strung bows with the
metal bands from the Passover wine barrels. The assistants
provided us with popguns—for a fee, of course. But they were
so skillfully constructed they could actually shoot a fly, if only
the fly would sit still and wait for us to fire. We also had other
weapons, Jewish weapons that could scare only infants to
death. Our food supply was no trifle either. Everyone brought
what God had blessed him with and what his mother had
generously provided. On Lag B'Omer we came to *kheder*
armed from head to toe, our pockets stuffed with all sorts of
goodies: *khalle* and biscuits, goose fat and eggs, whiskey and

cherry brandy, chicken legs and hunks of duck, gizzards and livers, sweetened tea, nuts, oranges, and jams, as well as some kopecks in cash. Each of us wanted to outdo everyone else and bring the most of the best treats and get in good with the assistants. The assistants showered us with praise, declared we were topnotch lads, and swept our goodies into their sacks. They lined us up like troops and ordered:

"Hold hands, Jewish children, and march across the bridge to the meadow to meet the Sea Cats and wage war with them."

"Hurray, the Sea Cats," we all cried in unison. We joined hands and swiftly went forward, with the pride and confidence of authentic heroes.

3

We called the young primer pupils the Sea Cats because they were short little tots, just learning the *aleph-beys*. To those of us already studying the Torah these little kids looked like flies or ants. We fancied that we could demolish them with one huff. We felt certain that the minute they saw us armed from head to toe with swords, bows and arrows, and popguns, they would surely kick up their heels and run for the hills. Such stout warriors as we Torah students could not be dismissed lightly. The tiny primer tots were scared to death of us, afraid of even setting foot within sight of us. We Torah students were nothing to trifle with.

Actually, we had never fought the Sea Cats. But we were convinced that with one glance we would make rack and ruin of these little pipsqueaks and finish them off. In addition to making short shrift of them, we would take spoils of war— we would split up all their treats and let them go sue us.

Because of our stout hearts and great confidence in our own strength, we pushed one another forward and slapped one another's shoulders and backs, while the assistants urged us from behind to quicken our pace.

"Why are you crawling like bedbugs?" they asked. Yet they themselves frequently stopped to unpack their bags. They tasted the various goodies and praised our treats and cherry brandy.

"Excellent brandy," they said, passing the bottle around, guzzling—*glub, glub*—in great big gulps straight from the neck of the bottle. "Good stuff! Topnotch liquor!"

The assistants licked their fingers and lagged behind us, motioning to us from the distance to keep moving. Ever onward.

Although the wind grew sharper, we went farther and farther into the big meadow. Clouds darkened the sky, and a cold, heavy rain lashed our faces. Our hands swelled and turned blue with cold. Our soaked boots squished in the mud. We had already stopped singing. We were tired and hungry—starved, in fact. We decided to sit down to rest and grab a bite to eat.

"Where are the assistants?" one of us asked.

"The hell with them! It's the food we want! Where's the food?"

And the gang began to mutter complaints against the assistants.

"They have some nerve nabbing our gizzards and livers, biscuits and eggs, our bit of cherry brandy, and our few kopecks. The nerve of them, leaving us stranded here in the cold, in the deserted meadow, dead hungry. To hell with the assistants!"

"May they drop dead in their boots!"

"The plague strike all the assistants in the world!"

"May God get even with them!"

"Shh! Pipe down! Here comes our enemy! Here comes the foe!"

"Little pipsqueaks with big sticks."

"The Sea Cats. The Sea Cats."

"Hurray, here come the Sea Cats."

As soon as we spotted them, we let loose like hunger-maddened wolves, ready to trample them and tear them to pieces. However, tragedy struck. An awful tragedy, which no one could have foreseen. If something is not destined to be, neither wit, strength, nor skill are of any avail. Just listen to what happened.

4

Although the Sea Cats were midget-sized pipsqueaks just learning the *aleph-beys*, they were evidently no fools. Before they met us in the big meadow to do battle, they prepared themselves by training at home. Then they filled their bellies, stuffed their guts, took along warm clothing and rubber galoshes, and armed themselves from head to toe no worse than we, perhaps even better. They too had swords, bows and arrows, and popguns. They didn't wait for our offensive but attacked us first and began to break our bones. They bustled in on all sides so quickly we didn't even have a chance to look around and see what we were doing. We didn't notice at first that they weren't alone but were accompanied by their assistants, who incited them with cries of:

"Get even with those Torah lads. Clobber those long-legged louts."

Naturally, we didn't take this lying down. Like heroes, we faced the little pipsqueaks, slashing them with our swords; we drew our bows and aimed our popguns at them. But, alack and alas, our swords were as blunt as—wood. By the time we made a move with our bows and arrows, we were already on the defensive. I won't even talk about the popguns! What good were popguns if the enemy refused to wait until he was popped, but dashed toward you and, while you stood helplessly by, knocked the popguns out of your hands?

A bad fix! So we chucked away all our weapons—swords, bows and arrows, and popguns—and began to fight the way God intended us to fight—that is, we entered the fray with our hands and fists. The only trouble was that we were tired, hungry, and frozen. We fought with no order, no plan, and no leader, for our assistants had remained behind. They were in their cups, blast them, soused from our bit of cherry brandy. And with ever-increasing strength the little pipsqueaks, warmly dressed and stuffed to the gills, swarmed all over us from three sides. They beleaguered us with blows, slaps, and punches. The very same punches which we planned to dole out to them, they doled out to us. And their assistants were in the lead and never ceased inciting them.

"Get even with these Torah lads. Punch 'em, beat 'em—get those long-legged louts."

It's hard to determine who first turned tail to the enemy. I only know that we ran home helter-skelter with all our might, right back to Kasrilevke. And the little pipsqueaks, damn them, ran hot on our necks after us, hooting and jeering and laughing at us behind our backs:

"Down with the Torah lads, down with the long-legged louts!"

5

We came home tired, hungry, sleepy, tattered, beaten, licked, whipped, done for. We heroes figured that our parents would surely have pity on us and offer us some honeycake to ease the pain of our blows. But it turned out that we had been deluding ourselves. They hadn't even given us a thought. Thank God, we all escaped without a whipping for our torn jackets and ruined boots. But the next morning the rebbi, Reb Nissel the Short, gave it to us for the bruises on our foreheads and the blue shiners beneath our eyes. We were taken and—we're ashamed to admit—laid facedown, one by one, and whammed where we ought to be whammed. In other words, if you didn't have enough, here's some dessert for you.

But we were thoroughly disappointed with our assistants, may all trace of them perish from the earth! When parents punish a child, they do it perhaps out of a sense of duty. When a rebbi lays you down and whips you—well, that's what he's a rebbi for, and that's what the whip is for. But the assistants, blast them! Not enough that they glutted down all our treats, may the worms glut them down, dear God! Not enough that they left us alone to the mercy of God in the middle of the meadow, but during the whippings they even held our legs to prevent us from kicking and squirming around.

And that's how our Lag B'Omer festivities ended. It was a dark and gloomy holiday, a lost Lag B'Omer.

THE PENKNIFE

1

Listen, Jewish children, I'm going to tell you a story about a penknife. It's not a concocted tale, but a real one that actually happened to me. I never wanted anything as much as a penknife. There was no treasure in the world I wanted as badly as a knife to call my very own. I'd keep the knife in my pocket, take it out whenever I wished, and cut anything I wanted. And I'd tell my friends all about it. I had just begun to go to Yosl's *kheder* (he taught the youngest children), and I already had a knife. Well, it was almost a knife. I had actually made it myself. Plucked a goose feather from a feather duster, cut off one end, flattened the other, and pretended it was a knife that could cut.

"What sort of feather is this, the devil take it? What sort of business is this running around with feathers?" asked my father, a sickly man with a yellow, wizened face. "There's a fine how-do-you-do! Feathers! What nonsense!" And he fell into a fit of coughing.

"What do you care what the boy plays with?" said Mama, a short woman who wore a silk kerchief. "The man gets excited for nothing, a plague upon my enemies."

Later, when I moved up to the study of the Pentateuch with commentaries, I almost had a real knife, which I also made myself. I found a piece of steel in my mother's crinoline and ingeniously set it into a piece of wood. I diligently sharpened the steel on a pot—and, naturally, cut all my fingers.

"Just look at him. See how he's bloodied his fingers, your

pride and joy," Father shouted, grabbing me so forcefully that my bones rattled. "What a child!"

"A thunder strike me!" said Mama. She took the knife away and threw it into the oven, paying no heed to my tears. Now there'll be an end to it, woe unto me."

Nevertheless, I soon got myself another knife, this time a real honest-to-goodness knife. The wooden handle was round and potbellied; it looked like a barrel and had a bent blade that opened and closed. Want to know how I got it? I scraped up the capital by saving my breakfast money and bought the knife from Shlomo for ten kopecks—seven kopecks cash, three on credit.

How I loved that knife! How I adored it! I came home from school dead tired, hungry, sleepy, and beaten up. (You see, I had just begun studying with the Talmud teacher, Motti the Angel of Death. . . . We were on the chapter "An Ox That Gored a Cow." And since one animal bumped into another, naturally I had to get whacked.) First, I removed the little knife from under the black cupboard where I had hidden it. (I couldn't take it to school, and I didn't dare let anyone know that I had a knife at home.) After that, I smoothed and slit a piece of paper in two and sliced a straw in half. Then I cut my piece of bread into tiny pieces, speared them with the tip of my blade, and finally transferred the bread to my mouth.

Later, before going to sleep, I cleaned the knife, scoured and polished it, took the whetstone I had found in the attic, spit on it, and quietly set to work sharpening the blade.

Father, a skullcap on his head, was bent over a sacred text, studying and coughing, coughing and studying. Mother was in the kitchen, busy with the *khalle*. But I did not stop sharpening my little knife for an instant.

Suddenly Father jumped up, as though from sleep.

"Who's squeaking over there? What's going on? What are you doing, you apostate?"

He approached, bent over my whetstone, grabbed me by the ear, and fell into a fit of coughing.

"What is this? Knives?" Father coughed, taking the knife and the whetstone away from me. "What a young lout! Too lazy to pick up a book and study, hah?"

I began to wail. Father helped things along with a few smacks, and Mama, her sleeves rolled up, dashed in from the kitchen crying:

"Stop it! What's going on? Why are you hitting him? For goodness' sake, what have you got against the child? Oh, woe is me!"

"Knives," Father shouted and coughed. "A snip of a child. . . . What a lout. . . . Can't you pick up a book? . . . You're eight years old already. . . . I'll give you knives, you empty-headed scamp. . . . Knives all of a sudden!"

God Almighty, what did he have against my little knife? How had the little thing sinned against him? Why was he so angry?

My father, I remember, was almost constantly ill, always pale and yellow, and in a perpetual rage at the world. He blazed with anger at the most trivial thing and was ready to trample me. Luckily Mama kept a wary eye and saved me in the nick of time.

They threw my little penknife so far I couldn't even find it after an intensive eight-day search. I sincerely mourned my misshapen knife, my good little knife. How dark and bitter was my lot in *kheder!* I came home day after day with swollen cheeks, with red ears mercilessly tweaked by the hands of Motti the Angel of Death—all because an ox bumped into a cow. To whom could I turn? I was as lonely as an orphan without my misshapen knife. Absolutely no one was aware that I wept silently in bed after I came home from *kheder*. I had a quiet cry, dried my eyes, fell asleep, and returned to *kheder* the following morning to resume studying about the ox that gored the cow. Once again I'd catch the blows doled out by Motti the Angel of Death, and face Father's anger, his cough, and his curses. I had no moment of leisure, saw neither pleasant mien nor smiles. No one ever smiled at me. I was lonely and forlorn. All alone in the entire world.

2

A year, perhaps a year and a half, passed. I almost forgot that misshapen little penknife. But as it turned out, I was destined to be plagued by knives throughout my childhood. As ill luck would have it, another little penknife came into my life. It was brand-new. So help me, a beauty! There was nothing like it. It had a white bone handle, two expensive, razor-sharp steel blades, and it came in a brass case studded with red brass tacks. I tell you, it was out of this world. The best on the market.

How did I get hold of such an expensive penknife, an item which I couldn't possibly afford? Well, it's a long, sad, but interesting story. So listen carefully, please.

We had a lodger, a German Jew. A contractor named Hertz Hertzenhertz. Can you imagine my opinion of him if he mumbled Yiddish, but was bareheaded, beardless and without earlocks, and, sad to relate, even went about in a highly untraditional, short gaberdine? How could I keep a straight face when this Jewish *goy* (or *goyish* Jew) spoke to me in his fractured Yiddish—a queer dialect that was more German than Yiddish?

"Vell, my dear boy, what Tauro portion are vee reedink zis veek in shul?"

I giggled and hid my face in my hands.

"Tell me, tell me, my dear boy, vat ve're reedink von ze Tauro."

I exploded with laughter and ran away.

A year later, however, I was already familiar with our Jewish German and liked him very much. It no longer bothered me that Hertz Hertzenhertz didn't say his prayers and ate without ritually washing his hands. At first I couldn't understand why he was not struck down. How come God permitted him to live? Why didn't he choke while eating? Why didn't his hair fall out? My rebbi, Motti the Angel of Death, told me himself that this Jewish German was a transmigrated soul, a Jew who had become a German and who might later reappear as a wolf, a cow, a horse, or even a duck. A duck? That would really be something, I thought, pitying the poor German. Still, one thing puzzled me. Why did Father, who was an honest, God-fearing man, always seat him at the head of the table, and why did all others who visited us also treat him with utmost respect?

"How do you do, Reb Hertz Hertzenhertz?" they would say. "A hearty welcome, Reb Hertz Hertzenhertz."

Once I even asked Father about this, but he pushed me away and said:

"Get along. It's none of your business. Why are you roaming around here, the devil take it? Are you too lazy to take a book in hand?" And he fell into a fit of coughing.

Again a book? God Almighty! I, too, wanted to be part of things. I, too, wanted to hear what Herr Hertzenhertz was talking about.

I stole into a corner of the living room, listened to Hertz Hertzenhertz laughing loudly, and watched him smoking his thick, black, aromatic cigars. Suddenly Father came over to me and smacked me.

"You here again, you empty-headed simpleton? What's going to become of you, you heathen? God Almighty, what's going to become of you?" And he fell into a fit of coughing.

But Hertz Hertzenhertz stood up for me. "Oh, leaf him alone. Let ze boy be."

But to no avail. Father chased me out anyway. I picked up a book, but had no desire to read it. What to do? . . . I wandered from room to room till I came to the nicest one of all—the one where Herr Hertz Hertzenhertz slept. Oh, how bright and cheerful was his room! The lamps glowed, and the mirrors sparkled. A big silver inkwell and several fine pens were on the tables, as well as several knicknacks—and a penknife. And what a beauty! If only I had such a knife. How happy I would be. What things I would carve. Yes, it must be put to the test. Was it sharp? Yes, it cut a hair. Sliced it right in two. Boy, was that a knife!

In no time the knife was in my hand. I looked from side to side and slipped the knife into my pocket for a moment. . . .

My hand trembled. . . . My heart beat so loudly that I could hear it going tick-tick-tick. I heard someone coming, a pair of boots creaking. It was Hertz Hertzenhertz. What should I do? I'd better keep the knife in my pocket now. I'd put it back later. Now I had to leave the room and run away.

I could not eat supper. Mama touched my forehead. Father looked sternly at me and sent me to bed. . . . Sleep? Do you think I could close my eyes? For all intents and purposes I was dead. What was I to do with the knife? How could I put it back?

3

"Come here, my precious little gem," my father said the next morning. "Have you seen the knife around?"

At first I was petrified. I fancied that he knew, that they all knew. . . . And I almost blurted out— Huh? The knife? Here it is. . . . But I choked up and with a trembling voice answered:

"Wha . . . what knife?"

"Wha . . . what knife?" Father mimicked. "Wha . . . what knife! The golden knife! Our lodger's knife. You lout, you scoundrel!" And he fell into a fit of coughing.

"Why are you picking on the child?" Mama intervened. "The child doesn't know a blessed thing about it, and you keep harping away, knife, knife, knife."

"Knife, knife. What do you mean he doesn't know?" Father raged. "All morning long he's been listening to us yelling, knife, knife, knife. The entire house is being turned upside down for that knife, and he asks, 'Wha . . . what knife?' Get along, move on, go wash up, you empty-headed lout, you heathen." And he fell into a fit of coughing.

Thank God they didn't search me. But what next? The knife had to be hidden in a safe spot. Where could I hide it? Oh, yes! In the attic. I pulled the knife out of my pocket and slipped it into my boot. I ate without knowing what I was eating. In fact, I was choking.

"What are you rushing for, the devil take it?" Father asked.

"I'm rushing off to *kheder*," I answered and felt my face becoming red as fire.

"Suddenly a scholar! What do you say to our new saint?" he grumbled, furious at me.

I barely managed to finish eating and say grace.

"Well, how come you're not going to *kheder*, my little saint?" Father asked.

"What are you chasing him for?" Mama said. "Let the child sit for a while."

A minute later I was up in the attic. The white penknife, placed in some dark corner, lay there and said nothing.

"Why are you clambering around up in the attic?" Father yelled. "You lout! You're almost Bar Mizvah, you bathhouse dunderhead!" And he fell into a fit of coughing.

"I'm looking for something," I replied and almost keeled over out of sheer fright.

"Something? What something? What sort of something are you looking for?"

"A b-b-book . . . an old T-T-Talmud."

"What T-T-Talmud? In the attic? You rascal! Come down, and you'll get what you deserve. You simpleton! You blockhead! You oaf!"

But I was more concerned about their finding the knife than about Father's anger. One could never tell. Perhaps this would be the day they'd choose to go up to the attic to hang up laundry or paint the rafters. I would have to remove the knife from the attic to a better hiding place. . . . I walked about in perpetual fright. Each one of my father's glances showed me that he already knew, that he would soon accuse me of taking our boarder's penknife. Then I thought of a perfect spot for it. An excellent spot. Where? In the ground. I stuck it into a little pit by the wall and, as a marker, covered it with straw. When I came home from *kheder*, I immediately slipped out to the courtyard, slowly removed the knife, and scarcely had my fill of looking at it when I heard my father's uproar:

"Where in heaven's name are you? How come you're not saying your evening prayers, you common clunk, you lowdown tramp?" And he fell into a fit of coughing.

But my father's continuous persecution and the rebbi's murderous smacks and whacks could not be compared to the joy I had upon coming home from *kheder* and seeing my only beloved friend, my precious knife. But, ah, me, that joy was mixed with pain and embittered with melancholy, fright, and loads of terror.

4

Summer. The sun set, the air cooled somewhat, and the grass smelled sweet. Frogs croaked, and puffs of rainless clouds flew past the moon, seeking to swallow it. The silvery moon played hide-and-seek; it seemed to float on and on, yet remained in one place. Father sat down in the grass, half-naked, wearing only his morning gown and his ritual fringes. He held one hand to his chest, raked the ground with the other, looked at the starry sky, and coughed. His face was deathly white as he gazed at the moon. He sat on the very spot where the knife lay buried but knew nothing of it. Oh, if he had only known! What would he have said? What would my punishment have been?

Aha, I thought, you threw away my bent knife, so now I've got a better one. You're sitting on it and don't even know it. Oh, Father, Father!

"Why are your eyes glittering at me like a cat's?" my father said suddenly. "How come you're sitting there with your hands folded like a rich merchant? Can't find something to keep you busy? Isn't it time for you to say, 'Hear O Israel'? May you *not* go to the blazes, you young lout! May a strange death *not* befall you." And he fell into a fit of coughing.

When Father said, "May you *not* go to the blazes, may a strange death *not* befall you," that was a sign that he was not very angry. On the contrary, it showed he was in a good mood. And indeed he was. One *had* to be in a good mood on such a lovely summer night when everyone was lured out into the delightfully fresh air. Everyone without exception was outside —Father, Mama, even the younger children, who played in the sand, looking for small stones. Herr Hertzenhertz also wandered bareheaded about the courtyard. He smoked a cigar, sang a German song, looked at me, and laughed. He was laughing at me, apparently, because my father had picked on me. But *I* laughed at them all. Soon they all would go to sleep, and I'd slip out of the house into the courtyard—that's where I slept, for the heat inside was unbearable. Then I'd amuse myself and take my delight in my little knife.

Everyone was now asleep. Absolute silence. I got down on all fours and, quiet as a cat, stole out into the courtyard. The night was still, the air delicious. I carefully crept to the spot where the knife was buried. I dug it up slowly and examined it by the light of the moon. It shone, glistened like gold, sparkled like a diamond. I looked up and saw the moon eyeing me and my knife. What was it staring at? I turned around; it kept on following me. I hid the knife in my shirt. The moon's gaze was still on me. It surely realized what sort of knife it was and where I had taken it from. . . . Taken? Stolen is a better word!

For the first time since I had the knife, the terrible thought—stolen—entered my mind. In other words, I was a thief. In plain and simple terms—a thief. The Torah, the Ten Commandments, declared in capital letters:

"THOU SHALT NOT STEAL."

Which was precisely what I had done. What would they do to me in Gehenna for this deed? Ah, me! They would chop off the hand I'd stolen with. They'd beat me with iron rods. I'd be sizzled on a hot frying pan. I'd burn forever. . . . Yes, I had to return the knife. I had to return it to its place. I must not keep a stolen knife. Tomorrow I would return it.

With these thoughts in mind, I placed the knife next to my breast. And I felt that it singed; it burned me. Yes, I would rebury it in its hiding place until tomorrow. The moon still gazed down at me. What was it staring at? It saw; it was a witness. . . .

I crawled slowly back to the house and into my bed and tried to sleep. But I could not. I tossed and turned from one side to another. At dawn I finally dozed off and dreamed of knives, iron rods, and the moon. I awoke early, prayed with great devotion, gulped a quick breakfast, and went straight to *kheder*.

"What's the big rush to *kheder?*" Father yelled after me. "What's chasing you? You won't lose much Torah by coming a bit later. Better say the grace properly, and don't skip anything. You still have plenty of time to be irresponsible, you ruffian, you renegade, you heathen." And he fell into a fit of coughing.

5

"How come so late? Well, look here," the rebbi scolded me. He pointed at my friend Berl the Redhead, who stood in a corner with bowed head. "You see, you scoundrel. Know that from this day on he will no longer be known as Berl the Redhead, the name he's had to this day. No, sir. Now he'll have a far finer name. From now on he'll be called Berl the Thief. So shout it out, my lads: Berl is a thi-ief! Berl is a thi-ief!"

The rebbi intoned these words in singsong pattern, and all the children chorused:

"Berl is a thi-ief. Berl is a thi-ief."

I stood there petrified; a cold wave surged over me. I didn't know what it all meant.

"Why the tight lips, you heathen?" the rebbi turned to me with an unexpected whack. "How come you're so quiet, you pagan? Don't you hear them all singing? Sing along with all the rest: Berl is a thi-ief. Berl is a thi-ief!"

My hands and feet shook. My teeth chattered. But I sang along:

"Berl is a thi-ief. Berl is a thi-ief!"

"Louder, heathen!" the rebbi spurred me on. "Louder, louder!"

Along with the entire chorus, I caterwauled: "Berl is a thi-ief. Berl is a thi-ief!"

"Shhh!" the rebbi cried suddenly, banging the table. "Pipe down! Now the trial's going to begin." And he chanted in Talmudic singsong, "Oho, Berl the Thief, come over here, my lad, and make it snap-py. Tell me, my boy, wha-at's your na-ame?"

"Berl."

"Berl wha-at?" the rebbi sang

"Berl . . . Berl . . . the . . . Thief!"

"That's the spirit, my dear lad, now you're a love-ly lit-tle bo-oy. And now Berele," the rebbi continued chanting, "live and be we-ell, and have vigor of body. Now if you please, take off all your garments. That's the way. Snap it up. Quicker. I beg you, just a little bit quicker. That's it, Berishke, my darling."

Berl stood there as naked as the day he was born. All the blood had drained out of his face. He did not move. His eyes were lowered. He looked like a dead man. A corpse.

The rebbi, still chanting, called one of the older students:

"Come now, Big Hershele, move to this side of the table, and make it snappy. That's it. Let's hear the story from beginning to end. Tell us how our Berl became a thief. Now listen carefully, my lads."

Big Hershele began to tell the story. Berl had got hold of the charity box named after Rebbi Meir the Miracle Worker, into which his mother dropped a kopeck or two every Friday evening before lighting the candles. Berl got hold of the locked charity box and with a tar-tipped straw drew out every last kopeck in the box. Then his mother, Zlate the Hoarse, caught on, opened the charity box, found the tar-tipped straw, and straight off snitched to the rebbi. Right after the rebbi's whipping, Berl admitted that for the past year he had been swiping kopecks out of the charity box and buying himself two honey-cakes and figs every Sunday . . . and so on and so forth.

"And now, children, pronounce judgment. You know what to do. It's not the first time we're doing this. Let each one declare what punishment should be meted out to a thief who steals kopecks from a charity box with a tar-tipped straw. Little Hershele, you begin."

The rebbi cocked his head, closed one eye, and cupped his right ear. Little Hershele answered loudly:

"A thief who steals kopecks from a charity box should be whipped till the blood begins to flow."

"Moshe, what do you say?"

"This is what should be done," said Moshe plaintively, "to a thief who steals money from a charity box. He should be stretched out on the ground. Two boys should sit on his hands, two on his feet, and two should beat him with well-salted rods."

"What do you say, Kopele?"

Kopele wiped his nose and squeaked out his judgment:

"A thief who swipes kopecks from a charity box should have all the kids come up to him and sing right into his face loud and clear: You're a crook, you're a crook, you're a big fat crook."

Everyone burst out laughing. The rebbi put his thumb under his throat like a cantor and summoned me with the traditional melody used to call a groom to the Torah.

"Step forth now, bridegroom Reb Sholom ben Reb Nakhum, to chant the Maftir. Tell me, Sholomke, my pet, what punishment do you suggest for a thief who takes kopecks out of a charity box?"

I wanted to reply, but my tongue did not obey me. I shivered as though in a fever. I felt as though I were being strangled. A cold sweat covered me from head to toe. My ears rang. I no longer saw the rebbi, my friends, or the stark-naked Berl the Thief. I only saw knives—an endless array of white, open, multibladed knives. The moon hung suspended by the door. It smiled and gazed at me as though it were human. My head spun. Everything was revolving—the *kheder,* my friends, the table, the books, the moon suspended on the door, all the knives. My legs were being cut away beneath me. Soon I'd keel over. But with effort I braced myself to keep from falling.

At night I came home. My face burned, my cheeks flamed, and my ears buzzed. I couldn't make out what people were saying to me. Father said something. He was angry and wanted to slap me. Mama stood up for me. Spread her apron like a hen taking her chicks under her wings. I didn't hear a thing. I didn't want to hear. I just wanted night to fall quickly so I could make an end of the penknife. What should I do with it? Confess and return it? Then I'd end up like Berele. Return it secretly? What if they caught me? The solution was to throw it away and be rid of it. Where could I throw it so they'd never find it? The roof? They'd hear a bang. The garden? They'd find it. Aha. I had an idea. I knew where to throw it. Into the water. I swear, that was a great idea! Into the water. Into the well. Right here in our courtyard.

The idea pleased me so much I decided I wasn't going to deliberate too long. I grabbed the penknife and dashed to the well. I wasn't holding a knife, I imagined, but something hideous and despicable that I wanted to get rid of—and the quicker, the better. Still, I regretted losing the knife—it was so expensive. I stood for a minute lost in thought. I fancied I was holding a living thing, and my heart grieved. After all, it had cost me so much effort; it was like destroying a living creature. But I plucked up my courage and let it slip out of my fingers. Plop! The water splashed and then fell silent. Good-bye knife! I stood for a while at the well, listening. Not a sound. Thank God. Finally had got rid of it. Nonetheless, my heart felt heavy. It hurt me. After all, there was nothing like that knife.

I went back to bed and saw the moon gazing at me. I fancied it had seen my every move. I heard a distant voice saying, "But you're still a thief. . . . Catch him . . . beat him . . . he's a thief . . . a thi-ief!"

I slipped back into the house and lay down to sleep. I dreamt I was running, floating, flying in the air with the knife. The moon noticed me and said, "Catch him. Beat him. He's a thief. A thi-ief!"

6

A long, deep sleep. Oppressive dreams. A fire burned within me. My head hummed. Everything was red as blood. Fiery rods struck me. I wallowed in blood. Snakes and scorpions writhed about me, mouths open, ready to swallow me. I heard a sharp blast near my ear—the shrill retorts of a ram's horn. Someone stood over me, chanting rhythmically: "Beat him. Beat him. Beat him. He is a thi-ief!" I cried, "Help! Take the moon away from me. Give the moon the knife. . . . What have you got against Berele? He's not to blame. It's me who's the thi-ief, the thi-ief!"

The rest I don't remember.

* * *

I opened one eye, then the other. . . . Where was I? Apparently, on a bed. What was I doing here? Who was sitting on a bench next to the bed? Oh, it's you, Mama?

Mama!

She didn't hear me.

Mama! . . . Mama! . . . Ma-maa. . . .

What did this mean? I was sure I was shouting. . . . Wait. I listened. She was crying. Crying softly. I also saw Father's yellow, sickly face. He was bent over a book. He said something softly and coughed. He sighed and groaned. Apparently, I was already dead. . . . Dead? But then I felt my eyes brightening. My head felt better. So did the rest of my body. One ear buzzed, then the other. . . . *Zzzzing.* I sneezed—*haptshoo!*

"God bless you. Long life to you. Many years of good health. *Mazel tov.* Congratulations. Oh, dear God, thank you!"

"He actually sneezed. Thanks to the Almighty Lord!"

"We have a great God. The boy will be well, God willing. Blessed be He, and blessed be His name."

"Quick, let's call Mintzie the *shokhet*'s wife. She's an expert at charms to ward off the evil eye."

"Better call the doctor. The doctor."

"The doctor? What for? Nonsense. There is a better doctor. The Almighty is the best doctor in the world. God, blessed be He, and blessed be His name!"

"Move on, folks. Please disperse a bit. It's awfully hot. For God's sake, move on."

"Well? I told you we should pour out a wax image* of him! So who was right, hah?"

"Thank God. Praised be the Lord. O God, God, blessed be He, and blessed be His name."

People swarmed around me; they stared at me. Everyone approached and tapped my forehead. They said charms over me; they whispered to me; they licked my forehead and spat; they tended me. They poured hot soup into me and stuffed me with spoonfuls of fruit preserves. Everyone hovered over me, caring for me like the apple of their eye. They fed me broths and duck-

---

* A folk belief that pouring out a wax image of someone was beneficial—Tr.

lings like a baby; they did not leave me alone. Mama always sat next to me and repeated the entire story. I had fallen to the ground virtually lifeless, and they had to lift me up. I lay delirious for two weeks, croaking like a frog, babbling continually about whippings and knives. . . . They thought that I was quitting this world, God forbid. Then suddenly I sneezed seven times and returned from the dead to life.

"Now we know what sort of God we have, blessed be He, and blessed be His name," said Mama with tears in her eyes. "Now we know that if we call to Him, He hears our sinful requests and our guilt-ridden tears. . . . We shed plenty of tears, your father and I, until finally God showed some pity. Almost lost a child, God forbid. Almost lost a child on account of our great sins. May we suffer what God intended for you. Who prompted all this trouble? What was it all about? A boy, a thief, some Berele whom the rebbi beat up in *kheder* till he was bleeding. When you came home from *kheder,* you looked half-dead already, may I suffer all your ills! What a murderer that rebbi is; what a brute! May God get even with him, dear Lord! . . . No, no, my child. If we live and be well, and you rise from your sickbed, God willing, we'll get you another teacher, not such a hangman, such a murderer like this Angel of Death, may his name and memory be blotted out!"

This bit of news delighted me no end. I hugged Mama and kissed her.

"Dear, dear Mama."

Father approached slowly, touched my forehead with his cold pale hands, and said softly, without a trace of anger:

"Oh, you've given us quite a fright, you little rascal." And he fell into a fit of coughing.

Even our beardless Jewish German, Herr Hertz Hertzenhertz, bent over my bed with a cigar between his teeth, patted my cheek, and said in German:

"Gut, gut! You're helsy, you're shtrong and helsy now."

Two weeks after I had recuperated, my father said:

"Well, my boy, now go to *kheder,* and pay no more mind to knives or other such nonsense. . . . It's high time you grew

up. In three years, God willing, you'll be Bar Mizvah, may you
live to be a hundred and twenty." And he fell into a fit of coughing.

With these sweet words Father sent me to a new *kheder,* run
by Reb Khayim Koter. This was the first time that I had heard
such kind and gentle words from my usually irascible father.
In an instant I forgot all his persecutions, all his curses, all his
smacks—it was as though they had never happened. If not for
embarrassment, I would have hugged and kissed him. Still,
how can one possibly kiss one's father?

Mama gave me a whole apple and two kopecks to take to
kheder, and the German, too, pinched my cheek and presented
me with two kopecks.

"Gut boy!" he said. "Eggzellent boy."

I took a Talmud folio, kissed the *mezuza,* and went to *kheder*
like a newborn man, calm, clearheaded and pure of heart, spir-
itually refreshed, with honest and pious thoughts. The sun
greeted me with its warm rays. A light breeze blowing at my
earlocks sounded like a bird chirping. I felt as if I were uplifted, flying. I felt like running, dancing, leaping. Oh, how good
it was to be alive when one was honest, when one was neither
thief nor liar!

I pressed the Talmud folio close to my heart and ran eagerly
to *kheder.* I swore that I would never ever take anything that
wasn't mine, that I would never ever steal, that I would never
ever deny anything, but would always be honest—absolutely
honest.

Monologue

A BIT OF ADVICE

Upon returning home from a journey, I received the following message:

"For three days now some young man has been coming to see you every morning and evening without finding you at home. He says it's very urgent."

Probably a writer with a manuscript, I thought as I sat down at my writing desk. No sooner had I begun to work than the bell rang. I heard the door opening. Someone was fussing about in the hall, removing his galoshes, coughing, blowing his nose—obviously a writer was present. By now I was curious to have a look at this character. Praise the Lord, he finally entered. Rubbing his hands, he greeted me elaborately, retreated a few steps, and offered up several reverential flourishes and obeisances. Then he introduced himself, muttering some outlandish name—the sort that goes in one ear, out the other.

"Have a seat," I said. "What can I do for you?"

"I've come to you on a very urgent matter. I mean, it's urgent as far as I'm concerned. Extremely urgent. It's actually a matter of life or death, and I've got a feeling that only you will be able to appreciate my problem. Since you're such a prolific writer, I've got a feeling you know it all and understand everything. Anyway, that's what I think. I mean, that's not what I *think*—I'm *convinced* that it's so."

I looked the odd creature over. A typical small-town intellectual—a writer. A pale young man with huge, black, sad eyes, the sort of eyes that plead with you to have pity on a lost, lonely soul. I don't like such eyes. I'm afraid of them. They never laugh; they never smile. They're always looking inward, immersed in their own ego. I despise such eyes.

"All right, let's see what you've brought," I said, laying down my pen. I leaned back in my chair and waited for him to pull out a sheaf of papers from his pocket, no doubt a three-part novel as long as the Jewish Exile, or a four-act play whose personae are named Murderson, Honestman, Devoutheart, Bitterroot, etc., names which indicate at once the type of man you're dealing with. Perhaps he even had a new cycle of odes to Zion:

> For the mountains he is longing
> Thereward where the eagle flies
> There where olive trees are blooming
> And the prophets reached the skies. . . .

How well we know these ditties! We're quite familiar with the sort of doggerel whose rhymes make you gag and whose metaphors flit before your eyes, buzz in your ears, and inspire only spiritual desolation.

But imagine the surprise! This time I was dead wrong. The young man did not place his hand on his chest pocket, did not pull out a sheaf of papers, had no intention whatsoever of reading me a novel, a play, or a cycle of odes to Zion. He merely straightened his collar, coughed until he'd cleared his throat, then declared:

"I've come here to you for no other purpose, you see, than to pour out my bitter heart to you and seek your advice. A man like you will certainly understand me. Since you're such a prolific writer, I've got the feeling you know everything. Only you can give me the proper advice. And believe me, I will do whatever you advise. I give you my word of honor. I hope you'll pardon me if I'm taking up too much of your time. . . ."

"Never mind. Let's hear what you've got to say," I said, relieved. I felt as though a stone had rolled off my heart. The young man moved his chair closer to the desk and began pouring out his bitter heart, at first slowly and calmly, but then with ever-increasing fervor.

"As you can no doubt see, I happen to be a young man from a little village. I mean, the village isn't *such* a little village, it's a rather good-sized village, one could very well say a town— but on the other hand, compared to your town, it is still a village. I would assume that you're familiar with this particular village, but I don't want to mention it by name, because, who knows, you're likely to write it up. So that's why, for a number of reasons, it wouldn't be right for me to mention it.

"Do you want to know what I do? What I mean is, at the moment I'm not actually doing *anything*. I'm still being fed, that is, by my in-laws. I mean, I'm not just being fed by them, but actually living under one roof with them, completely supported by them. For my wife, I want you to know, is an only daughter—that is, she's a one and only child. Except for that one daughter, they have no other children, and they are quite able—with absolutely no difficulty—to provide for us and support us for ten more years. I want you to know they're well heeled. I'm not exaggerating when I say that you might even consider them loaded. As far as we're concerned, they're rich magnates, nabobs, moneybags—there's no one richer in town.

"I'm sure you know my father-in-law. Anyway, that's what I think. But it wouldn't be right to mention his name. I want you to know he's the kind of man who likes to make his influence felt. For publicity's sake. For example, he gave the biggest donations for the victims of the Bobruisk fire. For victims of the Kishenev pogrom he offered more than anyone else. Back home, in our village, he's rather tightfisted, but he likes to make an impression abroad and be in the public eye. He's nobody's fool, if you get what I mean. He realizes quite well that here in town they respect him anyway, so who does he have to show off for? So he decides to thumb his nose at them all. He himself declares that he can't spare a penny. When someone comes to him for a contribution, he turns white as a corpse and says, 'What? You here again with outstretched palms? Here, take my keys, go to my cupboard and take whatever you want.'

"But do you think that he actually makes a move to take out his keys? Pardon me, but if you do, you're dead wrong. The keys to his cupboard are safely locked in a desk drawer. What's more, the key to the desk drawer is buried somewhere. That's the sort of chap my father-in-law is. Surely a man gets the reputation he deserves. But just between you and me, in our village he's known as the Swine. Behind his back, of course. To his face they flatter him so much it's enough to make you sick. Nevertheless, he takes it all at face value, strokes his belly, and lives absolutely grandly. What do I mean, grandly? Grandly isn't the word for it. Imagine! He never has to lift a finger; he lives in splendid fashion, eats excellently, and sleeps well— could anyone ask for more? After his nap he orders his carriage harnessed up, and they go out for an airing, sloshing through the mud.

"Comes the evening, people gather from all over, this one with a story, that one with some gossip or some concocted tale, and they besmirch all the villagers and poke fun at each and every one. Then they pass around the big samovar and sit down with Shmuel-Abba the *shokhet* to play dominoes. I want you to know that Shmuel-Abba the *shokhet* is a young man with earlocks, but he's a modernized chap, with a white collar and polished boots. He doesn't run away from young women, has a fine pair of pipes, sings well, subscribes to a newspaper, and is a topnotch chess and dominoes player. And when they sit down to play dominoes, they can play away the entire night, and you have to sit there and look on and yawn till you practically dislocate your jaw. So why don't you pick yourself up, you ass, and go to your room and sit down to read a book or scan a newspaper? But nothing doing. Why? It isn't fitting and proper. If a stranger is sitting there, how can you pick yourself up and suddenly leave? That's the sort of move that enrages my father-in-law.

"Of course, when it comes down to saying something, he doesn't say boo. But he gets all puffed up like a turkey and refuses to answer any of your questions—you can talk till you burst. And my mother-in-law immediately follows suit. And since both in-laws are looking daggers at their son-in-law—dammit to hell, my wife jumps on the bandwagon, too. After all, she's an only daughter. Mama and Papa's one and only. Her parents are her soul, her life, says she. And they in turn consider her the apple of their eye. You've never seen anything like it.

"In case she's the slightest bit indisposed, they call the doctor straight off, and everyone's in a dither. So is it any wonder then that a creature like her gets all puffed up and thinks that the entire world was created only for her sake? And what's more, you ought to know that she isn't overly bright. I mean, if you talk to her, she doesn't strike you as a fool, no fool at all; you might even say she's clever, quite clever, in fact, and sharp-witted—she's got a man's head on her shoulders. But what's the rub? The fact that she's pampered and mollycoddled, that wild she-goat! Day and night it's either giggling or a sudden plop down in bed with a crying fit like a little baby. 'What's the matter? What is it? Why are you crying? What do you want?' But go talk to the wall! Well, what can you do? That alone wouldn't be half bad. A woman cries till she stops crying. But the only trouble is—my mother-in-law. As soon as my mother-in-law finds out, she comes running, the Turkish shawl on her shoulders, wringing her hands and wailing her dirges. And I want you to know she's got a voice like a man. 'What's the matter, daughter dear? Is it *him* again, that murderer, that cutthroat, that assassin? Ah, woe is me! Does he care that you're my one-and-only darling? Is it his belly that hurts? Is it his blood that's being sucked dry?'

"Pour it on, blah blah blah. Like sand out of a sack. It seems to me she'll always grind away, she'll never stop sawing away at my heart and gnawing at my soul. And I've got a wild urge to take her by the Turkish shawl, crumple it up in my hands, trample it with my feet, and rip it into a thousand pieces. But on the other hand, if you look at it in another light, what do I actually have against her shawl? It's a shawl like any other Turkish shawl they bring her from Brod. I'm sure you're familiar with those speckled and fringed shawls, colored and checked with red, yellow, green, white and black. . . ."

"If you don't mind, young man," I interrupted him in mid-sentence, "I thought you said you wanted my advice on some urgent matter."

"I hope you'll pardon me," he said, catching his breath, "if I'm taking up too much of your time. But all this was necessary, you understand, as background for the matter at hand. I wanted you to become familiar with our household and our family's status. And only when you get to know all this, will you begin to understand my predicament. . . . Well, then, as soon as, God forbid, she's feeling a bit indisposed—my wife, I mean—my mother-in-law begins to grumble, and my father-in-law orders the carriage harnessed up, and they send for the doctor, the new doctor. That's exactly what he's called in town—the new doctor. I don't want to mention his name, the devil take him. Now here's where the real to-do begins, and it's precisely about this that I wanted to speak to you and ask your advice."

The odd creature stopped for a minute, wiped his perspiring face, moved the chair a bit closer, and prepared to continue talking. He was holding something in his hand. There are people who have to hold something when they talk, or else they can't tell a story. On my writing desk there is a display of various knickknacks and novelties, among them a miniature bicycle and a cigar clipper. Visitors are so enchanted by this little bike that everyone who comes to see me picks it up straight off. My visitor also fell in love with it. At first, while talking, he gazed admiringly at the little bike; then he picked it up and finally tried spinning the wheels. In short, once he had it in his hands, he did not let go of it. And while holding it, he continued his story:

"Well, then, the new doctor. Our town, for your information, has as many doctors as there are stray mutts on the street. There are Christian doctors, and there are Jewish doctors, big ones and small ones. There are also Zionist doctors—that is, they specialize in Zionism. But the doctor I'm telling you about is still quite a young man, a very homey sort, the son of a tailor —I mean, once upon a time his father was a tailor. Now he's no longer a tailor, for since his son became a doctor, it's beneath his dignity for him to be a tailor. I mean to say, just the opposite.

It's beneath the doctor's dignity to have a tailor for a father, and the sort of tailor to boot who among tailors has the reputation of being a mere hem stitcher. For instance, the father himself, I want you to know, is a small, cockeyed chap with a crooked finger who always wears a cotton-padded gaberdine. He's got a voice like a rattle-clacker and goes around day and night prattling away. 'My son the doctor had some case yesterday. Boy, that was some case! If he only wants to, that doctor son of mine, can he practice medicine!' He chews everyone's ears off with his son the doctor. And if that isn't enough of a plague, this doctor, for your information, happens to be a woman's doctor, a gynecologist. So wherever there's a secret, this cockeyed tailor drums it all over town. So woe unto that young woman or girl who falls into that doctor's hands and his tailor father's mouth. . . . Once the following incident took place in our town. A girl happened to be—"

"If you don't mind, young man," I interrupted in midsentence once more, "it seems to me you wanted to consult with me and ask my advice."

"I hope you'll pardon me if I'm taking up too much of your time. But I've begun telling you about the doctor because it's he who is actually the Angel of Death here. If it weren't for him, I'd be in paradise. For what do I lack? My wife, I want you to know, is a good-looking woman; you might even say a beauty. I also want you to know that we don't have any children yet, and she's also an only daughter, a one-and-only child. One hundred and twenty years later, if you know what I mean, it'll all be hers; I mean, mine. I've got plenty of respect, too— no complaints on that score—as befits a rich man's son-in-law. And thank God. I've got no worries about a good seat in *shul,* or a Maftir on Sabbath, or a drink if there happens to be a circumcision anywhere. Also when it comes to making the circuits with the *esrog* and *lulav* I'm right behind my father-in-law. Naturally, the cantor leads the parade, followed by the rabbi, my father-in-law, then me, and only then the rest of the congregation. And, forgive the proximity, even when I enter and undress in the bathhouse, the bathkeeper raises a fuss. 'Step aside, folks, make room! Here comes the rich man's son-in-law!'

"But I swear to you in all sincerity that all this nettles me. I despise all this tumult. What am I saying, despise? Everyone loves flattery, and no one refuses honor, so what's the rub? Enough's enough, especially since it's not I who am being honored. Why pick me? Just because my father-in-law is a rich man? Let them flatter *him;* let them lick *his* boots, if you'll pardon my expression, until they burst. What's it got to do with me? They're wild savages, I tell you. Stark raving mad. And I've got to live with this family as in a prison, for they don't let me get together with just anyone—it isn't fitting and proper for the rich man's son-in-law. Bring this up to my father-in-law? Fat chance! Talking to him is like talking to a blank wall. For your information he's a coarse chap, extremely coarse, a thorough-going boor, may he forgive me for saying this. But just as he's not within hearing range, so may it not harm him. And my wife? She's a wild goat, an only daughter, as I've mentioned. She's laughing one minute, weeping the next. A rash of giggles one moment, and plop down crying on the bed the next— and the doctor is called in.

"The new doctor, the devil take him. Thinking of him makes me sick unto death. Believe me, there are times when I feel like either grabbing a knife and stabbing myself or running to the river and drowning; that's how much that doctor nauseates me."

The young man fell into a reverie and grew melancholy.

"Are you trying to suggest that you suspect her of something?" I said, choosing my words carefully.

"God forbid," he said, jumping up as though scalded. He pushed his chair even closer. "How can I possibly say that I suspect her? A Jewish girl? She's a pure and virtuous woman! I'm talking about him, I am. About that nifty doctor, may hellfire consume him. And not so much the doctor as his dandy daddy, blast him, the cockeyed needle stitcher with the cotton-padded gaberdine. Day and night he prattles on and on and drums reports all over town. And do you think there's any substance to his prattling? Stuff and nonsense! Absolute rubbish! The creature has a tongue, so he wags it. Believe me, it wouldn't bother me any more than last winter's snow. The only trouble is that men have ears, and ears have got the habit of listening, and if you listen carefully, you get to hear everything you didn't want to hear in the first place. Especially in our town—a village, for your information, composed solely of world-famous long-tongued backbiters.

"If our village sets to blabbing about someone, he may as well bid the world good-bye. Imagine! In my presence they watched their tongues, but while my back was turned, I kept hearing remarks that made my ears perk. So I began to keep my eyes peeled, my ears cocked. I looked beneath the surface of words, and—what is there to say?—I could find nothing, absolutely nothing. Except for one thing. I noticed that when the doctor enters the house, she becomes a new person. Her face lights up; her eyes sparkle. What I mean is, her person doesn't change. She has the same face, the same eyes. But there's a different expression there. Do you get what I mean? An entirely different expression and a new sparkle! I was dying to ask her, 'Tell me just why is it, my darling, that when he steps into the house, you become a new person?' Guess what her reply was? She tickled off such a round of giggles that I thought I'd sink into the ground. And right smack after this burst of laughter she plopped into bed with such a fit of weeping that her mother with the Turkish shawl came running and began to revive her, filling the air with her storehouse of groans. Her father, meanwhile, made a dash for the carriage and sent me to get the doctor. As soon as the doctor arrived, she felt better immediately. The color came back to her face, and her eyes began to glitter like diamonds in sunlight.

"Just try to picture this nifty little tale. When I have to set foot in his house, believe me, I feel as if I'm stepping into kingdom come. Entering hell is probably far pleasanter. Not to mention looking at his face—oh, that noble, sensitive puss of his. His face is so beet red it's practically blue. And each of his pimples, every single one of his pimples, is studded with tiny blisters. And he's got the habit of perpetually smiling. He smiles like an unwashed cadaver. He keeps right on smiling whether there's good reason for smiling or not. There's always a smile on his mug, and he's just palsy-walsy with everyone. Not to mention me. To me he's always sugarsweet, so tender you could apply him to a third-degree burn. His kindness to me is endless and boundless. I wasn't feeling too well recently, had one of those fashionable ailments—influenza. You should have seen how this chap worked himself to the bone tending me. It wasn't even normal. It's remarkable. The nicer he is to me—may God not punish me for saying this—the more I hate him. I can't stand looking at him, especially when he's at our house and the two of them are making moon eyes at each other. . . . It seems to me that if I could take him by the scruff of the neck and chuck him out of the house, I'd feel a lot better. I can't stand his eyes and the way he looks at her. I can't stand his smile and the way he smiles at her. And I promised myself once and for all that this has to come to an end. How much humiliation can a man take? The entire village, I want you to know, is talking about me. There's no other solution for me except a divorce. I see no other way out. But what's the rub? Is it practical? My father-in-law is a rich man. With a one-and-only daughter. One hundred twenty years later, if you know what I mean, it'll all be hers; I mean, mine. But who needs the damn thing? What did I do before I met her? What do lots of other young men do? In short, there's no other way, right? Isn't a divorce the only way out?"

Here again the odd creature caught his breath, wiped the perspiration from his face, and waited to hear what I would say.

"Well, I, too, think that there's no other recourse for you except a divorce. Especially since I see that the love between you two isn't sizzling, and I understand that there are no children anyway and that you're the talk of the town. So what do you need this whole pack of troubles for?"

While I was speaking, the odd creature kept turning the wheels of the little bike and gazing at me with his deep, sad black eyes. When I finished, he drew even closer and began with a sigh:

"You mention love. Well, what's there to be said? I don't hate her. Why should I hate her? Quite frankly, I like her. In fact, I love her madly . . . and as for your remark that I'm the talk of the town, let them talk; let them rave and rant until they burst. I'm so infuriated with that doctor I feel a fire burning within me. At him and at her. How come she lights up when she sees him? Tell me, I beg you, how come she doesn't get red and gay when she sees *me?* In what way am I any worse than he? Is it because he's a doctor and I'm not? If they had educated me like they educated him, perhaps I, too, would have been a doctor, and maybe even a better one than he. Believe me that in the little letters of Sacred Writ yours truly can hold his own with him, and when it comes to the Hebrew language, I might even put him in my pocket.

"But on the other hand, I thought, what ill have I actually seen in her that I want to give her a divorce? Is it the new doctor? What would I do if, instead of a doctor, some other plague would have come along? And where is it inscribed that a young woman can't strike up an acquaintance with a doctor? So there's one reason for you. Second, what would become of me, for instance, if I went through with the divorce? For, you see, I happen to be an orphan, all alone in the world, with neither relative nor close friend—so go now and become a poor bachelor, then remarry, and for all intents and purposes start from scratch all over again. And how do I know that next time around I'll be better off? Suppose I tumble into a worse hell? Here at least I've got used to the pickle I'm in, and I'm still the crown prince as they say, the rich man's son-in-law. And one hundred twenty years later, if you know what I mean, it'll all be hers; I mean, mine. . . . You get the picture? Why should I take chances and speculate? The whole thing's just one big game, a lottery. Right? Isn't that so? What do you say? Isn't it just one big game? Isn't it a lottery?"

"That's just the way I feel," I replied. "It's just one big game, a lottery. Concord is certainly better than discord or divorce."

I was overjoyed that my advice tended more to concord than divorce. I hoped that I would now be through with him. But the upshot was that he grabbed hold of the little bike, pulled his chair right up to mine, and shouted at point-blank range:

"Concord? Perhaps you're right. But all I have to do is think of him, blast him to hell—I'm referring to the pimply-faced doctor! His daddy, the cockeyed hemstitcher, I want you to know, keeps drumming the news all over town anyway that the rich man's daughter is about to get divorced. How's that for low-down malice? If only the scoundrel wouldn't blather so much! But so long as they're already talking about it in town, what have I got to lose? As they say—a broken pot is done for. So long as it was a secret, you couldn't do a thing, except pinch your cheek to keep the color high. But now, when everyone is talking about the divorce, I think it would be downright mean on my part not to do anything. There's no choice left except a divorce. Right? What do you say? Don't you agree?"

"That's just the way I feel," I replied. "As long as everyone knows and everyone's talking about a divorce, it *is* rather inconsiderate of you to stay married. You've no alternative except a divorce."

"In other words," he said, moving his chair almost on top of me, "you feel that I've definitely got to give her a divorce. Give the matter some serious thought. Pretend you're the rabbi, and I come to you with my wife for a divorce, and you ask me, 'Tell me, young man, why are you divorcing your wife?' What sort of answer can I give you? My answer'll be that I'm divorcing her because she looks at the doctor and the doctor looks at her. Well? Is that a reason? I ask you, can I blindfold them? What would people think of me then? Come on, you tell me? Upping and divorcing a beautiful young woman, an only daughter, a rich man's one-and-only child, one hundred twenty years later, if you know what I mean, it'll all be hers; I mean, mine. . . . Well? What would people say? Crazy, right? What? Am I wrong? They'd say I was stark raving mad! Right?"

"That's exactly what I say—stark raving mad!"

At this point the odd creature moved so close that our legs looked as though they'd been intertwined. In place of the little bike which he had ruined, he picked on my inkwell. He heaved a sigh and resumed his explication:

"For you it's easy to say that the next chap is stark raving mad. I'd really like to know what *you* would have done, for example, if all this had happened to you. That is, if *you* had a boor for a father-in-law, a mother-in-law with a Turkish shawl who is eternally grousing, and a wife, may she live and be well, who is always running to doctors, and if the town would have pointed a finger at you, saying: 'There goes the she-goat's young husband!' If all this were your lot, it seems to me that you would jump up in the middle of the night, divorce her, and scoot away to the four winds. Well, wouldn't you?"

"That's exactly the way I feel," I said. "In the middle of the night I, too, would jump up, divorce her, and scoot away to the four winds."

"Naturally," he said, "it's easy to say jump up, divorce her, and scoot away to the four winds. It's easy to say, scoot away. Scoot how, by what means, where to? Into the earth? And what about the fact that she's an only daughter . . . a one-and-only child . . . and one hundred twenty years later, if you know what I mean, it'll all be hers; I mean, mine? . . . Consider that nothing? . . . Anyway, what have I got against her? What do I actually have against her? . . . Go ahead, tell me. What have I got against her?"

"That's exactly the way I feel," I said. "What *have* you got against her?"

"But after all," he said, "what about the doctor? Have you forgotten about the doctor? As long as I see this Angel of Death, I can't bear looking at my wife; I can't stand the sight of her face."

"In that case," I said, "you should divorce her."

"But let's be practical," he said. "What can a young man like me do in today's bitter times? Go ahead, you tell me. You be the wise man."

"In that case," I said, "there should be no divorce."

"No divorce? Then what about the doctor? Whenever—"

"Then get divorced," I said, hoping to bring the matter to an end.

"Divorce? Let's be practical. After all—"

"Then don't divorce her."

"Then what about the doctor?"

I don't know what happened to me. All the blood suddenly rushed to my head and I felt faint. I lunged for the odd creature's throat, pressed him to the wall, and screamed in an unearthly voice:

"Divorce her, you hear, you bastard! Divorce her, divorce her, divorce. . . ."

Hearing our screams everyone in my house came running.

"What's up? What happened?"

"Nothing. Absolutely nothing."

I spotted my cadaverous face in the mirror and hardly recognized myself. Afterward I had to beg my guest's pardon several times. I pressed his hands and told him a thousand times to forget what had occurred between us.

"Sometimes a man loses his temper," I told him.

The odd creature was a bit confused, mixed up; he admitted that a person isn't always his own master, that on occasion a man does lose control of himself.

Then, in the same manner he had entered my study, he departed. The same bow, the same few steps backward, the same reverential obeisances, the same rubbing of the hands.

"Pardon me if I've taken up too much of your time. Many thanks for the advice. . . . I'm very grateful to you. . . . Be well. . . . Thanks again. . . ."

"Don't mention it. . . . Have a good trip. . . ."

Railroad Yarns

IT'S A LIE!

"You're headed for Kolomeya, right?"

"How do you know it's Kolomeya?"

"I heard you talking with the conductor. Do you live in Kolomeya, or are you just visiting?"

"I live there. Why do you ask?"

"No special reason. Just like that. Is Kolomeya a big city?"

"What's the difference if it's big or not? It's a city like all other cities in Galicia. A nice place, a good town."

"I mean, are there any fine people there, any men of substance?"

"There are all sorts. There are rich men and poor men. Naturally, the poor outnumber the rich."

"Same with us. For every rich man, knock wood, there's a thousand paupers. Say, isn't there a rich merchant named Finkelstein in Kolomeya?"

"There is. Why, do you know him?"

"Actually, I don't know him personally. I just heard about him. Isn't he called Reb Shaye?"

"That's right. Why do you ask?"

"No special reason. Just like that. Is this Reb Shaye really as well off as folks say he is?"

"How should *I* know? I didn't count his money. Say, how come you're asking so many questions? You trying to establish his credit?"

"No. I'm just asking. I've heard it said that he's got a daughter."

"He has *three* daughters. Oho, so it's a match you're interested in? Do you know how much dowry he's going to give his daughter?"

"I'm not talking about dowry, you understand. I'm talking about his house. What sort of household does Reb Shaye Finkelstein have? What's it like?"

"What sort of household do you expect it to be? It's like any other Jewish home—it's Jewish, decent, and Hasidic. Indeed, a very beautiful Jewish home. In fact, it's even been said that, lately, as far as kosher food is concerned—but it's a lie!"

"What's a lie?"

"Whatever they say is a lie. Kolomeya, you ought to know, is a town jam-packed with liars."

"Then for this reason alone I'd like to know what they say about his home."

"Rumor has it that it's not what it used to be. For example, on Passover they used to eat only handmade extra-special-kosher matzas. . . . Reb Shaye himself used to travel twice a year to his *rebbe*. But today—well, today the place is no longer what it used to be."

"Is that all?"

"What more do you want? Expect him to shave off his beard and earlocks and feast on pork chops in the market square?"

"No, but from the way you said, 'Rumor has it,' I thought God-knows-what! The main thing is that Reb Shaye himself is an upstanding and respectable man. What I mean is—he *is* a decent human being, isn't he? That's what I mean!"

"What's the difference if he's decent or not? He's a man like all other men. A fine man. And—why not admit it?—a very fine man. In fact, rumor has it that he's a bit . . . but it's a lie!"

"What's a lie?"

"Everything they say about him is a lie. Kolomeya is a town where people love to talk about one another. That's why I don't want to repeat anything, for that would be slander."

"But when you know it's a lie, it's no longer slander."

"People say that . . . he's a bit of a . . . wangler."

"Wangler? Every Jew is a wangler. A Jew wangles! Aren't you a wangler?"

"But this wangler is in a class by himself. There's a story making the rounds that he . . . but it's a lie!"

"Well, then, what's the story?"

"But I tell you it's a lie!"

"Then I'd like to know the lie that's making the rounds."

"They say that he's gone bankrupt three times. But it's a lie! I heard it from only one person."

"Is that all? Did you ever hear of a businessman who doesn't go bankrupt? A businessman does business until someone else gives *him* the business. If a businessman dies before he's gone bankrupt, it's a sign that he died before his time. Right? Isn't that so?"

"You think all bankruptcies are alike? People say that his bankruptcy was particularly nasty. He salted away some money, then thumbed his nose at the world. Get it?"

"Apparently he's nobody's fool. Well, besides that, is there anything else?"

"What more do you want? Expect him to murder someone? Become a hooligan? Actually, there is a rather unpleasant story about him . . . but it's a lie!"

"Well, what's the story?"

"It's about a nobleman . . . but it's a lot of claptrap."

"What's the story with the nobleman?"

"There was a nobleman . . . signed notes . . . oh, the stories Kolomeya can concoct! Sheer lies! I *know* it's all one big lie!"

"Since you know it's a lie, it won't harm him."

"It's been said that Reb Shaye had some business dealings with a very rich nobleman, with whom he had pull, and plenty of it. Meanwhile, the nobleman died, and Reb Shaye presented two of his notes. This caused an uproar in town. How had Reb Shaye got hold of two of his notes, when it was a known fact that during his entire lifetime the nobleman had never signed anything? Kolomeya, for your information, is a town which has eagle eyes and beagle ears."

"Well?"

"Well, what? So he had a pack of troubles."

"Is that all? Jews always have troubles. Did you ever see a Jew who doesn't have a pack of troubles?"

"But word had it that Finkelstein had a threefold pack to carry."

"A threefold pack? Namely? What were the three troubles he was supposed to have?"

"First, there was a little incident with a mill, they say. . . . But that's definitely a lie."

"No doubt it caught fire, and people said that he himself fiddled with the matches while it burned, for since the mill was dilapidated, he had had it insured so as to be able to build a new one, right?"

"How do *you* know that that's what happened?"

"Actually, I *don't* know. But that's the way I picture it. That's how it had to be."

"Anyway, that's the talk of the town in Kolomeya. But it's a lie. I can swear it's a lie!"

"I don't care if it *is* true. What other troubles did you say he had?"

"*I* say? It's what everyone in town says. But I consider such common talk just plain faultfinding and trumped-up charges."

"Trumped-up charges? What, for instance? Counterfeit money?"

"Worse!"

"What could be worse?"

"I'm ashamed to tell you the things that Kolomeya is capable of dreaming up! Those empty-headed idlers! Those loafers! Perhaps they even concocted it so as to extort some money from him. You know! It's a small town—and a rich man has enemies."

"There was probably an affair with the maid."

"How do *you* know? Who told you?"

"No one told me, but I can guess! That trumped-up charge must have cost him a pretty kopeck."

"Take it from a friend—may we both earn every week what it cost him, despite the fact that he was absolutely innocent. You know how it is in a small town. . . . A rich Jewish merchant.

. . . He's doing good business. . . . People begrudge it to him. . . . It's as simple as that. They just begrudge it to him."

"Possibly. Does he have nice, decent children? I think you mentioned three daughters?"

"Three is right. Two married and one still single. Fine children, very fine children. People say of the eldest one that . . . but it's a lie!"

"Namely? What on earth can they say about her?"

"I tell you it's a lie."

"I know it's a lie. I just want to know what *sort* of lie it is."

"Listen, if you were to sit down and give ear to all the lies flying around in Kolomeya, three days and three nights wouldn't be enough. Rumor has it that the oldest one doesn't have a marriage wig but parades around with her own hair. But I can tell you for a fact that it's an out-and-out lie, for she's neither sophisticated nor educated enough to scorn a marriage wig. Concerning the middle daughter, they dreamed up a story which said that even before she married, she . . . but the things that Kolomeya can dream up. It's a lie!"

"Tell me, just so I can get an inkling into what Kolomeya can dream up."

"I told you that Kolomeya is a city jam-packed with liars, slanderers, and tongue waggers. Don't you know that? In a small town, when a young girl strolls with a young man on a dark night, there's a tumult. They want to know how come a young girl can be permitted to walk all alone with a young man at night."

"Is that all?"

"What more do you want? Expect her to elope with him on Yom Kippur to Czernowitz and pull the same trick that they say her younger sister pulled?"

"What sort of trick did the youngest one pull?"

"I swear it isn't worth repeating all the stuff and nonsense that makes the rounds in Kolomeya. I hate to repeat lies. . . ."

"Since you've already told so many lies, why don't you tell me this one, too?"

"It's not *my* lies I'm telling, Reb Jew, it's the next fellow's.

. . . And I can't understand why you're asking me so many questions about each and every individual like a district attorney. You strike me as being the sort of chap who likes to draw, squeeze, and suck the blood from a man's bones, yet you yourself don't volunteer a word. Pardon me for being blunt; but you strike me as being a Russian Jew, and the Russians have a terrible character trait—they love to creep into the next fellow's boots and heart. . . . The Russian Jews, apparently, are no mean slanderers themselves. . . . And anyway, we'll soon be in Kolomeya . . . and I have to start packing. . . . So if you'll pardon me. . . ."

THE TENTH MAN

In our compartment there were nine of us. Nine Jews. We just lacked one man for the required quorum of ten. Actually, there *was* a tenth man. But there were doubts whether he was Jewish or not.

A quiet beardless man with gold-rimmed pince-nez, he had a small, freckled face, a Jewish nose, a mustache with a most un-Jewish upward swirl, protruding ears, and a red neck. Throughout the trip he kept aloof; he looked out the window and whistled nonchalantly to himself. He was hatless, of course, held a Russian newspaper on his lap, and did not say a word. An honest-to-goodness gentile. An authentic Russky. But then again—was that really a gentile sitting there? He didn't look like a gentile. And furthermore, no Jew could ever fool another Jew. A Jew can recognize a fellow Jew a mile away, even on a moonless night. Good heavens! How could one not recognize that distinctive Jewish face. So he *was* Jewish. I'd have bet a gold coin that he was a Jew. But on the other hand, suppose he wasn't? Nowadays one could never tell.

We decided it was the same old story all over again. The poor fellow wanted to pass for a gentile. Well, let him have fun. But what should we do if we lacked a tenth man? Someone in the car had to recite the Kaddish, the mourner's prayer, for it was the memorial day for a loved one. Do you think it was just the usual memorial-day Kaddish for a father or a mother? Not at all. It was one for a child. A son. The man had buried his only son.

"I begged the authorities to let me give my son a proper Jewish burial," he told us, "and finally they allowed me to remove his body from the prison. But I swear he was as innocent as a babe. They sentenced him much too quickly. Frankly, he *was* a devil of a chap among his group, but he certainly didn't deserve to be hanged. Nevertheless, hang him they did. And so, gone forever! And his mother went right after him. That is, she didn't go so quickly. She suffered plenty. Tormenting herself and me, making me old and gray." He paused, then added, "How old do you think I am?"

We all looked at him and wanted to guess his age. But it was impossible. He had youthful eyes, but gray hair; a wrinkled forehead, but a sad and smiling face. All told, he was an odd creature. His jacket was a bit too long. His hat was set back on his head. His beard was rounded. And eyes! What a pair of eyes he had! Once you saw those eyes that laughed and cried simultaneously, you would never forget them. If he would only complain or shed a tear or two. But no! On the contrary, he was merry and lively—a strange creature, indeed!

"Well, then, where do we get our tenth man from?" said someone, looking slyly at the man who was whistling. But the latter pretended not to hear. He looked out the window and whistled a popular tune.

"How come you're looking for a tenth man?" another passenger called out. "Don't we have a quorum here?" And to avoid the evil eye, he began "not-counting" with his finger, "Not-one, not-two, not-three—"

"Don't include me," the whistler exclaimed—in Yiddish.

We all were thunderstruck.

"Aren't you a Jew?"

"I am a Jew, but I don't believe in these things."

For a while we all sat stupefied, looking at one another without a word. Only the father who had to say Kaddish did not lose his presence of mind. With his tragicomic smile he addressed the whistler:

"May you live to be one hundred and twenty! You deserve a gold medal."

"Why a gold medal?"

"I'll tell you—but it's a rather long story. If you agree to be the tenth man for our quorum—it'll take me just a minute to say Kaddish for my son—I'll tell you a fascinating story."

And the merry mourner took out a kerchief, girded his jacket with it, stood facing the wall of the train and began the afternoon service:

"Happy are they who dwell in thy house. . . ."

I don't know about you. But I must admit that I like a weekday afternoon service. I consider its Silent Devotion far sweeter than ten artistically rendered cantorial selections with their Sabbath trills, frills, and holiday manner. The father chanted the Silent Devotion from the bottom of his heart. All of us—including the tenth man, I believe—were deeply touched by his tender and poignant praying. Listening to a father saying Kaddish for his son was no trifle, either. Moreover, the father's voice was so sweet and gentle it pervaded one's very being. And his recitation of the Kaddish! Oh, that Kaddish! Only a stone would have remained unmoved.

In brief, it was an afternoon service to remember. After the prayers the father unbound the kerchief from his waist and sat down opposite the tenth man. With his usual tragicomic expression, he began to tell the story he had promised, stroking his beard all the while and speaking slowly, like a man who had all the time in the world:

"Actually the story which I want to tell you, young man, is not one story, but three. Three brief anecdotes—"

The first took place in a village, where a farmer and his wife had leased a farm. Many gentiles lived there, but no other Jews. The farmer was the only one. Nevertheless, he made an excellent living. As they say—it pays to live among gentiles. The only thing they lacked was children. For many years they were childless. So they didn't enjoy life. Only when they were old did God have pity. The farmer's wife became pregnant and gave birth to a boy. What joy! A male heir! So, of course, they had to arrange a circumcision, just as God has bidden. On the eighth day the farmer harnessed horse to wagon, rode to town, and brought back the rabbi, the *shokhet,* the *shamesh,* and five other Jews. Naturally, the farmer's wife prepared a magnificent lunch. Everything was in perfect order. But suddenly they gave a start—no quorum. The tenth man was lacking. What had happened? That country bumpkin of a farmer had included his wife in reckoning up a quorum. Naturally, they all considered this a huge joke. But before anyone realized, time had flown. What was to be done? It was a large village. There were many gentiles, but not one Jew. A hopeless situation. Then they give a look, and there was a half-covered wagon approaching the inn. In the wagon sat a Jewish drayman. Albeit a drayman, but nonetheless a Jew.

"Welcome! How good to see you!"

"Hearty greetings."

"Come in, and you'll be the tenth man."

The joy was indescribable. Now see what a great God we have. An entire village of gentiles could be of no help. Yet along came one Jew, a simple drayman, and the problem was solved.

The second story, my dear fellow Jew, happened not in a village, but in a town. In fact, in a Jewish town. One Friday night, after candles were lit. I returned from the synagogue and recited the Kiddush. I washed. Sat down to the table. Suddenly one of the candles tipped over. We pushed the Sabbath loaf over to it. Didn't do any good. The wick fell on the tablecloth and started burning. What now? Put it out? It was forbidden on the Sabbath! All the neighbors came running—the entire street! Tumult. Chaos. Pandemonium.

"Friends, we're lost!"

We give a look, and there was Fyodor the Sabbath *goy*.

"Fyodor dear," we said to him in Russian, "do you see the light there?" And Fyodor, gentile though he was, understood what we were driving at. He spit on his hand, and with two coarse, peasant fingers he took hold of the burning wick and snuffed out the flame. Well, I ask you. Can God's wonders be properly appreciated? So many Jews, knock wood, and yet no one could do a thing. Yet along came one gentile and saved an entire town.

Now here's the third story. This happened to the *rebbe*. The *rebbe*, long life to him, had an only son, a talented boy with all the virtues, as befits a *rebbe*. So naturally they married him off young. He took a wife with a dowry, and his father-in-law even promised to support him indefinitely in order for him to pursue his sacred studies. So he sat and studied. Everything would have been fine and dandy were it not for the draft. But at first glance what had the *rebbe*'s son to do with the draft? First of all, he was an only son. Secondly, if it came to a payoff, money was no problem. But bad times came, alas! They began to take only sons of Jewish parents, and money was out of the question. Not even ten thousand rubles. The authorities were adamant, the doctors heartless. It was awful! No ifs and buts, my dear young man, they brought the *rebbe*'s son to the physical stark naked. For the first time in his life he stood bareheaded. And that precisely turned out to be his stroke of good fortune. For it seems they found that his scalp was scurfy—God spare you the like—and this disqualified him. And it was no put-up job either. Perfectly natural. They speculated that it had remained with him from childhood. He had always been a stubborn child. Never let his hair be washed. So, naturally, what with that scurfy head they showed him the door.

"Having heard these three tales, I now ask you, my dear young man: What good are *you*? A Jew is what you are, a gentile is what you'd like to be, but most of all you're a scurfy lout. Well, don't you deserve a gold medal?"

At the next station our tenth man disappeared.

Kasrilevke Characters

BOAZ THE TEACHER

1

The day Mama took me by the hand and brought me to Boaz's *kheder* for the first time, I felt like a young chicken on its way to the *shokhet*. It flutters with fright, poor thing—not comprehending, but sensing that the future isn't all chicken feed.

Mama had good reason, then, to console me. She said that the Good Angel would drop me a kopeck from the ceiling, gave me a whole apple, a kiss on the forehead, and asked Boaz to go a wee bit easy on me. "The child, you see, has just got over the measles."

Then, as though offering him a fragile and expensive crystal dish, Mama turned me over to Boaz, and went home pleased and happy. And I, the ex-measly child, now alone, cried a bit at first but then dried my tears and assumed the responsibility of Torah studies and ethical conduct. I looked forward to the Good Angel, who soon would surely throw me a kopeck from the ceiling.

Oh, that Good Angel! That Good Angel! If only Mama had not mentioned him! For when Boaz approached and grabbed hold of me with his dry, hairy hand and sat me down at his table, I felt so dizzy I thought I would pass out. And when I looked up to the ceiling, my reward was a right good yank at my ear.

"What are you looking at, you little bastard?"

Naturally, I blubbered, "Ma-ma," and then had my first real taste of the rebbi's blows.

"A little boy should not look where he's not supposed to. A little boy should not bleat for his Ma-ma like a calf."

2

The one (and only) pedagogic method utilized by the rebbi was whipping. Why whipping? He explained this quite logically by citing a parable about a horse. What makes a horse run? Fear! Of what was he afraid? The whip. And a child was no different. A child must fear—God, the rebbi, his parents, sins, and evil thoughts. In order for a child to be imbued with the correct amount of fear, he must be laid down properly, with pants lowered, and given two dozen lashes.

"Ah, backside whacks. Don't spare the rod. There's nothing better! Long live the whip!" said Boaz, slowly taking the whip in hand. He never rushed; he inspected it from all sides, as though examining an *esrog*. Then he set to work, calmly and methodically, keeping rhythm by nodding and chanting a little ditty:

> Backside
> whacks.
> Backside
> smacks.

Wonder of wonders! Boaz never counted the lashes, yet he never made a mistake. He was never in a rage when he dispensed the whippings. Boaz was not the sort to get angry. He lost his temper only when a child didn't let himself be whipped but squirmed out of his hands and kicked his legs. That, you see, was an entirely different matter. When this happened, Boaz's eyes would become bloodshot, and he would whack away without singing and without keeping count.

"A little boy must lie still when the rebbi whips him. . . . A little boy must behave even when he's being smacked. . . ."

Boaz also became furious when someone laughed during a beating (there are some kids who laugh during a spanking—it's a sort of sickness, folks say). He considered laughing something terrible. Boaz had never laughed in his life and hated to see others laughing. The most munificent rewards would have been offered for anyone to step forward and swear under oath that he had seen Boaz laughing. But Boaz wasn't the laughing sort. His face wasn't even built for it. Boaz's face in laughter would surely have been uglier than anyone else's face in tears. (Yes, such faces do exist.) And, anyway, what sort of pastime was laughing? Only idlers, bums, nincompoops, and rogues specialized in laughter. But people who worried about making a living, who bore the responsibility of Torah studies and ethical conduct, could spare no time for laughter. Boaz never had any time, for he was either teaching or whipping, practicing his calling as a whipping teacher or a teaching whipper. Actually, it was hard to draw the line between the two and discover where teaching ended and whipping began.

Nevertheless, for your information, Boaz never whipped us unjustly. There was always a good reason for it: He whipped us for not learning, for not wanting to pray, for not obeying our parents, for not paying attention, for looking out the window, for turning around, for praying too quickly, for praying too slowly, for talking too loud, for talking too softly, for a torn lapel, for a missing button, for a rip, a scratch, a dirty hand, a spotted Siddur; he whipped us for chewing candy, for running around, for pulling a trick, and for this, that, and the other thing.

These whippings were given—as the Yom Kippur prayer has it—"for sins committed knowingly." There were also whippings "for sins committed unknowingly"—that is, lashes on account. In advance. Every Friday and before every holiday and school vacation. "If you don't deserve the whipping now," we were told, "God willing, you'll deserve it later."

We were also whipped because friends or strangers had snitched on us to the rebbi. Sometimes we got an explanation when we were smacked: "You realize, of course, for what good deeds you're getting this."

Sometimes we got a whipping just for the fun of it. "Let's see how a little boy lets himself be whipped."

In a word, the whip and lashes, fear and tears, prevailed in our foolish child's world—and there was no recourse, no cure, no ray of hope of ever getting rid of this living hell.

And what about the Good Angel which Mama had once mentioned? Where was he keeping himself?

3

I must admit that on occasion I doubted that fine story about the Good Angel. I was quite young when a spark of heresy stole into my heart, when I began to wonder if perhaps Mama had fooled me, when I learned to feel hatred. I was much too young to hate, but nevertheless, I already hated my rebbi, Boaz.

How could I not hate him? How could one not hate a rebbi who did not let you raise your head? It was forbidden. Don't stand here! Don't go there! Don't talk to him! How could one not hate a man who didn't have a spark of compassion, who rejoiced at another's pain, bathed in his tears, and smeared himself with his blood?

One would think there was no greater humiliation than a whipping. But was there anything more embarrassing than being stripped stark naked and told to stand in the corner? No, even that wasn't enough for Boaz. Boaz demanded that you strip, remove your shirt and underwear, lay yourself facedown without any help—and leave the rest to him.

> Backside
> whacks.
> Backside
> smacks.

Boaz did not give the whippings unaided. His assistants— he called them his choirboys—helped him. Naturally, they were under his strict supervision so that not a blow would be missed.

"Better a little less Torah than a few less lashes," Boaz asserted, offering a commonsense explanation of his theory. "Too much learning only confuses a little tyke. But an extra smack never hurts. Let's look at it more closely. When you study with a child, it goes right to his head. This confuses the thoughts and dulls the brain. But whipping him has exactly the opposite effect. By the time the sensation travels from that nether region through the rest of the body to the brain, the smack has meanwhile purified the blood and cleansed the brain. Now do you understand?"

Boaz never ceased purifying our blood and cleansing our brains. Alas, we stopped believing in that Good Angel from up above. We finally realized it was only a fairy tale trumped up to fool us into going to Boaz's *kheder*. We sighed and groaned over our lot, which was as miserable and bitter as the Exile. We muttered and talked and sought means for ending this awful tyranny.

4

During the melancholy moments of twilight, when the bright day slips away and night comes softly bearing its sad secrets, when shadows climb sheer walls and spread in all directions— during the melancholy moments between the afternoon and evening prayers when the rebbi was in *shul* and his wife was preparing yeast dough and fussing with the goat and the milk pitchers—all the children gathered around the oven in *kheder*. We sat cross-legged on the floor, huddled together like a flock of innocent lambs, and there, in the dark, we discussed the fearful Titus, our Angel of Death, Boaz. The older boys, who had been his pupils for a year or more, told horrible tales about Boaz and swore by all that was holy that he had whipped more than one boy to death, that he had driven three wives to their graves, that he had buried his only son—as well as other wild stories that made our hair stand on end.

The older boys spoke, and the younger ones listened attentively. Black eyes gleamed in the darkness. Young hearts fluttered. We all agreed that Boaz the teacher had no soul. He was a human being without a heart. Such a person was a wild beast or a demon, whose removal would be a praiseworthy deed.

Thousands of plans, foolish and childish schemes of getting rid of this Angel of Death, flitted through our young minds. How silly we were! Each one held these inane plans hidden in the depths of his heart. We prayed to God for a miracle— that either flames consume his Siddur or his whip blow away

. . . or . . . or. . . . No one wanted to utter the last possibility, afraid of saying it out loud.

Our imaginations were ablaze. Fantasy transported us. Dreams, beautifully sweet dreams, tangled with reality. Dreams of freedom—of running down hills, splashing barefoot in the river, playing horse and rider, jumping over fences—beautifully sweet and trifling dreams, destined not to be realized. For just then the familiar cough was heard, the thump of familiar soles, the shuffling of down-at-the-heel shoes. Our blood froze; our limbs became petrified. We sat down to study the Torah and prayed with the same enthusiasm that a convict displays while climbing the scaffold. We studied, but our lips whispered: "Lord of the Universe! Will the end of this Amalek, this Pharaoh, Haman and Gogmagog ever come? Will we ever be rid of this dark and burdensome tyranny? No, never!" we foolish children decided. "Never, ever, ever!"

5

"Fellows, I've got a nifty little plan for getting rid of our Gogmagog," said Velvel during one of those melancholy twilights. He was an older boy, a thoroughgoing rascal, whose eyes glittered like a wolf's in the dark as he spoke.

The entire gang gathered around Velvel to hear his nifty little plan for getting rid of our oppressor. Velvel began with a lengthy sermon: It was impossible to stand Boaz any longer. That demonic Ashmedai bathed in our blood. He treated us worse than dogs. A beaten dog at least has the opportunity of screeching, but we dared not even do that. And so on and so forth. Then Velvel called to us:

"Fellows, listen to me. I want to ask you something."

"Go ahead," we all said in unison.

"What if one of us suddenly got sick?"

"Aw, that'd be too bad," we replied.

"No, you got me wrong. What I mean is this. For example, if one of us got sick, would he go to school, or would he stay home?"

"Naturally, he'd stay at home," we all called out.

"But what happens," Velvel continued, "if two of us get sick?"

"Two of us would stay at home!"

"What about three?" Velvel continued—and we didn't weary of answering:

"Then three of us would stay at home."

"But what happens—just for the sake of argument—if all of us get sick?"

"Then we all would stay at home."

"Then let all of us get sick," Velvel said triumphantly.

"God forbid," we said. "Are you nuts or just plain crazy?"

"I'm neither nuts nor crazy. But you're definitely a bunch of asses. You think I really want us to get sick? We just pretend, so we don't have to go to *kheder*. *Now* you get it?" Velvel said.

We began to understand his plan. We began to like his plan and to consider what our ailments would be. One said toothache. Another, headache. A third, bellyache. A fourth, worms. But the upshot was none of these—not toothache, headache, bellyache, or worms. What then? Each of us would complain that our feet hurt. Because a doctor could diagnose all the above-mentioned sicknesses. But if you told him that your feet hurt and that you couldn't move them—let him come and examine them!

"Remember, fellows," Velvel said, "tomorrow morning don't you dare get out of bed. And to make sure we all stick together and none of us comes to *kheder* tomorrow, let's all shake and touch a fringe of our *tsitsis* to seal the bargain."

We all shook hands and touched the fringes. Each one of us went home that night, cheerful and buoyant, singing like soldiers who had found a way to overpower their enemy and win the war.

Children! We're coming to the most interesting part of our story. I know you're curious to find out how this childish plan, this crazy strike of ours, ended. I know you want to know if we stuck to our bargain and kept our word. How did people react when they saw that so many children had suddenly fallen ill? What did our parents say?

What did the rebbi do? Did we succeed in carrying out our plan?

Unfortunately, I can't tell you anymore, dear children, for it's the eve of a holiday, and I have to break off just at the climax and leave the ending for another time. . . .

But since we're at the point of saying good-bye, I just want to tell you briefly that Boaz is still alive. But, alas and alack, what a life it is! Years have passed since he last taught a class. What does he do? How does he make a living? Ah, me, he has to go begging from door to door. If you meet him someday (you can recognize him by his limp), give him a donation, won't you? It's a pity. The poor man is down-at-the-heels—a has-been!

VELVEL GAMBETTA

1

Everyone knows that Gambetta,* the famous Jewish lawyer, was blind in one eye. And since Velvel, too, was a Jewish lawyer, blind in one eye, he was nicknamed Gambetta. The only drawback was that the first Gambetta lived in Paris, and the second—Velvel—in Kasrilevke. On the other hand, perhaps it was an advantage, rather than a drawback. For let's not fool ourselves—what would the Gambetta of Paris have done in Kasrilevke? And what would the Gambetta of Kasrilevke have done in Paris? It was far more sensible for the French Gambetta to live in Paris and for our Gambetta to live in Kasrilevke, where he has presumably remained to this very day.

First of all, our Velvel Gambetta had a reputation for being a brain. Had he not been a Jew, it was said, he could have been a prime minister. And I think it's much better to say that a man *could* have been than that he *is*. For if he already *is*, it's over and done with, but if not, he was still in the running. Second, Gambetta earned a good, honorable living here. Well, actually, it wasn't always honorable, for honor and respect weren't always rendered. Occasionally, there were even insults—against which no mortal is immune. Can *anyone* brag that he has never ever encountered disrespect? Just show me the wizard who always manages to avoid insults! I'm not even talking about com-

---

* Léon Gambetta (1838-1882) was a French statesman, born of a Genoese family said to have been Jewish. At sixteen he lost an eye and, at twenty-one, began the practice of law. A member of the French Chamber of Deputies, Gambetta became the president of this body in 1879. Like the hero of Sholom Aleichem's story, Gambetta was a controversial and occasionally flamboyant figure—Tr.

ing to blows. For no man on earth can be forewarned regarding an unexpected smack.

But why do I mention blows out of the blue? Because it so happens that this story begins with an exchange of blows. If not for the blows, Velvel wouldn't have lost an eye, he wouldn't have become a lawyer, and he wouldn't have been nicknamed Gambetta. I wouldn't have had a subject, the printer a job, and you a story. But since the good Lord performed a miracle and there *were* blows, everything followed in due course, glory to God, and you've got a story to read. Praised be the name of Him who lives eternally, amen.

2

I know that as soon as you hear of blows being exchanged—Jewish smacks, that is—you immediately think of a *shul*, trustees, *shamoshim*, and various synagogue honors. You might ask where else can Jews beat one another if not in a holy place? And when can a Jew drub his fellow if not on Simkhas Torah when the Torah circuits begin? Not a bad guess, but, unfortunately, this time you're dead wrong. You can't always guess right, you know. It did not happen in the synagogue itself, but in the foyer, and not on Simkhas Torah, but during the intermediary days of Passover, and the whole to-do wasn't precipitated by a synagogue honor but by the word "subscriber."

I'm sure you all know the difference between "subscriber" and "subscription." But during Passover one young chap in the synagogue (I think it was Ephraim-Yosel, Moishe-Ber's boy) bragged to his friends that he was a paid-up member in the lending library. Here's the way he put it:

"All right, fellows, I now have the pleasure of informing you that I have just become a subscription."

To which one of his friends retorted:

"What do you mean you're a subscription?"

"I've enrolled in the municipal library," said Ephraim-Yosel.

"In other words, you're a subscriber," replied the other, "and not a subscription."

"What's the difference—subscriber or subscription?"

"There's a big difference," said Ephraim-Yosel's friend. "They're as unalike as Passover and pass-under, as different as shark and gefilte fish. By the same token, a subscriber is a subscriber and a subscription is a subscription."

While speaking, the latter used his hand to demonstrate which was subscriber and which subscription. Well, actually, he did not *do* anything with his hand; he merely moved it like the man who wanted to define "massive" by pressing his friend's hand and grunting that massive means MASS-IVE. But even such a handy explanation did not impress Ephraim-Yosel, who still asserted:

"I don't give a damn what any of you say—I'm still a subscription."

"Subscriber," the other corrected him.

"What's the difference?"

"So you still don't see your mistake, huh?"

"Who asked you to correct me?" said Ephraim-Yosel.

"If you're wrong, I'll correct you."

"How do you know I'm wrong? Perhaps, it's just the other way around."

"Because I know."

"You don't know a damn thing."

"And you're a damn fool."

"And *you're* an impudent smart aleck."

"And you're a son of a bitch, your father's a filthy swine, and your uncle's a lousy crook."

"And *you're.* . . ."

But it was hard to catch the subsequent abuse because the punches flew from both sides. Had friends not intervened, they would have bitten each other's noses off. But just when the bystanders were breaking up the brawl, the most serious damage was done: One tore the other's gaberdine in half, and the other unintentionally jabbed his elbow into his opponent's eye—at which the latter emitted an unearthly screech and passed out. When they tried to revive him, they saw that his eye was swollen. A tumultuous uproar broke out, and they sent for a doctor. When the doctor announced that the eye was gone, the tumult became even greater. My God, an eye knocked out!

Blinded! But all the screaming was just so much eyewash, for when the shouting was over, the wounded man still remained with only one eye. And the latter was none other than Velvel.

3

This saga of the eye obviously took place during the era when the Enlightenment was already so deeply entrenched in Kasrilevke that secular books and municipal libraries could be mentioned publicly. For by then times were already different. Gone were the cellars and attics, gone were secret hiding places where one would surreptitiously read the works of Yitzhok-Ber Levinson, Abraham Mapu, Peretz Smolenskin, and other Hebrew writers. Now it all was done in broad daylight. So rejoice Kasrilevke youths. Congratulations! You've been released into God's world! Doors and gates are wide open to you. Make haste, you rascals. Grab your places, but take care to excel—for soon a cloud will come, and they will slam the school doors right in your face. In vain will be your knocking and your screaming. You'll tear your hair and say: "Woe unto lost chances—there once was a time, ah, me—those were the years."

It was during that very era that our Reb Velvel began dabbling with culture. He became an avid reader and learned so many foreign words that he practically knew the entire dictionary by heart. If not for the accident to his eye, perhaps he might have entered a university and received a degree in medicine or law like other young men; he might even have achieved worldwide fame. But because of that mishap, he had no opportunity to progress. However, since he liked reading and foreign words and had an excellent hand and a good head, he took to legal counseling. After studying the necessary books and learning the entire code of law by heart, he hung a shingle on his door—COMMERCIAL ADVOCATE—and drew the insignia of a scribe—an inkwell and a large pen—which served strict notice that the office would accent writing and eliminate idle chatter and small talk.

Velvel's depositions were so noteworthy that one would have

had to traverse the entire globe to find a finer example of legal writing. So said Velvel himself, as well as all other connoisseurs of legal style. In fact, people stood in awe of his depositions and affidavits. When he took pen in hand, the fear of death came over them, for he wrote and wrote—it gushed out of him as from a broken pipe. He wrote everywhere and to everyone, the regional governor and the ministers of the land included. He skipped no one.

But don't get the impression that Velvel was a common informer or a scoundrel, God forbid! Not at all! The world has a plentiful supply of informers and scoundrels. Don't breathe a word of it, but the greatest concentration can be found among us Jews. One man tattles on another because the latter has deprived him of his livelihood. Another squeals because his *neighbor* has it too good. A third tells on his fellow villager because he *himself* doesn't have it too good, poor soul. Then there's the kind that turns informer just like that, for no good reason at all—simply out of pure geniality. Just for the fun of it. Because he'd like to see what sort of fuss his blabbing would trigger. Of course, none of the talebearers I've listed ever signs his name. They can be compared to those sneaky mongrels who always attack you from behind, nip your ankle, and either draw blood or rip your coattail. Only then do their tails droop and they go on their merry way.

4

No, Velvel Gambetta was not that sort of writer. He was a self-made lawyer, who developed a unique system for doing business. Called "tracting," it consisted of contracting, protracting, distracting, and extracting. After signing the initial contract, Velvel would protract the case, distract his clients, and extract his fees. And the more he "tracted," the happier he was. He also adored writing lots of affidavits and depositions—one after the other, one atop the other—such an infinite amount that the only tangible result a client ever saw was more legal paperwork.

"Well, Reb Velvel, what's new with my case?"

"What should be new? We have to file an affidavit, and everything will be swell and dandy."

"So why don't you file it?"

"I can't file this particular affidavit until I deposit a deposition stating that I filed the previous affidavits."

"So how come you don't deposit the deposition?"

"That's just what I'm trying to tell you. I have to file an affidavit to get an affidavit that I filed the affidavits."

"Apparently there's no end to your filing, Reb Velvel."

"If you don't like it, find yourself a better lawyer."

But it was all stuff and nonsense. The client would not look for another lawyer, and Velvel would continue to file affidavits and tract as long as the "traction" was good. For he was still the best lawyer in Kasrilevke. For instance, take the others. Yosel the attorney had a sharp tongue—at home that is. But where it counted he was tongue-tied. Mendel the fat advocate was a boor, an ignoramus, a downright embarrassment in a court-room. Quite often the judge threw Mendel's petition right back at his face and said, "Take up shoeshining and stop scribbling petitions." Counselor-at-law Soloveytchik did have some know-how. To hear him tell it, he supposedly had three full semesters under his belt—but he was a scoundrel, an out-and-out thief. Yerakhmiel the legal adviser was a decent chap, but a big shot with a buttoned lip. Everyone despises a tight-lipped individual, but a chatterbox, especially if he's a lawyer, everyone adores.

5

There was just one more particular in Velvel Gambetta's system—witnesses. Witnesses and more witnesses. Every case had loads and loads of witnesses. For two reasons:

First of all, the witnesses enabled him to contract, protract, distract, and extract as much as he wanted, since among loads of witnesses there was always one sick, a second traveling, and a third who simply forgot to appear in court. Second, with the witnesses themselves he played a strange game, otherwise known as Velvel's politicking.

But here I must interrupt for a moment and tell the reader a secret (which I hope will travel no further). Our Velvel frequently had dealings with both sides. In other words, he displayed his knack of simultaneously being the lawyer for each of the opposing sides. Obviously, neither of the two were supposed to know this—and each thought that Velvel represented him alone.

Do you want to know how he accomplished this feat? Quite simply. Imagine that Reb Duvidl came to Velvel and asked him to file an affidavit against me, stating that I'd done thus and thus to him. Before starting proceedings, however, Velvel promised Duvidl that for that mean stunt I'd be fixed in such a fashion that even Siberia would seem like paradise. And he railed out against me: "What the devil! Is *that* what he did to you? Just let me get hold of him, and I'll tell him a thing or two. That's it. I *am* going to get hold of him. In fact, I'll send for him right now, that bastard!"

At which Velvel sent for me and stated:

"Well, what do you say to that rascal Reb Duvidl? Not enough that he's cursed you up and down, but he also wants to start proceedings against you. In fact, he was just here. Naturally, I told him that *you* are in the right and not him. But you know me, I'm no common flatterer, and I'm not going to undertake to handle this affair either."

At this, I interrupted him, of course, and asked, "Why not?"

"I don't want to," he answered. "Duvidl's just been here. It isn't right."

So I tried to talk him into it. "Forget his being here. After all, *I'm* here now."

To make a long story short, this kept up until I convinced him to become my lawyer.

That's when the merry-go-round of witnesses would begin. Velvel himself set up the witnesses for both sides and managed the negotiations so skillfully and with such class that the witnesses were finally led to squabbles, invective and— why not?—fisticuffs. That's when he *really* had something to do. Another brand-new case. The insulted and beaten witnesses naturally had *their* witnesses who saw the punches be-

ing thrown, and since *they* all patronized Velvel, master at
law, they, too, finally ended up with squabbles, invective, and
fisticuffs. Resulting in more work for Velvel.

6

Velvel Gambetta had one fault (did you ever see a man without faults?): He couldn't get along with women. No wife could
stand him more than a year—or at most, a year and a half.

From which one may infer that Velvel had not one, but several wives. Do you think he had several at once? Heaven forbid! Kasrilevke had not as yet reached such a sophisticated
state of civilization whereby a Jew could afford to be like his
big-city brethren who followed the fashion of having several
wives concurrently. Kasrilevke Jews thank God if they can
endure one wife. They said that even *one* wife who had fine
taste and knew the tailor and the dressmaker could make a
man old and gray. Not to mention what she could do if she
thought she could play piano or, in addition to knowing the
latest card games, had read one book in her life and seen two
or three plays. In that case, woe unto the poor husband. During the winter he would have to have open house at least once
a week, as well as provide a summer cottage for his wife and a
high-school education for his children. In short, such a poor
chap is only to be pitied. The only thing we can do for him is
heave a great big sigh.

Now let's return to Velvel and his wives.

Velvel Gambetta's first wife, Breindl, was one of our own
—from Kasrilevke, that is. She was Yossi the candler's daughter, as fine a Jewish girl as you could find. People envied Yossi
that match. With such a small dowry she had managed to nab
an intellectual, the master at law himself. But the upshot was
that soon after the wedding Yossi's daughter began saying
that she didn't want to live with him. Why? She was afraid.
Afraid of what? Afraid he would sue all the stores. Which
stores? Whose stores? And how could this possibly concern her?
But go argue with a woman! That business with the lawsuits

and the stores gave her no peace. Though you tore her to pieces, she still wanted no part of him.

Obviously, Kasrilevke was not satisfied with an excuse like that. Lawsuits? Stores? How, what, and wherefore? There was a secret here, probably the kind that could not be revealed in polite company. All sorts of stories began to make the rounds in the village; they were whispered from ear to ear and told in strictest confidence. While listening to these stories, the men checked to see if any women were around and then exploded into gales of laughter.

"What's so hysterical?" the women asked. "Tell us. We'd like to laugh, too."

The men's reply was another salvo of laughter. At this point the women began to take offense and snapped:

"Just look at those asses making fools of themselves. Come on, out with it. What's the big joke?"

And that's when the laughter really began. They held their sides, doubled over with laughter, and actually rolled on the floor.

7

In short, Velvel Gambetta divorced Yossi's daughter (incidentally, she married again and is now in America). But Velvel didn't remain single for long. He soon remarried and brought back a provincial girl (never before married), lived with her for a year, and quietly divorced her. Then he set out for Berdichev and returned with an elegant *madame,* decked out in hat, gloves, and so forth. He paid social calls, furnished his house anew, and established weekly at-homes with young people who played the latest card games. But neither the house nor the furniture nor the latest card games helped one bit. One fine morning they went to the rabbi for a divorce, and back to Berdichev went the elegant *madame,* decked out in hat, gloves, and so forth.

The next time Velvel Gambetta departed from town to get married again, the Kasrilevke wags, who loved to poke fun at everyone, had some advice for him. Why did he have to bother traveling to get married and then divorce his wife back home? Wouldn't it be better to arrange a marriage and a divorce then and there at one and the same time?

To which Velvel replied that there were far too few sages of their ilk in the world. The only thing that surprised him was why such geniuses still went barefoot and wore hand-me-downs. He aimed so many other barbed shafts their way they didn't know which way to flee. He then promptly set out for Warsaw and brought back a hellcat with false teeth and a queer-looking headdress, who spoke Yiddish with an outlandish and totally unfamiliar dialect.

First of all, she chattered quickly. What am I saying, quickly? Before she had uttered the first word, five or six others tumbled over one another in the rush to take off, fearing that they'd miss some rare opportunity. Hardly had they flown the coop than a dozen others stood lined up, preparing for flight.

That was number one. Second, she had a squeaky voice, appended a variety of groans onto everything she said, and delivered all her remarks in an odd mixture of clashing synagogue melodies. To top it off, she cackled like a magpie as she displayed her false teeth and shook her headdress to and fro. In a word, it was pure delight. People in Kasrilevke loved to watch this false-toothed "Warsaw beauty," and they roared with laughter as she rattled on in her squeaky, singsong dialect. Folks said that with her around, Kasrilevke didn't need a theater.

So it was really a shame that she didn't last too long in Kasrilevke. Only one summer. For when the High Holy Days rolled around, Velvel divorced her and she returned to Warsaw.

But Velvel Gambetta never again remarried; in fact, he has remained single until this very day.

Maybe you know a nice Jewish girl for him?

ISSER THE SHAMESH

1

When I think of Isser the *shamesh* I am always reminded of Alexander the Great, Napoleon Bonaparte, and other heroes of the past.

Isser was nothing to sneeze at. He was a man who led the entire congregation, substantial householders included, by the nose. A man who had the entire village in his side pocket; who served everyone, yet was everyone's master; who had an angry countenance, ferocious eyebrows, a copper beard, a mighty pair of paws, and a huge walking stick. A formidable man, indeed.

How did Isser rise to his position? Ask me another! Some people are born inert. They're the sort whose status in life never changes. They never seem to budge from the niche you first saw them in. When I was a child, I couldn't tear myself away from Isser. One thing always intrigued me. What was Isser like before he became Isser? That is, when he still had not developed those ferocious eyebrows, the huge, crooked nose constantly stuffed with snuff, and the copper beard that started out so thick and dense and ended up so sparse and wild? What did he look like when he was a barefoot lad studying in *kheder* and getting whipped by *his* rebbi? What was Isser like when his mother held him in her arms, nursed him, cleaned his nose, and cooed, "Sweet little Isserl, my heir, my pride and joy, may all your pains be mine instead"?

So ran my thoughts when I was a boy, and I was unable to tear myself away from Isser.

* * *

"Get on home, you little bastards, an ill wind take your parents," Isser said, not even letting me look at him.

There was only one of me. So how come Isser referred to me in the plural? How come I deserved the extra *s*? Isser, you see, could not stand having anyone stare him in the face. Isser hated kids. Couldn't stand the sight of them. "Children," he said, "are a pack of troubles. They're rotten pests; they're malicious and spiteful. Kids are wild goats jumping into gardens. Kids are dogs nipping your coattails. Kids are pigs crawling on the table. Kids should be in a perpetual fright and have the seven-year itch."

And indeed we *were* in a perpetual fright and *had* the seven-year itch.

What were we afraid of, you ask? Well, try *not* to be afraid when Isser took you by the ear, dragged you to the door, and kicked you out, saying:

"Go home, bastards, an ill wind take your father and mother."

Want to complain to Mama? Well, go ahead and try. Do you want to know what would happen? I'll tell you precisely. You'd come home and show your mother your tweaked ear. Mama would run to Father crying, "Look, look at your one and only. Look at the way that murderer, that gangster, tore his ear off." Father would then take your hand and bring you to *shul* straight to Isser the *shamesh,* as though to say: "Here, see what you've done to my one and only! You almost tore his ear off!"

Isser would then raise a fuss and say, "I bid you and your little bastards a hearty adieu. Good day!"

You see? For him a one-and-only child was bastard*s*. What would Father do next? He would pull his hat over his eyes and go home. Mama would ask him, "Well?" and Father would reply, "I gave that wicked Haman a piece of my mind. What more could I have done to him?"

Actually, it wasn't very nice for Father to tell such a whopping lie. But there was no choice if one was at the mercy of a tyrannical *shamesh.*

2

One can say that the entire village was at the mercy of that tyrant. Isser could do—and did—whatever he liked. If Isser didn't feel like heating the *shul* in midwinter, you could burst a blood vessel arguing, but he'd pay no more attention to you than to the snows of yesteryear. If Isser wanted morning services to begin early, no matter when you arrived, you'd be late. If Isser didn't want to call you to the Torah for months on end, you could try to catch his eye from today till doomsday and cough yourself blue. He would neither see you nor hear you. The same was true if you lacked prayer shawl, Pentateuch, holiday prayerbook, *esrog,* or Hoshana Rabba willows. Since you were nobody special, Isser would bring it to you not when you wanted it, but whenever the spirit moved him.

"Worshipers are a dime a dozen. Like stray mutts," he grumbled. "But me, I'm one and only, one single *shamesh,* God bless me, for so many people. They drive you nuts!"

Isser thrashed about, gesticulated, insulted everyone. If rubbed the wrong way, Isser would show the door even to the most respected householder, who'd leave in such a dither he'd miss the doorway. "Better not annoy me," Isser would say. "I don't have time to talk to you. There's plenty of you and, God bless me, only one of me."

So no one annoyed him. They were content if he didn't pick a fight with them.

Naturally, no one would ever dream of asking Isser what became of the money that people donated when they were called to the Torah, or the proceeds of the *yohrzeit* candles, or the contents of the charity box, or other monies pertaining to congregational affairs. If, after all, Isser was the master of the *shul,* to whom did he owe a rendering of accounts? And the congregation was pleased that Isser left them alone and did not throw the keys to the *shul* at their faces and say:

"Why don't you take care of this *shul* yourselves? Keep an eye on the wood, water, lights, and matches. Wash a towel once in a while. Repair a prayer stand. Buy a Siddur, and rebind a book of penitential prayers. See that there's enough Purim rattle-clackers, *dreydls,* Hanuka candles, *lulavs* and *esrogs,* willow branches, this, that, and the other thing."

Everyone knew quite well that all these items not only cost money but brought in profits; nevertheless, no one dared poke his nose into the matter. That was the *shamesh's* domain. That was his income, his source of livelihood.

"A fine income I have from you. . . . All I have is a head-ache. . . . Water for kasha is what you give me," said Isser, and everyone held his peace.

Yes, all kept silent, although they knew very well that Isser was stashing away money. Everyone knew very well that the *shamesh* was loaded. In fact, he may even have secretly extended little loans—for security, naturally. He had his own little house, and a cow as well. He guzzled brandy daily, and out of a water glass at that. He wore a fur-lined coat in winter, praise the Lord, just like the richest householder. His wife's leather boots were always fully soled, and she had recently ordered a new cloak for herself—at the congregation's expense.

"With our blood, a plague upon her, dear God!" the congregants muttered softly behind Isser's back. But when the *shamesh* approached, the topic of conversation suddenly changed.

Isser got the point. He knew that the congregation was dying to fire him. But he paid no more attention to them than Haman does to the Purim rattle-clacker. Isser had them in the palm of his hand. Isser knew exactly what he had to do.

3

Isser was smart enough to realize that if one can't please everybody, one ought at least to curry favors wisely. Hence, he was in cahoots with the trustees, the handful of big wheels in town. He kowtowed to and obeyed these worthies and didn't mind doing an extra favor for them. The way he buttered them up was sickening. Especially when new trustees were up for election. Then Isser did not sit still. Whoever has not seen Isser at election time has never seen anything magnificent. Hat askew, huge walking stick in hand, Isser plodded through the mud in his long boots. Perspiring, he strode from one trustee to another, busily conniving and transporting endless shipments of slander and intrigue.

Isser had always been a master at fostering intrigues. He could have made two walls clash. He incited people so skillfully to mutual animosity that the entire congregation would be at odds, bickering and cursing, and almost come to blows. But Isser remained absolutely nonchalant, innocent as a lamb. Isser, you see, was not a bad navigator at all. Keep fighting, he thought. Poke each other's eyes out, folks—and you'll forget all about the *shamesh*.

Making people forget about the *shamesh* was a prime necessity for Isser, for people had recently begun taking him to task, insisting that he give a complete account of the *shul's* money. Who were the instigators? The youngsters, the small fry, the very same "little bastards" he had always hated and pestered to death.

The saying has it that children grow up and old people become children. Several generations came and went. Young kids became big billy goats. The little bastards became rich little villagers. The little villagers got married and became great big villagers. And they grew old—and Isser still remained Isser. But suddenly, a new young generation sprang up—a strange new generation, made up of pests, brats, and rogues—God protect us from such fresh young louts.

"What sort of lord and master is Isser? Isser is just a *shamesh* who's here to cater to *us*, not we to *him*. How much longer will this long-legged old Isser rule over us? Let's see the accounts! We want a complete reckoning!"

Thus demanded the new generation, composed solely of pests, brats, scamps, scoundrels, and rogues. And they said this right smack in the middle of the courtyard. Out loud, too. At first Isser played dumb, pretended to be hard of hearing. Then he chased them from the *shul*, extinguished the lights, and locked the door. Then he incited the householders against them, concocted all sorts of slanders about them. He declared that these rogues ridiculed their elders and made fun of the trustees. To prove his point, he displayed a poem written (and lost) by one of the scoundrels.

It was only a silly little jingle. But what a hullabaloo this poem raised in town! Oh, my, what a revolution! Isser would have been better off had he not found the poem and not shown it to the trustees. Indeed, this very poem was the beginning of his downfall. Instead of taking the poem with a grain of salt, the foolish trustees spread it all over town. They passed it from hand to hand until the entire congregation had learned it by heart, and some wags set it to a popular old tune. The ditty was sung all over. Tradesmen sang it at their workbenches. Cooks, by the ovens. Girls sang it while sitting outside, and mothers used it as a lullaby. . . . A silly jingle has a strange power. While the throat is singing, the brain is busy working. It cogitates and ruminates until it discovers something. Thoughts spin and peck at one's mind until finally something is pecked out and thought becomes deed.

The incident that the poem triggered was a neat, but short one. So listen! It may come in handy someday.

4

An assortment of scoundrels, scamps, and troublemakers pestered Isser without letup; they searched and rummaged, then finally launched their attack. One fine morning they climbed up to the *shul's* attic and discovered an enormous treasure. An endless supply of wax candles, about two hundred pounds of tallow, two dozen brand-new prayer shawls, all kinds of prayer books, books of penitential hymns, lamentations, and other fine items that are more valuable to a *shamesh* than to you. With great to-do this treasure was brought down from the attic. Just picture the scene! On one side stood Isser with his crooked nose, ferocious eyebrows, and copper beard that started out dense and thick and ended up sparse and wild. On the other side stood the scamps, scoundrels, and troublemakers with their treasure. But don't think this fazed Isser, God forbid. Isser was not the sort of chap who readily lost his presence of mind. He just stood there wondering what in heaven's name such items were doing in the *shul's* attic.

Early the next morning the following announcement was chalked onto the *shul's* fence:

YOHRZEIT CANDLES SOLD HERE AT COST PRICE!

The next day there was another announcement. The third day another. Isser had a job on his hands. Every morning he had to stand holding a wet rag and erase the pesky pronouncements that sprouted every which way along the old *shul's* fence. What's more, the young scamps secretly placed packs of letters about Isser and his few cohorts in the prayer stands, and the congregants found new ones there every Sabbath.

Isser had a hard time. He convinced the trustees to post in the *shul* itself a proclamation written on parchment with huge letters:

Whereas owing to our great sins, there have recently appeared in our midst young people who are vain of mind and empty of spirit, spoiled brats who publish false reports about the most prominent people in town;

We, therefore, herewith proclaim in the name of the trustees of the great synagogue that from this day henceforth we will pay strict regard to these matters, and the ones we catch will be dealt with according to the law.

Naturally, the youngsters immediately tore down this proclamation, and in its place a new one sprang up. But the youngsters didn't sit on their hands and tore this one down, too. So a third proclamation was put up. And then the congregants found in their prayer stands more letters about Isser and his trustee cohorts. In brief, there was a period when everyone was writing: the trustees composed proclamations, and the wags and young rebels wrote letters. They kept this up until the approach of the High Holy Days, when new trustees were up for election. A battle began between the two sides. On one side stood Isser and his patrons, the old trustees, and on the other, the young troublemakers and their candidates. Each side tried its utmost to sway the rest of the congregation. One with passionate speeches and fiery sermons, the other with sweet talk and promises of roast duck and gizzards, a host of campaign pledges. Do you know who won? You'll never guess! The young scamps, scoundrels, and troublemakers. The new trustees were chosen from among the young men with short coats, wags, paupers, and—ah, me, the shame of it—working people. Imagine, common workingmen!

5

You've realized, I'm afraid, that the story is coming to an end. How long can it be dragged out? Do you want me to tell you how our new trustees dealt with the old *shamesh?* How they took poor old Isser and with song, honors, and hullabaloo paraded him through the streets on Simkhas Torah? Do you want me to describe how the scamps, jokers, and troublemakers marched around town with the entire treasure of candles and tallow, and all the prayer shawls and liturgical books that they found in the attic of the old *shul?* I'm sure you don't. I'm certain you won't ask me to describe such events.

Experiencing revenge over one's enemy is fine. But bathing in his blood—never. I can only tell you a few things:

This year I came home for the High Holidays. Hadn't been home in ages. Much water had passed under the bridge. But still I found the old *shul* at the same spot. The same Holy Ark, the same curtain, the same pulpit and chandeliers. But the people had changed so radically that I could hardly recognize them. The old people had died long ago, and many new tombstones with fine inscriptions had surely been added to our cemetery. The young people now had gray beards. There were new trustees. There was a new cantor, a new *shamesh.* New melodies, new customs. Everything was new.

On Hoshana Rabba, when the new cantor and the new choir were beautifully chanting "Hark, the Herald Proclaims" and the congregation began to beat their willow branches (apparently that custom had become permanent), I noticed an old, bent, white-haired man with a crooked nose, ferociously thick eyebrows, and a beard that started out thick and dense and ended up sparse and wild. I was attracted to this little old man, went up to him, and stretched out my hand.

"Greetings! Aren't you Reb Isser . . . the *shamesh?*"

"The *shamesh?* What *shamesh?* Haven't been *shamesh* for ages. I'm like a beaten-down willow branch."

That's what the old man told me in a trembling voice and pointed with shaking hand to his own beaten-down willow branch that lay at his feet. A bitter smile played on his white beard that started out thick and dense and ended up sparse and, even now, still wild.

Satire

THE LITTLE REDHEADED JEWS

Book One

1

*[The Little Redheaded Jews—Their Familial Lineage—
Their Manners and Gestures—Their Life and Means of
Livelihood—Their Sabbath Afternoon Promenades—Their
Physiognomy—Their Cuisine]*

Remote from our villages, behind the Hills of Darkness and
beyond the Sambatyon River, resided a people called the Little Redheaded Jews.

Since these faraway Redheaded Jews, cut off from the rest
of the world, hardly had contact with a soul, they were not
only uncivilized and exceedingly boorish, but frequently quite
barbaric. They were so estranged from Judaism, Jewish history, Yiddish, and Hebrew that only a handful understood a
word of the holy tongue. Except, of course, for such Hebrew
terms as "free loan," "ready cash," "let's eat," "bottoms up,"
"welcome, stranger," "are you a nut or a nitwit?," "son of a
dog," and other such phrases which had become part and par-
cel of their quaint Yiddish vernacular.

Nevertheless, a few moments of conversation sufficed to
stamp them as the world's greatest sages. Besides knowing
everything there was to know, they loved to rib, mock, and
deride one and all. Although many of them considered themselves keen thinkers, illustrious philosophers, astute critics,
and profound scholars, they were actually prodigious wind-
bags. But crowning all these attributes was—God save us!—a

frightfully fierce obstinacy. One had to have Job's patience to argue with these Redheaded Jews. Contradicting them was absolutely impossible. Their vainglory and self-puffery were beyond description. Everyone considered himself topnotch and put the next fellow at the bottom of the scale.

Marrying off a child they deemed a major tragedy. No one was good enough, neither the future spouse nor his family. Therefore, most of them sought matches in other towns. Everyone looked for his equal abroad. So long as he wasn't a local boy, even a bathhouse janitor would do. Of course, this finicky attitude provided brisk business for the matchmakers, who jumped at the chance to deal with living merchandise. Of the latter there was quite a lively turnover, knock wood, and it provided the matchmakers with an honorable livelihood.

First appearances that the life of the Redheaded Jews was sweet and jolly were quite deceptive. Among them were a few wealthy men who had lucrative business contacts with some of the landed gentry. Most of these rich Redheaded Jews were merchants: They manipulated the best trade in the world. They kept bamboozling and maneuvering until they had outmaneuvered not only others, but themselves as well, and they refused to die until they had gone bankrupt at least once. When they made money, they blustered and bragged; nevertheless, when they expired, they were buried in complimentary shrouds. Those who loathed swindle devoted themselves to free loans; in other words, they freely lent money, but charged interest because Rabbi Meir, of blessed memory, had ordained that taking interest on business loans was permissible. But owing to the frequent bankruptcies, the lender rarely saw his money again. He was content merely to collect interest, knowing that the principal was gone forever.

The usurers, however, fared much better: They were young husbands who were either still freeloading at their in-laws' tables or were now on their own. They prowled the streets, wearing their Sabbath cloaks in midweek, sniffing and weeding out the good risks from the bad. Once these small-time leeches had latched themselves onto you, they could not be dislodged until they had sucked you dry.

The religious functionaries also had an easy life—rabbis, rabbinic judges, *shokhtim*, cantors, *shamoshim*, mediators— fine Jews one and all, who devoted themselves to charity, collection boxes, and other communal affairs. And those individuals who were unfit for any other task and had no income became teachers—that is, they masqueraded as teachers: They sweated till they were blue in the face, sat with their pupils in dark, crowded and ill-smelling rooms, and screamed their lungs out from morning to night, beating, flogging, and crippling Jewish children.

The majority of the Redheaded Jews were poor workingmen, who toiled a lifetime for a crust of dry bread. The others, with nothing to do, knocked their heads against the wall. They were brokers, supposedly, and roamed about the marketplace twirling their canes and wondering how to provide for the Sabbath. Yet on the Sabbath it was impossible to recognize them. The men dressed up like lords; their wives and daughters, decked out like noble dames in silk and velvet, wore hats, gloves and kerchiefs, and hung the deuce-knows-what on themselves. And thus began their promenade.

Soon the street became inundated with multicolored dresses and rainbow-hued feathers. An outsider observing these strolling matrons and modern young ladies accoutered in a variety of hideous colors might assume that they all were children of nobility who knew nothing of noodle-pudding pans, baking boards, kitchen knives, potato graters, and kneading troughs. The outsider might surely imagine that these women hadn't the slightest inkling of how to prepare yeast dough, peel potatoes, salt meat, or pickle cucumbers. At that Sabbath post-noodle-pudding hour the street looked like a masked ball, like a circus swarming with overdressed clowns who, as everyone knew, would remove their bells, decorations, and particolored outfits at the end of their act and then crawl back into their old workaday patched and rumpled clothing.

The Redheaded Jews rarely ate meat, not because they were vegetarians, but because the kosher-food tax put meat beyond their means. Nevertheless, they had so many kinds of recipes they could fill a book. Here, for example, is a sampling of some of their meat-saving dishes: steamed groats, borscht à la Wallachia, kidney beans and dough pellets, fruit-and-raisin roll, corn porridge, potato pudding, honeyed buck-wheat, egg bows and chicken fat, garlic-flavored pancakes, cheesecake, poppyseed tarts, beets, and plums.

Their Sabbath recipes, however, were in a class by themselves. Naturally, they had about a dozen varieties of puddings —noodle, seven-layer, kneaded-dough, rice, raisin, stuffed-dumpling, strudel, and almond, not to mention pudding and stuffed neck of chicken, pudding and gizzards, and so on. They also had many kinds of *tsimess*—plum, carrot, parsnip, pear, apple, raisin, apricot, and bay leaf and spice.

But above all they fancied sharp spices—loads of pepper, strong horseradish, black radish, and onions prepared in various ways: onions and chicken fat, onions and radishes, chopped eggs and onions, onions and herring, liver and onions, onions and chicken skins fried to a crisp, and just plain raw onions.

And their looks reflected their cuisine. They often fell sick, were plagued by stomach ailments, and were continually under doctors' care. If the doctors here at home would take my advice, they would settle on the other side of the Sambatyon. I swear they would make money hand over fist. That would be far better than being crowded into one part of Yehupetz and Kasrilevke, fighting over patients, and continually snapping and leaping at one another's throats like a bunch of cats.

2

[The Capital City of the Redheaded Jews—Their Language —Their Oblique Manner of Speaking—Their Exaggerations —Their Billingsgate and Oaths—Their Names and Their Literature]

Although the Redheaded Jews were spread over many towns and villages, they considered Redville their capital. Why it was called Redville I don't know. If the mudholes which black-ened the roads all year around and dried up only in July were any criterion, the town could well have been called Blackville.

But the Redheaded Jews had a habit of obscuring their speech via a verbal game called black-is-white-and-sour-sweet. From their nicknames one gathered the rules of the game.

For example, a man called Brains was beyond shadow of a doubt—shred him to bits and he would remain—a perfect fool. Someone known as Honest-to-God was a notorious liar. Penitent was a hardened sinner, Manners an uncouth boor, Professor an absolute idiot, Good Risk a veteran bankrupt, Smooth Tongue a stutterer, and Matchless Fellow a firebug whose business went up in smoke once a month like clockwork.

The Redheaded Jews also loved to exaggerate and blow everything up out of proportion. For instance, if they wanted to call someone a fine human being, their eyes glazed, and they said, "He's got a heart of gold, that paragon. He's a diamond, a saint. He's a man without an ounce of gall." On the contrary, a bad man they described as "an evil monster, a Haman, a murderer, may all trace of him be blotted out forever and ever." A pretty girl was "a dazzling, ravishing, breathtaking beauty," but a plain one was dismissed with: "Phoo, she's as ugly as sin. Her homely face would stop a clock." If rich: "Wow, talk of wealth! That moneybags is so loaded he's got cash to burn. I wish I had a ruble for every thousand he owes!" If poverty-stricken: "He's a hard-up, down-at-the-heels, out-at-the-elbows, flat-broke beggar who starves seventy-seven times a day, not including suppertime."

But the most remarkable thing was that for them a mere wink served as a sure means of communication. One word sufficed for ten. There was no need for lengthy confabulation. An outsider eavesdropping on a dialogue between two Redheaded Jews would think they were talking a shorthand version of double Dutch.

Now for their billingsgate. Compared to their curses, the Biblical chapters of admonition are a blessing, a veritable compliment: "May you break and ache, shrivel and drivel, wither and slither, then desiccate, dehydrate, and evaporate!"

Nor were their oaths run of the mill. I'm sure you have never heard such solemn declarations as: "If what I'm telling you is not unadulterated, one hundred and sixteen percent truth, may I carry, miscarry, and be carried away, may I be pressed and impressed, depressed and repressed, suppressed and oppressed. May I turn forever and ever into a stone, a bone, a broom, a tomb, a lizard, and a gizzard."

The language of the Redheaded Jews would be a suitable research topic for some of our local linguists. Since these scholars are always bragging about their ingenuity, such a learned investigation would be right up their alley. I guarantee that it would well be worth their while.

Even the names of the Redheaded Jews were peculiar and clumsy. Since the enlightened Redheaded Jews loved to ape other people's ways and adored everything the next fellow possessed, they assumed foreign names. Avrom became Albert, Berel Benedict, Yosel Julius, and Feitel Philip. Among their aristocrats one might even encounter such names as Proboscis, Fleabitus, Grabitis, and Scoundrelius—anything, so long as it didn't sound Jewish. As for the fashionably modern womenfolk, they too changed their names. Those known as Hanna, Dvora, Peysi, Yentel, and Leya were henceforth called, respectively, Agnes, Dorothy, Pauline, Ethel, and Cleopatra. Copying the ways of others, whether in names, dress, or customs, became very chic among the Redheaded Jews. For example, if someone cut off his nose, within a day every single Redheaded Jew would be noseless—and then noses could be snapped up for a ruble apiece.

Several lines should also be devoted to the literature of the Redheaded Jews—their writers, storytellers, books, journals, and newspapers.

For the most part the newspapers applied themselves to polemics, or as they preferred to call it—criticism. The papers condemned one another, and the writers disputed. Their extremely significant polemics consisted of the following: One paper waited expectantly to see what its rival would print, whereupon it would say exactly the opposite. For example, take the two papers the *Rose* and the *Thorn*. The conservatism of the former was matched only by the radicalism of the latter. If the *Rose* commented: "Yesterday, a bright, warm, beautiful, and glorious day, the sun shone, and the birds tweeted," then the *Thorn* wrote just the reverse: "Yesterday, the most godawful day since Creation, was cold and dark, wet and nasty, slushy and slippery."

Every Sunday the conservative *Rose* presented a feature article which described the rich man's Sabbath noodle pudding and lauded it as a culinary achievement; the gazette gushed forth like a nightingale and warbled a song of praise to the rare delicacy. Aware of the *Rose*'s write-up, the *Thorn* issued a lead editorial fiercely attacking noodle puddings in general and rich men's puddings in particular and asserted that it was high time to extirpate this abominable dish which the peasants continually derided.

This, then, was the extent of their criticism, the purpose of which, however, was not to defame anyone, God forbid, or engage in personalities.

For example, here is what the *Rose* printed one day:

"Yesterday the *Thorn,* in its usual fashion, came out with an article, replete with filth and mudslinging. We shall not utter even one word of reply. We shall merely ask one question: Foul, scurrilous, naked, and indigent *Thorn!* How much longer will you prevail?"

To which the *Thorn* replied:

"Much time has elapsed since that base, cringing, and hypocritical rag, which has sold its soul to the devil and calls itself the *Rose*, has come out against us with such a cheeky, impertinent, and audacious editorial. We are ignoring it completely and have only two words in reply: Brazenfaced hussy! Bury your pages in a napkin and shut your trap forever."

Literati occasionally cannot come to terms. But the Redheaded Jews' literati could not agree on *any*thing at *any* time. Hence the reason why they heaped critiques upon one another. No matter what the *Thorn* wrote, its adversary, the *Rose*, said just the opposite. In reply, a journalist of the former presented a *Thorn*y critique wherein he ripped the *Rose* to shreds. Then the *Rose* bounced back to give the *Thorn* its comeuppance. And that's how full-fledged war often broke out between the correspondents. My Lord, rivers of ink were spilled!

3

[*The Mud of Bone-dry Avenue, Its History and Brick Houses—The Redheaded Jews' Olfactory Sense—Their Love Affairs*]

The streets of Redville were for the most part full of mud, dirt, and grime. The old-timers, in whom we must place credence, told an interesting story concerning the deep mud-holes. Once upon a time, on Passover Eve, a wagon laden with matzas sank into one of these holes in the middle of the market-place, and both the horse and the drayman were drowned. Seven weeks later, after Shevuos, all three were found—the wagonload of matzas, the horse, and the drayman. However, given the Redheaded Jews' propensity for tall tales, I have a faint suspicion that the entire incident was concocted.

But let's return to the streets of Redville. The town's main boulevard—and chief ornament—was called Bone-dry Avenue. I wonder why. After all, everyone knew perfectly well that during the muddy season Bone-dry Avenue was no less muddy than any other thoroughfare. I pored over ancient tomes and consulted various people, assuming the name to be an invention of the Redheaded Jews. But I discovered the following: Ages ago, a proclamation was issued that Bone-dry Avenue be paved with stones. Naturally, bids were placed. At first, the contractors undercut one another left and right. Later, in cahoots, they worked hand in glove and took hush money. But I have no idea what happened next. Despite all this, old-timers swore that long ago Bone-dry Avenue was not only a boulevard, but a phenomenon unprecedented in the annals of street paving.

"It was so noodleboard-smooth, so pepper-dry, so mirror-clean and shiny that it clearly reflected the beholder's image." Thus asserted the old-timers. But frankly I could not accept their contention. If in truth the street had once been paved with stones, why wasn't there even a hint of a pebble in the mud? Hence, we are forced to conclude that in all of Bone-dry Avenue's history it had never been paved. Then what are we to make of the old-timers' story concerning the proclamation, the bids, the contractors, and the hush money? Clearly, it was one enormous fabrication. But on the other hand, why engage in quibbling and idle speculation? If so they called it, well and good. Indeed, is anyone obliged to squabble with an entire town and contradict such obstinate people as the Redheaded Jews?

In any case, Bone-dry Avenue was the most beautiful street in Redville. There lived the richest nabobs, the foremost householders, the cream of society. Upon that street were to be found two-storied brick houses graced with tin roofs, verandas, balustered balconies, and red, green, and yellow shutters. But the architecture was rather outlandish. As if on spite, one house jutted out, the other was set back; one was too high, the other too low; and all were crammed together as though they wanted to shove one another out of the way and proclaim: "Hey, look at me!"

It did not matter that the windows and balconies faced the mudholes; the owners still considered them absolutely charming. But what about the ever-present odor? Alas, about that nothing could be done. The Redheaded Jews weren't such pampered fresh-air fiends. "Air-shmair," they shrugged; their sense of smell was on its last legs anyway. And since most of their noses were perpetually stuffed—God spare you the same—they had difficulty with the letters *m* and *n*, which they pronounced, respectively, as *b* and *d*.

The silence that pervaded the streets during the week was sheer pleasure. Summertime the windows were closed in order to keep the flies out, and the shutters were tightly shut lest, heaven forbid, a ray of sunshine enter. And everyone sequestered himself in his house. The market folk spent their days in the stores looking for customers. Not a living soul stirred on Bone-dry Avenue.

But with the advent of the Sabbath post-noodle-pudding

hour, the street became unrecognizable. Redheaded Jewish boys and girls promenaded on the boulevard, but not as in our villages, where they mixed the sexes helter-skelter. No, sir! The Redheaded Jews took a dim view of that. There the young boys and girls walked separately, one group opposite the other, just as in a folk dance. When they met, they made eyes at one another and, upon passing, accidentally on purpose bumped into one another, rubbed elbows, blushed, and giggled softly.

And so romances were born. They began with stares, imperceptible touches, occasionally even heartfelt sighs, and ended with—unlike romances in Yehupetz or Kasrilevke—most frequently they ended with . . . absolutely nothing.

4

*[The Redheaded Jews' First Meeting with an Outsider—His
Good Tidings—Uplifted and "Hurrah!"]*

One hot Sabbath during the summer, when the Redheaded Jewish boys and girls were promenading two by two along Bone-dry Avenue, an incident occurred which caused a flurry of excitement and a tumultuous uproar that spread from Bone-dry Avenue to the rest of the town. What had happened? The Redheaded Jews had spotted a unique individual, a strange sort of man. He wasn't a redhead. They had never encountered such a curiosity. They couldn't even imagine the possibility of a Jew's not having red hair. What an ugly monster! Everyone stopped to stare at this phenomenon. They pointed, exchanged glances, and asked one another:

"Who's that? What's that? Where's it from? What's it doing here? What an ugly monster!"

The "ugly monster" was, in fact, a handsome man in his prime. His forehead was high and broad, his hair and beard long, his countenance clear and smiling, and his eyes kindly and perpetually atwinkle. Apparently he had not noticed the furor he had created. He walked along the street as complacent as a man of means, his hands behind his back, his head high. Contemplating Bone-dry Avenue and its colored brick houses, he hummed to himself as if nothing untoward were happening. But as time went by, the tumult buzzing on the street crescendoed:

"Bzzzz. . . . Wow. . . . Who's that? What's that? Where's it from? What's it doing here? What a queer bird!"

In short, they decided to approach this creature and get all the pertinent information directly from him. But since no one wanted to be first, everyone was eager to send the next fellow.

"Go start a conversation with him. . . ."

"Why me? You go. . . ."

"Listen to me, just ask him. . . ."

"*You* ask him. Why me?"

"No, you just go up to him. . . . *I'll* do the talking. . . ."

"It'd be better if *you* went up to him, and then *I'll* do the talking. . . ."

Members of the crowd dickered at such length with one another that finally the newcomer was completely surrounded. Seeing that his way was blocked on all sides, he stopped and loudly addressed the crowd, his eyes smoldering like glowing embers.

"Sabbath greetings, my dear brothers and sisters. I see you're wondering about me, eager to know who I am, what I am, where I'm from, and what I'm doing here. Let me introduce myself to you. I am one of your brethren, one of your own flesh and blood, one of your ten million kinsmen who live on the other side of the Sambatyon River. Very likely you know far less about us than we know about you. I consider myself fortunate to have been chosen to bring you the good news that not only are we constantly thinking of you, but we are also active on your behalf—we want to take all the Redheaded Jews from this foreign soil, to which you were exiled two thousand five hundred years ago, and help you settle in your own land."

"Ha-ha-ha, Palestine, the Land of Israel, no doubt," several hundred persons thundered in laughter, sounding like a dozen cannon salvos.

"He's talking nonsense. . . ."

"He's from the other side of the Sambatyon. . . ."

"He wants to bring us to Palestine. . . ."

"Palestinian Jew!"

"Hurrah for the Palestinian Jew!"

"Hurrah!" interjected another few hundred souls. By now the street had become flooded with people. Everyone laughed, holding his sides and shrieking in one breath: "Hurrah for the Palestinian Jew!"

The newcomer, thunderstruck by the reaction to his good tidings, was unable to comprehend what was going on. He about-faced and retraced his steps. But the entire troupe of young men and women followed him; they hooted and whistled and shouted, "Hurrah!"

"Hurry and see the spectacle," they called to one another.

"There he goes, the Palestinian Jew."

"Hurry up, or God forbid you'll be too late."

After much anguish our newcomer finally arrived safely in his room at the Red Inn and locked the door behind him. The boisterous Redheaded Jews kept flocking around the inn. Convulsed with laughter, they catcalled and screamed:

"Hurrah for the Palestinian Jew!"

Luckily it was Sabbath; had it been a weekday, they would have smashed the inn to bits. Nobody wanted to budge and depart for home until the innkeeper, a robust redhead, stuck his fiery mop of hair out the window and bellowed:

"Begone, you redheaded devils, you broom-tailed witches in sheep's clothing, you loafers and idle bums. What hell-fired ill wind has got into you? We've got a visitor who's no different from anyone else—except for the fact that he's not a redhead. Big deal! Does that mean he's supposed to be hounded? So I'm telling you to beat it *now*, confound it, this very minute. And if not—the devil take your blasted fathers—I'll. . . ."

Only then did the crowd disperse, each one to his respective dwelling. For if there's one thing the Redheaded Jews adored, it was a colorful, down-to-earth, and peppery harangue.

5

*[The Redheaded Jews' Meeting—The Visitor's Speech—
An Impatient Interruption]*

Saturday night, immediately after Havdala, the visitor sent
invitations to the town's elite: to the rabbis, teachers, scholars,
and sages, to the rich nabobs, and even to some of the simple
artisans. They were told that the newcomer had a very important question of general concern to discuss with them at the
inn; it was an urgent matter which would affect their lives.

An uproar broke out in Redville.

"Some strange creature's come to town. One of the swarthy
Jews from the other side of the Sambatyon. Passes himself off
as a Palestinian Jew and thinks he can tell us the latest, up-to-
the-minute news. Let's go hear what he has to say."

Without waiting for a second invitation, Redheaded Jews of
all ages and from all classes promptly set out for the meeting,
not so much for the sake of the meeting itself, but because
everyone was eager to look at and hear a Palestinian Jew.

Soon the Red Inn was crowded to suffocation. The place
teemed with a horde of pushing and shoving Redheaded Jews.
Everyone wanted to be closer and take the best seats up front.
The room was so jam-packed the walls sweated. Although the
audience was crammed like sardines, more Jews kept swarming in. Finally, the innkeeper got an idea. First, in his usual
fashion, he roundly cursed the ancestors of the mob gathered
outside, and then he bolted every single entrance. Only then
did the visitor rise, greeted by deafening cheers and applause.

"Sshhh! Pipe down everyone! Shut up!" all the Redheaded
Jews cried out in chorus. And then they began sniffling, hawk-
ing, and blowing their noses, as though they hadn't blown them
in years. When all the handkerchiefs were put away, one man
in the rear coughed. Then another. Then a third. As ill luck
would have it, the coughing went from row to row until the
epidemic spread through the entire hall.

"What's the sudden coughing?" the rich men shouted. "Listen to that gasping! Couldn't you have wheezed yourselves dry at home? Come here to cough, have you? A hacking cough upon you beggars! What nerve!"

That moment it became absolutely still. For the Redheaded Jews feared the moneyed men like the seven-year itch. There, if a man of wealth said, "No coughing," all coughing ceased at once.

"Gentlemen," the visitor began, his eyes blazing, "I request your kind attention. Please hear me out, my dear, beloved brethren. Your fellow townsmen did not greet me too courteously. Apparently, I am not a welcome guest. They viewed me as a madman and jeered me with cries of Hurrah! They did not understand what I said to them. But do you think I'm angry or discouraged? Heaven forbid! I am only deeply distressed for you, my dear brethren, and disturbed by the people's low level and profound ignorance. But since you apparently represent the town's finest elements—among you good people I see rabbis, teachers, businessmen, intellectuals, and sensitive laymen—I assume that *you* will understand me. I want you to realize, my dear brethren, the trouble and self-sacrifice I had to undergo in order to get here. For you, my dear Redheaded Jews, are stuck away—if you'll pardon the expression—the devil-knows-where. To reach you, one must traverse many deserts and areas of wilderness, clamber over hill and dale, and wander in and out of thick forests. Not to mention crossing the Sambatyon. No trifle, you know, that Sambatyon River.

"I knew perfectly well the hazards of the journey. I knew that it would be costly in terms of time, money, health, and honor. Had I not undertaken this journey, I assure you that my children and I would be far better off. Nevertheless, my heart was drawn to you, my dear brethren, and so I renounced honor and worldly possessions and devoted myself to this sacred task. I wanted to see you, my dear Redheaded Jews, and convey to you heartiest greetings from your ten million brethren on the other side of the Sambatyon. Indeed, they are real flesh-and-blood brothers, who along with you serve one God and stem from the same source—Abraham, Isaac, and Jacob. I very much wanted to find out how you were faring and personally express the glad tidings that we are thinking of you and are active in your behalf. In fact we have plans for you which, God willing, should please you."

"What, for example? Let's hear what you have in mind. Why keep us in suspense?" all the Redheaded Jews cried out impatiently.

"We want to take you from here, my dear brethren," the visitor continued. "Understand? You've wallowed in the mud long enough. Too long have you been mocked and humiliated by all other peoples. The time has come to rise, cleanse and groom yourselves, and be like other nations. Just as your ancestors were taken from Egypt, we want to take you from here and settle you in your own land, the one that God promised your forefathers, Abraham, Isaac, and Jacob, the land of our holy temple, our priests and Levites, our kings and our prophets. And the name of this country is the Land of Israel, the Holy Land, Palestine, for which your ancestors sacrificed their lives and from which came forth the divine light, our Torah, that illuminated the whole world, opened everyone's eyes, and offered liberty and understanding to all people. . . . Yes, we have given everyone enlightenment and understanding—except ourselves. We have given everyone liberty, but we have masqueraded as slaves, servants, and lackeys. . . . Why are you staring at me like that? Why don't you speak up? I am talking to you! To you, pious Redheaded Jews—rabbis, teachers, and men of good deeds, Jews who devoutly wear ritual fringes, long gaberdines, and beards and side curls! No need telling you about the Land of Israel. After all it's Palestine, the Holy Land—Je-ru-sa-lem! In various prayers you recite: 'With mercy return to your city Jerusalem' . . . 'Bring your Divine Presence to Zion' . . . 'Jerusalem your city and Zion your dwelling-place' . . . 'May the memory of your sacred city Jerusalem' . . . 'Rebuild Jerusalem' . . . and, of course, the famous call: 'To next year in Jerusalem!' "

"Pah! Those are just prayers," shouted a few of the observant Redheaded Jews. "That's what we Jews are made for—to pray and serve God."

"Pray and serve God?" the visitor thundered. "The trouble is that you pray, but you don't know what you're saying. You talk, but you don't know what you're talking about. You're sick, but you don't know what's ailing you. You're living in self-delusion and in total lethargy. You're drugged with sleep. Dead to the world."

"Make it short and sweet!" cried the impatient Redheaded Jews. "Stop preaching! Make it snappy!"

"You want it short and sweet? You don't like preaching, eh? You hate to hear the truth, right? So I say, you all are drugged with sleep. That's why I've come to wake you, to rouse you from your heavy-eyed slumber, and shout in your ears: Arise, brethren, arise! The time has come. For two thousand years you have wallowed in the mud, unaware of your own misfortune, like the worm in the horseradish that can't imagine anything sweeter. Arise! Look about you. Consider your critical condition. I say you are on the brink of disaster, of terrible catastrophe. You grow weaker from day to day. You sink deeper and deeper into the mud and into the darkness. As time goes by, you become more and more ignorant, and you stifle in the oppressive closeness. You devour one another alive. . . ."

"The point! The point!" shrieked the impatient Redheaded Jews. "Come to the point!"

"You want to know the point? Are you in a rush? No time to spare? You're just like the Jews in my country. You've got the same traits. Your ten million brethren on the other side of the Sambatyon reacted exactly the same way. But at least we noticed our miserable condition in the nick of time. We saw that we would either be devoured or be given enough time to do the trick ourselves. We were given broad hints—that is, we were beaten and kicked. We learned that the world was an ocean and its people fish.

"We finally realized that although our prophets and poets wrote great poetry throughout the ages, their statements were actually meant for the distant Messianic future. But *we* felt that salvation was dependent on the deeds of our own hands.

We understood that if we wanted to live, we would have to be like everyone else, just as we were long ago.

"Studying our great history and our beautiful language, we realized that we were unjustifiably ashamed of the name Jew. We were a people as any other people. The only thing we lacked was a land, our own homeland. So we raised a tumult before the whole world. 'A land. A land. Give us a land!' We were all ready to go to one place; we began to talk of only one thing. But we decided first to cleanse and groom ourselves and our children. To become educated, to behave properly, to prepare ourselves and the entire people for the great task before us. We organized meetings and congresses; we collected money and established a fund; we taught our children and opened Hebrew and secular schools. . . ."

"Schools? We don't want schools! We don't even want to know about them!" several hundred Redheaded Jews cried out at once. They raised the roof; they clamored; they howled and whooped in a cacophony of voices, a symphony gone wild.

"No schools," yelled one.

"Schools," screeched another, "that's just what we *do* want!"

Then pandemonium broke loose.

"Schools!"

"We don't want schools. We don't want schools."

"Don't want to hear about it."

"Really? Then in that case I *do*. Schools. Schools!"

6

[The Visitor Rises—All the Redheaded Jews Talk at Once—
They Contradict, Wrangle, Outshout One Another—
They Go Home in Peace]

When the Redheaded Jews were silent, they were absolutely silent, but when they began to speak, they chattered about everything under the sun, gesticulating wildly and talking all at once. They yelled; they screamed; they squawked like magpies in the woods—they didn't shut their mouths. No human force could keep them still. Of no avail were the visitor's requests to let him finish what he had started to say; of no avail were the cries of "Shhh! Pipe down! Keep it quiet!" It was like preaching to the winds. They paid no more attention to the rich men than Haman does to the Purim rattle-clackers. The poor visitor had to break off in the middle of his speech, step down in humiliation from the rostrum, and listen to the Red-headed Jews chewing over and commenting on his remarks, each one according to his degree of understanding.

"He wants schools. . . ."

"Which is just what we *don't* want. . . ."

"On the other side of the river. . . ."

"Blathering about the Land of Israel. . . ."

"And that we need organizations. . . ."

"Which is just what we *don't* want. . . ."

"What do you say to his big, fat mouth?"

"Shut up! Who asked you to butt in, big shot?"

"When it comes to the Holy Land, let *me*. . . ."

"Believe me, those who say he's cracked are absolutely right. . . ."

"Pardon me, but you're an absolute jackass."

"Really, you mangy bastard? Take this! . . ."

"-nizations is what we need. . . ."

"Brilliant idea! What about money?"

"Money?"

"Hear that? They're talking about money," said the rich men, protecting their pockets. "Which means they're talking about us, right? Come on, let's go home."

"How about a round of rummy?" said some members of the Burn-the-Midnight-Oil Society.

"Naturally. Nothing but! By the way, where were you last night?"

"Last night we played poker at Brains' house until it was time for morning prayers."

"Really? Who gambled away all his money? Who went broke? Who broke the bank? Tell us, tell us!"

"Don't ask! We really got burned. At first, Manners was

riding high, as usual, and Matchless was sweating it out; then the Worrier beat the pants off Manners by showing four kings against three aces. You should have seen the look on his face. A pair of threes over a pair of deuces. Then three fours over three treys. Every time the Worrier showed his hand, Manners nearly dropped dead. This slaughter kept on until his money ran out. But you know who made out best of all? The Professor. He was playing knock rummy with the women. And a black day for them it was! He stripped them clean, then gallantly bade them good day! Come on, let's go, and we'll set up a game. A pity, time's awasting. Before you know it, morning'll be here."

"Heretics, heathens, bums," shouted the rabbis and the other religious functionaries, all of whom had gathered in one corner. "A bunch of pork-gobbling libertines want to lead us to the Land of Israel. Bareheaded and beardless, they want to bring the Messiah down to us. Fellow Jews, speak up! Let's hear from you! Help! God Almighty, help! Save us!"

But the greatest bloc of opposition came from the community of Redheaded Jewish intellectuals: researchers, scholars, philosophers, and would-be statesmen. They demanded proofs, "from the viewpoints of science, logic, history, politics and humanity," concerning the possibility of, and the precedents for, approaching an entire people and suddenly, like a bolt out of the blue, telling all the Redheaded Jews who for two thousand years had dwelled in peace on *this* side of the Sambatyon, who minded their own business and wouldn't harm so much as a fly on the wall: "Pick yourselves up, Redheaded Jews, pack up and cross the Sambatyon, and settle some wasteland populated by wild Turks."

"First of all, what will the other nations say; indeed, what about the Turks themselves? And whoever heard of such a thing?" they asked. "On the contrary, point out a historic parallel, and show us if it has ever happened before. Second, it's a slap in the face against civilization; it's a shame; it's an insult against all humanity. For the whole world is awaiting the time when the sun will break through the clouds and all dark corners will be illuminated; when all nations will become one nation, all peoples one people, all languages one language, all persons one person—"

"A fine how-d'ye-do! How about not being absurd? What do you mean all persons will become one person?" A young bespectacled scholar leaped up. "I can accept the fact that all peoples will become one people, but—"

"Hold your horses!" a bald highbrow interrupted. "Let's first logically reexamine the whole matter: What actually *is* a people? Let's define our terms. What does people *mean?* What's the origin of the word?"

"A people is called a nation," said the bespectacled scholar. "Nation is spelled N-A-T-I-O-N. . . . The *t* is pronounced like *sh*. . . . Is it any clearer now?"

"Your comment is so terribly significant," snapped a bushy-browed egghead, "that it ought definitely be expanded into a special monograph—"

"Or at least into a public disquisition," cried another brainy young intellectual, in ecstasy over his polysyllabic verbal contribution.

"Why a disquisition?" cried Specs, jealous of his colleague's use of such a big word. "A monograph is one thing, and a disquisition is another. A monograph is a tract, and a disquisition is—a disquisition."

"It's the same thing," Brainy said angrily. "There is absolutely no difference between them."

"There certainly is," said Specs.

"Excuse me," Brainy shouted, "but there is no difference whatsoever."

"Excuse *me*," Specs retorted. "They're as different as day and night."

"Will you stop it already?" roared another scholar. "Did you ever? When one says day, the other says night. Better use your energy to form a group to unite the Redheaded Jews. Then we'll be able to take action. That's just a wee bit more necessary than all your piddling research and philosophy and all your monographs and disquisitions."

* * *

It was past midnight, but the Redheaded Jews were still jabbering, screaming, yammering, squealing, and gesticulating wildly, as usual. The rabbis shouted: "Heathens, heretics, bums, and sausage snackers want to bring down the Messiah." The highbrows, scholars, and philosophers did not cease their intellectual labors: arguing and contradicting one another. All they wanted was immediate proof of how an entire people could be brought over the Sambatyon and settled in Palestine. Their view was that it made no sense whatsoever.

"For instance," some said, "take the history of other peoples."

"All other peoples are one thing," another highbrow shouted, "and the Redheaded Jews are another."

"No. They're all the same!"

"Not at all. They're absolutely different."

"Excuse me, but there's not a whit of difference."

"Pardon *me,* but they're as different as day and night."

"When will all this stop?" cried some of the intellectuals. "We ought to sit down and see what we can do for the people. All your research won't fill their bellies. Come now, if you're not happy with the plans concerning Palestine, let's hear what suggestions *you* have to offer. The people are waiting. They're looking up to you. Yet all you think about is research, philosophy, and politics."

"He's absolutely right," added a few of the poor people. "It's high time that they started thinking about us. It's about time they did something for us and for our children."

But no one paid attention to them. Everyone wanted to talk; no one wanted to listen. The deliberation dragged on and on until gradually the crowd began to disperse. The first ones to sidle out were the rich businessmen. After them came the members of the Burn-the-Midnight-Oil Society. On the way home they cracked jokes. They derided the visitor from the other side of the Sambatyon, they mocked the redheaded innkeeper, the rabbis, the eggheads, and they made fun not only of the new organization, the Redheaded Jews for Palestine, but of all the Redheaded Jews and the entire world as well.

7

*[The First of Elul Passes—The Visitor Departs—
The Status of the Householders and the Plain
Redheaded Jews]*

The rabbis could not stand the impious notion that the Redheaded Jews, who had hitherto awaited the Messiah, devotedly recited, "I believe," and loudly proclaimed, "To next year in Jerusalem," should suddenly begin to think of Palestine of their own accord. Consequently, without losing a moment, the rabbis picked themselves up at dawn and in a deposition before the municipal authorities declared:

"Whereas a stranger has come from the devil-knows-where to visit us and is inciting the people to revolt; and whereas the entire community will bear witness and swear that what we claim is true; and whereas it would harm the nation and violate the Law—for above all else we adore the Law—we hereby request that the authorities act in time in order to prevent the Redheaded Jews from being led astray. Moreover, whereas we do not know who the man is, what he is, what he does, and where he is from, he should be sought for questioning. For if what we suspect is true, he is surely either a counterfeiter, an escaped convict, a runaway, or just one of these hooligans who hoodwink you and lead you from the straight path direct to the underworld. One thing is beyond doubt—the man is not on the up-and-up."

No sooner said than done. While the visitor was still asleep, a bebuttoned official with a bulbous blue nose appeared at the Red Inn and addressed the innkeeper in the following fashion:

"Listen here, friend. We've always considered you a quiet, honest Jew. Finding you handling stolen goods or contraband is one thing we'd never have suspected you of."

Before doing anything else, the redheaded innkeeper, a worldly-wise man and a favorite among all the officials, ordered a bottle of whiskey and two tumblers to be placed on the table.

"Look what they're saying about you," said Buttons to him, sticking his nose into the deposition. "And who do you think swore this out? Nobody but your own damned Redheaded Jews. How else would we ever know what's going on among you, if your own people wouldn't tattle on one another?"

"Honored sir, exactly what is it you wish?" said the innkeeper, filling up both glasses. "But before you tell me, let's clink glasses and drink to our health. Good health—that's the main thing. And so"—he continued in Yiddish—"to life, Buttons! May all I wish you come true. . . . Now tell me what is it you want."

"Tell me, my dear man," said Buttons, "who is this queer fellow that stopped at your place during the Sabbath? Where is he from? What's he doing here, and what sort of speech did he deliver last night?"

"May you live and be well and always be sound of mind and limb," said the innkeeper. "But I don't understand a word you're saying. It's pure Turkish. First of all, I myself don't know who he is. Second, he left long ago. And third, no such person stopped at my place. So I don't see how I can be of any use to you. Here's to you! Health and long life! May we both be healthy, and may just half what I wish you come true."

"Oh, what a rascal you are!" Buttons laughed. "Actually, you should have been hanged from a tree a long time ago. Lucky for you, I like you—the devil alone knows why. I know you're lying like a dog. So listen here, you'd better own up and point out that individual to me, for I'd like to ask him a question or two."

"By all means. Do you think I'd hide anything from you?" replied the innkeeper and promptly ran up to the visitor's room to wake him

"Look sharp, Reb Jew. Get up. Get dressed. Pack up. And be quick about it. Kick up your heels, and run for dear life, because you're in hot water. I'm having the horse harnessed to the coach. So don't waste a minute, and go in peace. And for God's sake, don't even bother to look back. And when the Good Lord brings you home safely, don't forget to thank the

Almighty that he pulled you through without a scratch. . . .
No, no time for questions. Pack quickly, and slip away. You
don't know the Redheaded Jews, and you don't know who our
religious functionaries are. . . . Have a good trip, and best
regards to each and every one."

By the time everyone awoke the next morning, the stranger
had already departed.

Praised be God, the Redheaded Jews were subsequently
blessed with peace and tranquillity. The quiet there was sheer
joy. Everyone was preoccupied with his own affairs. The shop-
keepers sought customers; the moneylenders charged interest,
since interest on business loans was permissible; the leeches
collected usury; the workingmen worked their fingers to the
bone; the *shokhtim*, the cantors, and the teachers performed
their assigned tasks; and the speculators roamed the market-
place, sticks in hand, wondering where the next Sabbath meal
was coming from. The young intellectuals wrote articles for the
papers, assembled at Friday night meetings, and discussed
means of getting money to buy land in Palestine. No sooner
did the rich hear the word "money" than a flurry of restless-
ness overcame them.

"Imagine!" they said. "A pack of beggars, panhandlers,
teachers, and young eggheads want to buy up Palestine. Now
isn't that a laugh?"

The riffrafftocrats of the Burn-the-Midnight-Oil Society
were yes-men to all the rich magnates' suggestions and poked
fun at the new organization, the Redheaded Jews for Palestine. All the Burn-the-Midnight-Oilers did was play poker,
rummy, sixty-six, and that terribly challenging game turtle-
myrtle. The highbrows and scholars, too, met every evening
and continually analyzed the question of whether Palestine
would, God forbid, block progress or be detrimental to the de-
velopment of world civilization. And each question, each scien-
tific inquiry, spawned another. They debated; they sharpened their tongues; they exercised their vocal cords; they bick-
ered and contradicted one another. They always had something to discuss. Their investigations led them so far back that

their latest subject for scholarly consideration was: Which came first, the chicken or the egg? Another question deliberated was: Why did the egg yolk and the white constantly remain separated? Such were the profound matters that they pondered.

Meanwhile, what was happening with the poor? Not a blessed thing! The poor remained penniless and starved without fanfare from day to day. After all, there was no law against that. Death is in the hands of God and will come to one and all alike. Actually, the children of the poor weren't so bad off. They were free as birds, naked and barefoot, unwashed and uncombed, wallowing in the mire like a bunch of pigs. And (forgive the proximity) what about the rabbis and the rest of the religious functionaries? Them leave alone! Taking care of matters pertaining to Judaism, such as Passover brandy, the *eruv*, which permitted Jews to carry personal articles on the Sabbath, and the specially watched, extra-kosher matzas was enough of a task. It sufficed that the religious functionaries remembered to provide the Redheaded Jews with *esrogs* for Sukkos from the isle of Corfu—heaven forbid that they come from the Holy Land.

In brief, things were quiet, knock wood, on the other side of the Sambatyon. Peaceful and tranquil. A thick, silent, and dark night fell over the Redheaded Jews. They became drowsy. Shhh! Let's not disturb them. Let's tiptoe away and wish them good night and sweet dreams.

Good night, Redheaded Jews, and sleep well!

Book Two

8

[The Masters of the Land—Their Hatred of the Redheaded Jews—A Sudden Blow—Stories Told About the Catastrophe]

The Redheaded Jews were not the only pampered folk on the other side of the Sambatyon. Besides them there were other peoples: Arabs, Persians, Indians, Turks, Tartars, and the

like, all of whom considered themselves the authentic first
fiddle—the rightful masters of the land—and the Redheaded
Jews a mere bunch of nobodies, left over from the plagues. Although the Redheaded Jews countered by showing their importance and by bringing historical proofs that their status
was equal to that of the other old-timers, the others paid no
more attention to their arguments and proofs than to last
year's snow. So the Redheaded Jews were still considered
strangers, a burden tolerated, dredged up from the deuce-
knows-where.

For many centuries the gentiles and the Redheaded Jews
got along rather well—that is, the Jews were permitted to live
in absolute freedom in the places they had already settled. In
fact, the gentiles' attitude was: Since the Jews had settled there,
let them live in peace, dammit, with an assortment of ills,
aches, and plagues.

In the cities, too, special streets were set aside in their
honor. There the Redheaded Jews could do as they pleased:
open stores or taverns, sell whiskey, buy grain, become merchants and brokers, trade and deal, beguile, baffle, and bam-
boozle, lend money at as much interest as the traffic would bear.

Indeed, the latter was the cause of the initial hatred and
the Redheaded Jews' decline into disfavor. For when these
moneylenders were needed, the non-Jews were quite cuddly-
wuddly with them, but the tumult began later when the notes
fell due and the Redheaded Jews began adding up the IOU's
and demanding the interest payments.

"Leeches. Bloodsuckers. Exploiters! Brought your inherit-
ance here, have you? Loafers, parasites, chiselers. People who
don't sow or reap, yet eat their fill—who needs you? Who needs
you Redheaded Jews? Why don't you go back where you came
from?"

The Redheaded Jews heard all this and dismissed it with:
"Nonsense. They'll keep barking until they shut up. When
they need us, they'll come running back to us again."

The Redheaded Jews' view was that their strength lay in
cash: A Jew had to think of a livelihood; he had to make
money, and the more, the better. The Redheaded Jews, who

loved to poke fun at everything under the sun and rib everyone, including themselves, directed the following scathing
comment at their own kind:

"All people can be divided into two categories: louses and
louses. If you don't have any money, you're just a plain louse;
if you *do* have money, you're certainly a louse, for if you
wouldn't be a louse, you wouldn't have any money. But it's
better to be a rich louse then a poor louse; for as they say, if
you already indulge in pork, you might as well lick the platter
clean. For where there's money, there's honor, familial pedigree, Torah, and wisdom. In a word, money is everything.
Phoo on the fact that the rest of the world makes fun of us.
They call us tatterdemalions, bamboozlers, loafers, parasites,
exploiters.

"But let them jabber on. Who cares for their twaddle? We
know who we are. We're still God's favorites, the elect of God.
Of us it still is said: 'You have chosen us from among all the
peoples.' Take all their foolish remarks on the one hand, and
on the other—forgive the proximity—the various synagogue
honors. Can there be any comparison? Of course not. So let
them talk and let them write. We've survived worse Hamans,
and God willing, we'll survive the modern ones, too. We'll
still keep going to our *rebbe;* we'll still have the honor of
snatching a piece of his leftover bread and the joy of eating
the third meal of the Sabbath with him. And so, once and for
all, we'll live it up without worries or care, singing:

> The *rebbe* told us to be gay
> And have a happy time today.
> Dance till dawn, drink some wine,
> And all will have a joyous time."

And thus the Redheaded Jews eased their hearts.

Many years passed. One day a thick, black cloud suddenly
slipped over them. A flash of lightning which lit up the darkness was followed by a mighty rumble of thunder. Huge
hailstones began to fall on the Redheaded Jews, especially

on the poor of Beggarsville, alas, who lived in shanties at the edge of town. In a trice the Redheaded Jews were roused as though out of a deep slumber. Rubbing their eyes, they said:

"Huh? What? What happened here?"

"What happened here?" mimicked one of the Redheaded Jews. "In just one minute I'll tell you all about the neat little incident that happened here. A dispute over a Persian customer broke out between a Jewish clerk in a Jewish store and a Persian salesman in a Persian store. The Jewish clerk, a fellow called Yitzhok, decided to call the customer into the store. So the Persian salesman, one Parshandatta by name, shouted to the Jewish clerk, a fellow named Yitzhok, saying: 'Hey, Yid!' So the Jewish clerk, the fellow named Yitzhok, retorted with: 'Jackass!' So the Persian salesman, one Parshandatta by name, snapped back and said to the Jewish clerk, the one named Yitzhok: 'You're all a bunch of ragamuffins and garlic glutters.' At which the Jewish clerk, the one named Yitzhok, replied: 'And you're all a bunch of swine, sots, and thickheaded clods.' So the Persian, the salesman named—"

"What an endless tale!" someone interrupted. "This one said; that one said. That's not the entire reason for the recent storm. The pogrom took place because a noble landowner called Agag had mortgaged his estate, including his forest, mill, carriage, and horses, to our rich man. The nobleman kept paying interest until our man finished him off, foreclosed on him, and took away his estate, including his forest, mill, carriage, and horses, and made the nobleman stand up on his own two hind legs, so to speak. But the nobleman swore revenge—"

"Nonsense! That's not the real story at all," a woman interjected. "Listen to me. There's this countess called Vashti who's loaded. She's got an eighteen-year-old bum of a son who ran up lots of debts. Kept signing notes. It's around him that this sweet incident is brewing—"

"Fiddlesticks!" squeaked a poor old lady. "And that's why, folks, ducks walk around barefoot! Just because Vashti's sonny boy signs notes, why does my little shop have to be smashed up, my bedding ripped to shreds, and my kids frightened out of their wits? Did you ever? Not enough that they ruined me in the store, they had to come home and—"

The poor old lady ended her speech with a little squeal and wanted to talk about the extent of her misfortune. But no one let her continue.

"Off to the rabbi with you," the men silenced her, "go squeak over there—not here! Take your complaints to him."

Everyone had his theory about the cause of the outbreak. Everyone jabbered excitedly, gesticulated, and lost his head in the attempt to describe exactly how the pogrom had begun. Everyone literally snatched the words out of his neighbor's mouth.

"What did they have against me?" said the pug-nosed egg lady who supported a blind husband and seven children. "What did they have against me and my basketful of eggs? Ah, me, woe is me! What'll I do now? Oh, the troubles! The mi-se-ry!"

"I had one Sabbath dress," sighed a young woman, rummaging among the refuse of tattered clothing, broken crockery, feathers, and pieces of glass, hoping to salvage something. "They ripped up my pillows, broke my dishes, alas, and even smashed my chipped soup pot to bits."

"They made a pauper out of me," said one of the notions dealers from the Beggarsville section of town. Even during the good years a thief could have carried away his entire stock in his side pocket. "They poured oil, gasoline, and tar over my ribbons and then set them on fire. Made a mishmash of everything. Like this." And he moved his hands, attempting to describe the mishmash.

"That's nothing," complained a dry-goods merchant. "What about taking entire bolts of cloth and cutting them to ribbons? That takes brains and loads of good sense!"

"And *I* ask you, what am *I* going to do now, for instance, without a workbench?" cried a poor shoemaker with a face as yellow as wax.

"Benched is he who works not," replied a limping tailor, who still had pillow feathers in his side curls. "What's the good of a workbench if there's no work? People say that some form of public aid for us is under consideration, but this doesn't please me at all. They're deliberating too long. I'm afraid they'll consider it until there won't be any consideration left for *us*."

"What are you afraid of? It can't get any worse," the shoemaker replied and motioned silently to a poor woman standing in the street.

Arms folded, she shook her head and talked to herself in a hoarse voice: "O Lord God, Lord God, God, God Almighty!" The death of her child during the riots had deprived her of her reason. Impish little urchins occasionally ran over and mimicked her: One tugged at her skirt; another pulled her hair. Seeing this, the adults laced into the children for all they were worth:

"Off with you, you rascals, scamps, scalawags, the devil take you!"

The small fry retreated and dashed off like frightened magpies to the synagogue, where a circle of Redheaded Jews had gathered. One young man was telling a miraculous story about his grandfather, a man of more than eighty, knock wood, who was saved from the disaster only by virtue of his God-fearing piety. The young man gesticulated as he spoke, and the entire group listened intently.

"When the whole thing began," he said, "I immediately ran to my grandfather, long life to him. I come running, more dead than alive, look around, and there's my grandfather, long life to him, calmly sitting and studying, wearing his prayer shawl and *tfillin* as though nothing were happening.

" 'For goodness' sake, Grandpa,' I said, 'take off your prayer shawl and *tfillin,* and come quickly. Let's run away before they get here.'

" 'Go, my child,' he said to me. 'Go. I'll remain here.'

" 'For goodness' sake, Grandpa, what are you talking about? What if they get to you, God forbid? Come, Grandpa, hurry, hurry.'

" 'No one runs away from God,' he said. 'If I'm destined to die before my time, the Angel of Death will find me anywhere. No one fools him. So go, my child,' he said, 'go, and God bless you!'

"And imagine, the minute I set foot outside, I met—"

Suddenly a host of Redheaded Jews streamed out of the synagogue. The circle broke up. The young man's story remained unfinished. Everyone headed silently for the hillside cemetery. They moved quietly, with heads bowed. Old men wept silently and whispered verses from the Psalms.

Was it a funeral? Who was the corpse? Who had died? Well, actually, no one. They were merely carrying the torn fragments of sacred books to the cemetery in order to bury them as prescribed by tradition.

"Look down, O Lord, and see," the rabbi whispered as two round tears rolled down his yellow cheeks and disappeared into his beard, "see whom you have punished, alas, and for whom you have displayed your great might."

Up above the fiery sun blazed: It baked and scorched, roasted and singed the great dark spot on the earth known as Beggarsville.

9

[The Great Meeting in the Synagogue—The Rich Men Volunteer—The Young Men Talk of Emigration— A Committee to Be Formed—A Refusal]

An ancient, inflexible rule existed among the Redheaded Jews. Whenever fire or plague, riot or decree came upon them, all of them dashed to the synagogue to deliberate and decide on means to counteract the evil plight and dispel the misery. First of all, they repented. Each person thought that he, more than anyone else, was personally to blame. Since God did not punish gratuitously, one had to reconcile himself to the Almighty by praying, reciting psalms, and fasting. And since God was a father to all, He answered if one called to Him.

But the Redheaded Jews were stunned and perplexed by this new and undeserved misfortune which had suddenly befallen them. They sank into lethargy. They did not know what to do, where to go, or to whom to cry out. The tragedy was so great that the communal leaders did not even wait for any official invitations. The rich men volunteered to help; the householders went with bags from house to house. Everyone gave what he could: a loaf of black bread, a *khalle,* some flour, salt, pepper, onions.

But since it was hard to fill a sackful of holes, on the third day the Redheaded Jews in Beggarsville slowly began dying of hunger. Sympathetic people then intervened and raised a fuss: How come no one is doing anything? Which resulted in the decision to summon the town's most prominent men to a grand meeting in the *shul.* The poor Redheaded Jews now breathed easier. They got a new lease on life when they heard what the rich men had told the rabbi. The town's leading businessmen said that they would certainly be present at the meeting, God willing, and that they wanted something to be done for the sake of the poor. The rich men had explicitly agreed to render as much aid as possible; they didn't even care if it would cost money, so long as it wasn't too much. For lots of money, well, naturally, that was impossible, you see, for everything had a limit, everything must proceed with method and moderation, especially where money was concerned. Understand?

By the time word of mouth brought this news to Beggarsville, it was blown up out of proportion, enlarged like a rolling snowball. A rumor spread among the poor that the rich men had promised them hills of gold, no matter what the cost. The rich were prepared to give them the shirts off their backs; they were ready to go through fire and water for the sake of their poor brethren. In Beggarsville there was merriment and joy. Then all the poor people—men, women, and loads of little children— converged on the town and beleaguered the great synagogue from within and without.

That day every pauper felt like a man of means, like a pampered only child who is fondled, stroked, and dandled, carried on one's shoulders, fussed and fretted over. It was no trifle, you know. Their joy beggared all description: After all, they were poor Redheaded Jews—and from Beggarsville at that! Apparently they had now come upon the seven years of plenty. It was the most charming thing in the world to see how arrogant the poor had become. One couldn't even come near them. When a householder attempted to start a conversation with one of the paupers, he was forthwith greeted with a fiery barrage: "Have respect, you mangy lout. Remember who *you* are and who *we* are! You're just a plain householder, and we—*we* are the poor of Beggarsville!"

Later, when all the prominent householders, rich merchants, rabbis, rabbinic judges, and other communal worthies had assembled in the great *shul,* the *shamesh* went up to the pulpit and rapped three times for silence: "Shhh. Keep it still! Quiet down!" One of the rabbis then stood and delivered a lengthy sermon wherein he introduced a host of related Biblical verses and showed that:

"According to the Midrash and the Kabala, the authentic End of Days has arrived—that is, the Messiah is supposed to come now. He must come, for if he doesn't, we're done for. He *has* to come. He simply must! And since the Redheaded Jews are now in trouble, not to mention the Beggarsville paupers who have been left high and dry, it is the responsibility of every man in town to help however he can, whether with advice or money."

"But of course! Naturally," cried some of the rich men in unison. "Don't forget us! We, too, want to help as much as we can. We don't even care if it costs us some money, as long as it isn't lots of it, for lots of money, well, naturally, that's impossible, you see, for everything has a limit, everything must proceed with method and moderation, especially where money is concerned. Understand?"

It was beyond comprehension why the rich men were now so generous, so butter-soft you could have applied them to a third-degree burn. Their remarks clearly revealed that they felt some measure of guilt, that they had in some way sinned against the poor Redheaded Jews. The rich men were in such spirited good humor that they generously allowed the young eggheads to meddle in and set forth ideas already proposed in the newspapers.

"There is only one remedy," said the young intellectuals. "The one-and-only remedy to help the poor is emigration."

"What does that mean?" asked the rich men.

"Emigration means to emigrate," replied the young men, "to travel, to journey, to move from one place and settle in another."

"Where to?" asked the rich men. "To which countries?"

"Where to?" said the young men. "To India, Ethiopia, Iraq, and especially to Egypt, for in Egypt there's plenty of land and hardly any people. According to the papers, everything is cheap as dirt there. Practically free."

At any other time there would have been the devil to pay for remarks of that sort. The young men would have been given short shrift by the rich for daring to intrude among their elders. But having got a whiff of emigration, the rich men were pleased and wanted more. It smacked of getting rid of all the poor. And that was nothing to sneeze at!

"I swear the plan's not bad at all," said the rich men. "In fact, why don't we look into it? Egypt's not a bad sort of place."

"What are you talking about?" said the rabbi, in opposition. "Have you forgotten that every year at Passover we recite in the Hagada: 'Slaves were we to Pharaoh in Egypt'?"

"Never mind what we recite in the Hagada!" the rich men said sharply, implying that no further opposition would be welcomed. "How can you compare modern Egypt with the Egypt of the Hagada? My goodness, nowadays Egypt is more Palestine than it is Egypt."

Overjoyed that the rich men were on their side, the young people drew nearer and told of the recent articles concerning emigration and committees. The first step, they suggested, should be in the formation of a committee.

"There's a fine how-d'ye-do! Great bit of news. I'll give you committees," countered one of the Redheaded Jews. "What good are committees? Let's get down to brass tacks. Where will we get money to bundle off so many poor people, knock wood?"

"Money?" said the rich men. "Money is no problem at all. Everyone will pledge a monthly sum according to his means. Not lots of money, for lots of money, well, naturally, that's impossible, you see, for everything has a limit, everything must proceed with method and moderation, especially where money is concerned. Understand?"

"Emigration. . . . Egypt. . . . Committees. . . . Pledges," cried all the Redheaded Jews, outshouting one another. As usual, they waved their hands and made a tumult. Pandemonium broke loose.

When the poor people outside heard the news that there was talk of emigrating to Egypt and forming committees and soliciting monthly contributions, a black gloom fell over them.

"What's this?" they yelled. "Did they bring us here to form committees and cast ballots? What sort of merry-go-round is this? What good are all these formalities, emigrations, committees? What's the use of all this fuss and pie in the sky? Provide for today, God will provide for tomorrow. Send us to Egypt, to Goshen, send us packing to the blazes for all we care, so long as it's today, right *now!* For back to Beggarsville we cannot go. Our wives and children are sleeping on cold stones under the open sky and dying of hunger, and you're going to form committees for us? No, sir! Nothing doing! We don't want committees! Committees is one thing we do not want."

With this shout on their lips the poor people barged into the *shul;* they caused such a commotion that they raised the roof with their deafening uproar. At first no one understood what all the shouting was about. But when the rich men made out the words, "We don't want committees," they flew into a furor and exclaimed:

"Mind your manners! Behave, you measly beggars! It's on your behalf that the entire town has assembled. We're breaking our heads trying to make plans how to help you. We're trying to find the quickest way to ship you out of here, and you've got the gall to open up your big mouths. Beggars—back to your homes! Back in Beggarsville you can speak your mind to your hearts' content."

Epilogue

[Material for the Historian of Redheaded Jewry—A Letter from an Emigrant to Egypt—The End of the Redheaded Jews]

The future historian of the Redheaded Jews will be amazed by this chapter and will be ashamed to record some of the savage events described herein. He will refuse to believe that Jews, who are called "compassionate sons of compassionate fathers," actually exploited their brethren's tragic plight, absconded with communal funds, hoodwinked innocent souls, lined their own pockets, and profited from others' woes.

"Ah, me, alack and alas!" the historian will exclaim. "How heartless were those Jews who treated other Jews worse than animals and allowed sick women and tiny infants to sleep outdoors in rain and cold; those companies that promised to bring entire families to the free country of Egypt for a small fee, but actually took all their money and left them stranded in the middle of the desert; and those dandies and spendthrifts who promised poor Jewish girls the moon, but pulled the wool over their eyes and sold them to white slavers for huge profits.

"Oh, my oppressed brethren! How terrible it is when the beaten beat themselves and the bruised bruise one another," the future historian will say. But when he reads the newspapers of that period or the letters which the Redheaded Jews sent home from the "free country" of Egypt, he will really tear his hair.

Following is one of those letters:

My dear ones,

This letter is being written not with ink, but with bloody tears. Too bad that this happy land—may it fry in hell!—didn't sink into the earth like Korah before I got to know it. Too bad I didn't break a leg before I even budged from home. Too bad I didn't die a strange and miserable death before I ever set foot in this wasteland called Egypt. I'd need an infinite supply of paper and ink to describe all the anguish we've had since our first day here. All the tears our wives have shed could have filled the Sambatyon River twice over.

Our first misfortune took place on the Friday when the agents who brought us to the ship made off with our bundles which contained our prayer shawls, *tfillin* and candlesticks. Consequently, our wives could not light Sabbath candles, and they cried their eyes out—may their curses fall right on the heads of the committees. Then a fearful hurricane tossed the ship and churned up waves higher than houses. We were quite prepared to die, assuming that it was the end. We suffered for three weeks. Throughout the voyage we never tasted a morsel of warm food and saw only sky and water. Although we were sick and hungry, wretched and broken when we landed, they nevertheless kept us out in the rain for a full day and night.

And don't you think that then and there my wife, Esther, upped and decided to give birth? Before you knew it she had a baby boy, who soon died. My wife was deathly ill, heaven help us, and there wasn't even a spoonful of soup or jam to put new life into her soul. The next day they finally had pity on us. People from some committee or other came and took us away. We were driven into a stable and given soft rolls and oranges: after everyone got his roll and orange, we all were chased again.

Then they took our names and placed all of us on a ship. For one and a half days we sailed under a broiling sun, which scorched like the blazes. Finally, we were cast ashore. We saw neither houses, trees, nor grass—only sand and sky. That's where they wanted us to settle. They gave us work and told us to plow the earth, plant trees, and drag hunks of wood from the sea and build houses. The foreman they placed over us was an ill-tempered madman quick to give a blow at the slightest provocation. When we shouted blue murder, they tied each of us up and whipped us mercilessly. Finally, we managed to escape more dead than alive. We scattered in all directions, wherever our legs carried us.

Several of us arrived in Egypt. Here perhaps things won't be too bad, for one can make a living—that is, we're given work. For turning the wheel of a sewing machine from dawn to midnight we get a silver dollar. The children get half a dollar. In brief, things aren't too bad.

Everyone here is called Mister. Horses wear glasses, and men wear paper dickeys. The only trouble is no one here knows anything about Sabbath or holidays, and none of us understands the natives, for they don't talk here, they lisp. The devil knows what sort of language it is! What's more, these people haven't the slightest compassion. You can drop dead from hunger on the streets, and no one will even stop to look. For everyone is busy; everyone dashes hither and thither in a perpetual rush. The man who wants to go into business can sell anything he likes; he can peddle old clothes, matchsticks, shoe polish, or wax, and as they say, he can "make a living."

But I say I'm lucky, for others are worse off than I. Not long ago I bumped into Yenkel, Uncle Mordecai's son, and was struck dumb with amazement. He had changed so much I almost didn't recognize him. He got all dressed up like a mad organ grinder's monkey. He wore a short, long-waisted jacket, and a high fur cap which looked like a noodle pot.

"Yenkel," I said, "is that you?"

"Who else?" he said. "Of course, it's me, although I'm not called Yenkel anymore. Now my name is Mr. Jack."

"Well, how do you do, Mr. Jack? How are you making out in this fine land?"

"Not bad at all," he said. "At first things were terrible, but now, thank God, I'm making a living."

"What do you do?" I asked.

"Work in a laundry. Washing and pressing."

"Is that what you call making a living? Ah, woe unto me that my Uncle Mordecai's son has to slave away as a washerwoman, and in Egypt, of all places."

Then he told me what the rest of our gang of Redheaded Jews was doing. "They're all making a living, thank God!" he said. "Moishe, Shprintze's son, specializes in mending holes in underwear. Berel, Dobbe's pride and joy, bangs pegs into heels. Mindi's son Mendel, bakes bagels. Mottel, Ratzi's boy, sells brooms. Some still roam about without work and ask for handouts. As for the rest, I myself don't know what happened to them. Perhaps they're no longer among the living."

Both of us had a good cry, got everything off our chests, and promised to meet at least once a week. That will ease our hearts a bit, for our homesickness is so great it's gnawing the life out of us. Believe me, I'd exchange success, a million dollars, and all the grand opportunities here for one look at Beggarsville. Ah, me, if I only had wings, I would fly right over to you, my dear, beloved kinsmen. We think of you constantly and miss each and every one of you. Be sure to tell everyone the following: Don't you dare budge from your homes, for you'll regret it and you'll only bring down a bane upon your bones, like Peysi the widow, who met a bitter end with her two daughters, poor things! Like others, she was led to believe she could make her daughters' fortune and find fine husbands who would give them huge dowries and beautiful gifts—but the upshot really was that those dandies fooled them and transported the girls in chains to some unknown destination, where they were sold for huge sums to white slavers.

So for heaven's sake, beware of these dandies decked out in paper dickeys and golden watches who promise you the moon on a silver platter. Don't let yourselves be talked into anything. By *anyone*. And watch your daughters, especially, like the apple of your eye. Had I not been hoodwinked by the emigration committees, I'd at least be sure that in one hundred and twenty years my bones would be buried in a Jewish grave among my dear and beloved kin in Beggarsville.

My wife, Esther, may she live and be well, sends you all the best. And, remember, for heaven's sake—don't you dare budge from home. . . .

Such were the letters that the Redheaded Jews received from their fathers and mothers, sisters and brothers, friends and acquaintances who had gone abroad. And though for the most part one letter was more depressing than the next, the Redheaded Jews nevertheless looked forward to better news. They did not lose faith; they hoped that, God willing, they would soon get glad tidings of prosperity and joy.

Perhaps someday we shall know whether or not their hopes were realized. For curiosity's sake we may even take a trip, God willing, and see how our brethren, the Redheaded Jews, are faring in the new Exile of Egypt. But one thing is certain. Those Redheaded Jews who remained at home were no longer the same, for as soon as the stunning news reached them, there was an upheaval. As though awakening from a long sleep, they sobered up and began to comprehend their situation. They realized that they would have to abandon their old ways and begin to plan for the future. And only then did they understand what the onetime visitor had said about their land, Palestine. Suddenly their interest in that matter perked up. Heated discussions, hullaballoo, and excitement—in the typical fashion of the Redheaded Jews.

No doubt you want to know what the results were? What came of these discussions? Did the Redheaded Jews actually *do* something to better their lot? Or were they satisfied merely with words, words, and more words? Were the various opinions reconciled, and did they come to some sort of agreement? Or did everyone stick to his own idea? Did they ever conclude their discussions? Or did someone always shout, "We don't want it!" at the crux of the presentation?

But here the curtain falls, and for the time being, we must bid good-bye to the Redheaded Jews.

From America

MR. GREEN HAS A JOB

How do you do, Mr. Sholom Aleichem! I don't think you know me, but we're a bit related. Second cousins twice removed. Actually, I'm not related to you personally, but to your pal, Tevye the dairyman, and his kinsman, Menakhem-Mendel from Yehupetz.

Now you're interested, huh? You've stopped! Aha, now you want to listen. If so, then let's stand here on the sidewalk and chat for a while about our golden little land, America. And not so much about America as about its business: how you eat your heart out till God sends you the proper job. For if the Good Lord helps and you land the proper job, there's hope that in time you can work yourself up the ladder of success and become a Jacob Schiff or a Nathan Strauss. In a word—to become an allrightnik.

At the moment I can't say I'm an allrightnik. But, God be praised, I *do* have a job. The wonderful part of it is that I hit upon it all on my own. I can see that you're dying to know who's talking to you. If I tell you that you're listening to Mr. Green, you'll no doubt think: Green, Yellow, Blue? That doesn't tell you a thing. Here in America I'm Green. On the other side I was known as Greenberg. From where? From Odessa, you say? Right you are. From Odessa! From Yehupetz? From Yehupetz, too. And also from Kasrilevke, Teplik, Shpola, Uman, Berdichev. In brief, from all those far-flung places. I was in business like all other Jews, manipulating and brokering, until along came good times, and we were chased away and ended up here in the land of Columbus. And we kept on eating until we ate the last shirt off our backs. Then we sank into a different kind of hell. We took on all sorts of slave labor—but still things didn't work out.

Finally, one month before Rosh Hashana, on the first of Elul to be exact, I saw ads for cantors, *shuls,* and small prayer rooms. I noticed that the stores were displaying year-round and High Holy Day prayer books, *shofars,* and prayer shawls. I also noticed that everyone began buttering up to the Almighty, trying to get on the good side of Him for the sake of business. So I said to myself: Mr. Green, how long you gonna be a greenhorn? Why don't you, too, cash in on Elul, the High Holy Days, and the Ten Days of Repentance? But it's easier said than done. In order to cash in, there's got to be something to cash in on. What sort of work could I do? Pass myself off as a cantor here in America? No, for back home I had never been a shoemaker! A *shokhet?* No, for my father had never been a common drayman. I certainly couldn't be a reverend—you know, a *shamesh*—for I *did* know Hebrew and I *did* understand the meaning of the prayers. Could I become a strictly kosher butcher? No, for in the old country I hadn't been a fence for stolen horses.

Immersed in these thoughts and meditations, as your Tevye the dairyman says, I wandered into a *shul.* It was the first of Elul, the day of the new moon. The worshipers were reciting the Psalm "The Lord is my light and aid." After the service someone said:

"All right, who's going to blow the *shofar?*"

"The *shofar?*" I called out. "Me! I will."

So you'll ask me: How do I come to being a *shofar* blower? Here's the story. I never blew the *shofar* back home on the other side. Neither did my father. Or my father's father. But when we were kids, starting with Elul, we small fry, little rascals one and all, would grab the *shofar* and blow it and blow it just for the fun of it until the *shamesh* would douse us with cold water and drive us from the *shul.*

In a word, I could do the job. But like they say, the proof of the pudding is in the eating. So I took hold of the *shofar,* blew a few long, short, and quick blasts and ended up with one mighty blast which without exaggeration was heard on the other side of the Brooklyn Bridge.

Hearing such a blast, they asked me, "Where are you from, young man?"

"What's the difference where I'm from?" I said.

"How would you like to blow the *shofar* for us for the High Holy Days? Our *shofar* blower just died."

"If I could make a living from this job, I'd gladly take it."

"Making a living from blowing the *shofar* alone is rather difficult," they said, "unless you can do something else."

"Namely? What else would you want me to do?" I said. "Want me to be a driver, a garbage man, or a street cleaner?"

"Since you're a *shofar* blower, we can't expect you to do such low-class, menial tasks. The only thing we can do is give you a chance to blow the *shofar* in another *shul*."

This was a tempting idea and I thought: If I get a chance to blow the *shofar* in one more *shul*, I might as well take two *shuls*. And why not three? Downtown I went from one *shul* to another, from one prayer room to another, had tryouts in every place, showed my skill with the *shofar*, and made a big hit. For when I blow, everyone comes running from all the *shul*. Judges, Congressmen, and assemblymen have heard me, and all of them have said: "Wonderful!" Naturally, during my first year I only had one *shul* and two small prayer rooms. The second year—three *shuls* and five prayer rooms. This year, God willing, there are prospects for up to twelve prayer rooms, and I'll be able to make a nice few dollars.

But, alas, how can one man attend to so much business? Don't ask! This is America, you know, and here one must make the best of a situation. In one place I blow the *shofar* a bit earlier, in the next place a bit later, in the third, later still. I try to do my best in order to satisfy the public. For if I don't show up on time, I'm likely to lose my job and my reputation.

No doubt you're wondering, Mr. Sholom Aleichem, how come my English is so good. It's because of my kids. They're already one hundred percent Americans and don't want to talk one word of Yiddish. If you'd take a look at my boys, you'd never guess they were Jewish. Same goes for me. If you'd meet me after the High Holy Days, you wouldn't recognize me either. Me, just before the beginning of Elul, I cast off my stylish suit, grow a beard and look like a homey old-timer. But as soon as the High Holy Days are over, I shave, put on my hat and suit, and once more become the picture of a modern gentleman. What doesn't one do in America for the sake of business?

I can tell you by looking at you, Mr. Sholom Aleichem, that you're itching to write me up in the papers. You've even taken out your notebook. Well, it's okay by me. Go right ahead. In fact, I'll be much obliged to you. Because for me it'll be free publicity. What's more, I'll even ask you to put in my address:

Mr. Green
Cherry Street
New York City

And I hope that someday we'll bump into each other uptown. Until then—so long and good-bye.

OTHERWISE, THERE'S
NOTHING NEW

[A Letter from America to the Old Country]

To my dear friend Yisrulik,

May you and your wife and children be inscribed for a year of health and happiness, and may God's blessings come upon all Israel, amen.

We've been worried stiff because you haven't written us any letters. We've been walking around in a blue funk ever since that period of revolution,* constitution, and pogroms began back home in the old country. We're literally eating our hearts out. If the papers here in America aren't bluffing, then those revolutionaries probably made mincemeat of half the world already.

Every day we get wind of another sensational event. Last night I read a cable that they strung up Mr. Krushevan, that damned anti-Semite and president of the Fourth Duma. Let me know if that isn't a lot of hot air. And write me about your business. Are you still working for someone, or are you on your own? And how's Khane-Rikel? What's Hershel doing? And my cousin Lipa? And how about Yosil, Henikh's boy! And Bentsi and Rokhel? Zlatke? Mottel? And the rest of the tailors? Are you thinking of coming to America? Fill me in on all the details in your next letter.

Now for myself. Well, what can I say, pal? Everything's okay

---

* The revolution of 1905—Tr.

with me, the wife and the kids. Thank God, we're all making a living here. We work like horses, but at least we make ends meet. We're not salting away any money, but we've got two rooms and a kitchen. After work and come nighttime we paint the town red. Sometimes we go to a Socialist meeting, sometimes a Zionist meeting, and sometimes the Yiddish theater. We sweat and toil till we're blue in the face. But we're free. I can join any club I like, and if I feel like it, I can become a citizen and vote.

The only thing we miss is—home. We're homesick something awful. My wife, Jennie (we don't call her Blumeh anymore), doesn't leave me alone for a minute. She keeps nagging me to take a trip back to Russia and visit our beloved, dear ones in the cemetery. You'd never recognize Jennie. She's a regular lady rigged out in hat, gloves, and all the trimmings. I'm enclosing a snapshot of her and the rest of the family. What do you say to my oldest boy? That's Mottel. Now he's called Mike. He's an allrightnik. He works in a factory and earns ten, twelve dollars a week. If only he wouldn't gamble, he'd be a topnotch allrightnik. My other boy, Jack, used to work in a factory, too. He managed to pick up a bit of English and is now a bookkeeper in a barbershop. My third rascal, Benjamin, is a barroom waiter. He doesn't get wages, but he brings home between six and eight dollars a week in tips. My fourth boy, the one on the picture wearing a cap, is a loafer. He doesn't want to go to school but hangs around the street day and night playing ball. The girls are okay, too. They work in shops and have some cash in the bank. The only trouble is that I see neither hide nor hair of them. They step out *whenever* they like, go *wherever* they like, and with *whom* they like.

America's a free country. You're perfectly free to keep your opinions to yourself. You can't even tell your own daughter what to do. Take my oldest girl, for example, formerly Khaye, but now known as Frances. What a job I had with her! Without telling me, she fell head over heels in love and said "I do" with a good-for-nothing bum, a member of the Brotherhood of Pickpockets. He was a runaway from the House of Detention but told her he was a famous clothing manufacturer and realtor. The upshot was that he was a bigamist. He only had a sum total of three wives, none of them divorced. The trouble I had till I got rid of him! Now Frances just married a pushcart peddler and is on easy street. My other girls are still single. When they get engaged, they won't ask my permission either.

America's a free country. Everyone minds his own business as he sees fit, and that's that. Well, now that I've written you, pal, and told you what's doing with me, be sure to let me know right away what's what with you and what's going on back home. Best regards to one and all—and again all the best for the New Year. So long and lots of luck!

Your best pal,
Jacob (formerly Yenkel)

[*A Letter from the Old Country to America*]

My dear Yenkel,

I received your New Year's wishes right on the eve of Rosh Hashana. Thank you very much for your kind letter, and I wish you all the best for the coming year. God willing, I hope that we may soon see each other in joy, amen.

Now I'm going to answer your letter.

Listen, if you've already taken the trouble to send me New Year's greetings for the first time in two years, why don't you write Yiddish like a normal human being? How in heaven's name am I supposed to understand what you're saying: "worried stiff," "blue funk," "hot air," "salting away," "bluff," "hide nor hair," and other such words and expressions? You've asked me to spell out everything in detail. What can I say? There's really nothing new. Thank God, all is well now. The rich men are doing nicely, as usual, and the poor people are dying of hunger, like all over. Workingmen like us are sitting around without a stitch of work. But at least we're all safe from a pogrom. We're not in the least afraid of a pogrom. We've already had one, along with two encores—something which only Kishinev is noted for. In fact, the pogrom reached us a bit late, but to make up for it, we had one with all the trimmings. In short, I don't want to write too much. I can't, for there's nothing new to write about.

Dear Yenkel, I can only report one thing—I'm still alive! I've looked the Angel of Death in the face three times. But never mind. How does Getzi the dressmaker—remember him? —put it? *"Who by earthquake and who by plague?* In other words, if you're destined for lots of suffering, then at least God spares your life. . . ."* My heart went out for my wife and children, so I sent them away. They hid in the attic of a kindly peasant and lay there in all their glory two days and two nights without so much as a drop of water, a crumb of bread, or a wink of sleep. Things only quieted down, thank God, on the third day, when there was no longer anything to rob or anyone to beat. Then everyone slowly crawled down from the attics, alive and well, praise the Lord. No one from our family was hurt, except Lipa, who was killed along with his two sons, and Noah and Melekh, two workers with golden hands, and poor Moishe-Hersh who was dragged down from an attic, and Perl-Dvora, who was later found dead in a cellar with her tiny infant, Reyzele, at her breast. . . .

Including children, then, the grand total of our family's losses was seven dead. But how does Getzi put it? *"This, too, is for the best.* In other words, it could have been worse. As for better—the sky's the limit."*

You asked about Hershele. Don't worry about him. For the past six months, he's been unemployed, sitting in solitary confinement in prison. Why is he serving time? I suppose a safe guess would be that he was imprisoned for the notorious crime of holding his prayer book upside down! Rumor has it that they have greater honors yet in store for him. He'll be either hanged or shot. It all depends on his luck. For as Getzi says, "It's all a matter of luck." For instance, Yosil, Henikh's son, dropped dead just before they were able to cart him off to jail. Otherwise, there's nothing new.

Well, how come you didn't ask anything about Leybl, Nekhemya the carpenter's son? Remember him? He was an absolute good-for-nothing, right? Leybl-Stable he was called. Today he's living like a duke with lifetime tenure in the Petro-pavlovsk Penitentiary. But do you know who I feel sorry for? For Zlatke. They say she's gone mad for woes. No trifle, you know, losing two children in one week. Avrom, Moishe's son, is probably already in America. If you see him, give him my best regards, and tell him that his father's quite a considerate chap—he dropped dead before they proclaimed the new con-stitution. And our Mottel simply disappeared—no one knows where.

Lots like him have vanished. We don't even know what's be-come of them. Some ran away, some were killed, and some are resting up in prison or traipsing about in the Siberian snow, pushing wheelbarrows. But what do they care? Those stubborn characters were insistent. Either constitution or die, they said. But we workingmen don't know any underhanded tricks. How does Getzi put it? *"Spare me your honey, and spare me your sting.* In other words, don't do me any favors! I'll tie my own shoelaces, thank you!" A queer chap, that Getzi. One of his sons was killed in the war; the other one's in jail. Getzi him-self has got plenty of troubles, but when it comes to quoting a proverb or a verse from the Bible, he gets carried away.

Otherwise, there's nothing new. Thank God, all is well and, praise the Good Lord, we're all in the best of health, except for Khane-Rikel, who's been complaining about her heart, poor soul. No trifle, you know, being in constant fear of expro-priation. Of course, you probably don't know the first thing about expropriation. So I'll explain. They come into your house with a bomb, and it isn't filled with matza meal, you know, but with powder and nails. "Reach for the sky!" they shout. (Getzi calls this a Biblical stickup: "Lift ye your hands.") They empty all your pockets and take everything you own. And go do them something!

Once, two of these characters came into my place, pronounced that fine verse, and took my sewing machine. I also had a cow—but it died of its own accord. My girl, Brokhe, is an even greater pauper than ever before, and Alter, too, is a far cry from being rich. Leyzer was deported for lack of a residence pass not too long ago. He certainly deserved it, huh? Who asked him to be a Hebrew teacher? Mendel also improved his position: He upped and died, some say of tuberculosis, others of hunger. I say he died of both. Binyomin's pride and joy is in the army, and there's constant talk of cholera. That's all we need.

Otherwise, there's nothing new. And as for the request of Blumeh, or Jennie as she's now called, to take a trip and see her dear ones in the cemetery—now's not the time, Yenkel. Now's not the time. Put it off a year, when with God's help things will quiet down a bit and everyone will stop killing everyone else. That's when you should come, and then, the Good Lord willing, both of us will go to that holy field. God be praised, many more of our friends are there now. Not to mention casual acquaintances. And there's more arriving daily.

Otherwise, there's nothing new. Be well, and give regards to each and every one. As for America, I'm not coming there. Your America doesn't even begin to attract me. A land where people get stiff when they worry, where you walk around blue funks and hang around streets, where money is salted, where towns are painted red and faces blue, where Blumeh becomes Jennie and men have three wives—no offense meant, but from such a land one ought to run away. After reading your letter, I've come to the conclusion that if we get the constitution we expect, we won't need America, for we'll have a better America here than you have over there. But, Yenkel, don't you worry your head over it. We're going to get a good constitution like I'm going to wake up a millionaire tomorrow—blast that anti-Semite Krushevan with a pack of ulcers and plagues. I just pray that God inscribes us all—us here and you there—for a year of health and happiness.

Your friend,
Yisrulik

THE STORY OF A GREENHORN

America is a land of business, you say? Never you mind. That's the way it's got to be. But marrying for money and selling yourself for business—*that* I consider absolutely disgusting. I'm not preaching, you know, just stating cold facts: Ninety-nine percent of the greenhorns marry just for money and business. Well, this makes me mad as hell, and if I meet a greenhorn like that, I give *him* the business. Just leave it to me. If you want to listen, I'll tell you a fine story.

One day I sat in my office writing some letters when in came a young greenhorn, practically a boy. With him was his young wife, so help me, peaches and cream! As pretty as can be and as sound as a freshly picked apple.

"How do you do?" he said. "Are you Mr. Baraban, the business broker?"

"Have a seat? What's the good word?"

So the greenhorn opened up his heart and told me a long story. He's been in America for ten years. He was a pants maker by trade. He met a working girl with one thousand dollars' cash, and she fell in love with him. So he married her. Now he was looking for a good business, so he wouldn't have to work in a factory. For he had—God spare us all—rheumatism and so on and so forth.

I looked at the young woman and said to him:

"What sort of business would you like to go into?"

"I'd like to open up a candy store," he said, "for in a candy store she'd be able to help out."

There's a greenhorn for you! Not enough that he picked himself a juicy peach, over which even an atheist would gladly have said a blessing, not enough that she brought him one thousand dollars' cash; but he was also dying to have her slave away in the store so he could sit with his pals and play pinochle and so on and so forth. Just leave it to me. Boy, do I know these characters!

So I thought: A canker sore is what you're going to get from me, not a candy store. As far as I'm concerned, you can croak like a dog in a laundry. I'm going to make a laundryman out of you. How come I thought of a laundry? Because it just so happened I had a laundry up for sale. So I said to the greenhorn:

"Why bother with a candy store, where you'll have to work eighteen hours a day and hope that a schoolboy dashes in and buys a penny's worth of candy and so on and so forth? Just leave it to me. I'll give you a better business—a laundry in the Bronx. You'll work regular hours and live like a king."

I took a pencil and figured out that after the overhead, rent, two pressers, one delivery boy, laundry expenses, and so on and so forth, he would clear some thirty dollars a week. What could be better than that?

"What would that cost?" he said.

"So help me, it'd be a bargain for a thousand, but for you I'll make it eight hundred flat. Just leave it to me. The only thing you'll have to do is shell out those few dollars and pick up the key. Then you can even go around blindfolded, for believe you me, you'll be okay. Meanwhile, be well and come back in three days, for now I don't have any spare time and so on and so forth and so long!"

I went to my laundryman and brought him the glad tidings. The Good Lord had sent me a sucker, I told him, a greenhorn. If he had any sense, he could now get rid of the laundry for good money. So the next move was up to him and so on and so forth.

The crook knew what I was driving at and said:

"Bring that fish over to me, and everything will be swell and dandy."

Three days later my greenhorn and his wife showed up. They brought a deposit and, following the customary procedure, took the laundry for a week's tryout. Naturally, my laundryman saw to it that the week would be not only good but top-notch. And so the business was settled. The greenhorn forked over his few dollars, the laundryman gave him the books and the key, and I took commission from both sides, of course, and so on and so forth. For Mr. Baraban the business broker knows his business. As they say: *Finita la comedia.*

Finished? That's what you think! As far as I was concerned, the comedy was just beginning. For when everything was set-tled, all around, a blaze of sudden anger at that greenhorn swept over me. Why did that son of a bitch deserve a bed of roses—a gorgeous wife like that, a thousand dollars in cash, and a working business without headaches? I felt I had to get that laundry back at half price and sell it back to the laundry-man. How? I'm not called Mr. Baraban the business broker for nothing! There's nothing I can't accomplish if I set my mind to it.

So I went to a place directly opposite that greenhorn's laun-dry, rented a corner store from the agent, slipped him a ten-dollar bill as a down payment, and hung a sign on the window saying: A LAUNDRY WILL SOON OPEN HERE! Just as I expected, within twenty-four hours my greenhorn showed up, all hot under the collar.

"Hey, what's going on? I'm a dead man!"

"What seems to be the trouble?" I asked.

So he told me about the catastrophe. Some devil-knows-who rented a store directly opposite his and was opening a laundry.

"So what is it you want, greenhorn?"

"Find me a customer for the laundry, and I'll thank you till my dying day. I'll even remember you in my prayers," he said, and so on and so forth.

I calmed him down and told him that it wasn't going to be so easy to find a customer. "Just leave it to me," I said, "and I'll try my best. Why don't you come back in three days, for right now I'm up to my neck in business and so on and so forth and so long?"

Next, I contacted the former laundryman and told him the whole story.

"Here's your chance to buy back your laundry from the greenhorn at half price."

"How are you going to accomplish that?"

"What's it to you? Just leave it to me. I'm not called Mr. Baraban the business broker for nothing."

"Okay," he said.

"Will I get my commission?"

"Okay by me."

"It'll cost you a hundred."

"Okay."

And so on and so forth. Meanwhile, the three days passed, and my greenhorn showed up with his wife. The wife was a bit paler, but she was still as lovely as a sunny day.

"Well, what's new?" they said.

"What should be new?" I said. "You ought to thank God that I just about managed to scrape up someone interested in your laundry. The only hitch is you'll have to lose money."

"How much?"

"Don't ask how much you're losing. Better ask how much you're gaining. For no matter how much you get it'll be found money. You playing around with American competitors? Why, they can drive you to such expenses that you'll have to pick yourself up in the middle of the night and run off with just the shirt on your back."

Anyway, I so succeeded in frightening the wits out of them that they took half of what they paid for the laundry and, to top if off, even paid me commission, for I'm not obliged to trouble myself for nothing. And so—good-bye laundry!

But wait, I'm not through yet. If you've been listening carefully, you'll remember that I shelled out a ten-dollar down payment to the agent for a store and hung out a sign for a laundry. So the next question was: Why should I let ten dollars breeze into the winds without benefiting anybody? After all didn't Mr. Baraban the business broker sweat plenty for that ten-dollar bill? That's number one. Second, I was still mad as hell at that greenhorn. It rankled me that that bastard still had a few hundred dollars in his pocket and a wife that looked like a million. What did he do to deserve it? Mr. Baraban, the biggest business broker on the East Side, was stuck with a wife who, if you'll excuse the expression, was a downright monster and a Jezebel to boot, while that greenhorn—*him* God had sent a doll, you know what I mean, a sweetiepie, may a foul disease overtake him before he looks at her again.

So I didn't sit on my hands but wrote him a postcard asking him to come see me at such and such an hour, for I had a business proposition for him. He didn't wait to be asked twice and came at the appointed hour, bringing his little wife with him.

I asked my dear guests to be seated and told them the following:

"You don't know those American bluffers! If you knew the trick that that old crook of a laundryman played on you, your hair would stand on end."

"What did he do?"

"What did he do? He simply rented the store opposite yours and hung out that laundry sign just to scare you into selling his laundry back to him at half price."

Hearing this, the couple exchanged glances. They were as angry as all get out. Especially the young wife. Her eyes blazed like two burning coals.

"By rights you ought to get even with that thief in such a way that he won't easily forget you," I said.

"How can we get even with him?"

"Leave that bird to me," I said. "I'll fix his wagon so well he won't wake up for doomsday. Furthermore, you'll benefit from all this. You'll even be better off than ever before."

They looked at me like a pair of innocent doves and seemed to say, "From your mouth into God's ears—may you have a long and happy life" and so on and so forth. And I suggested the following plan: Why should they buy someone else's business and pay the next fellow an arm and a leg for it?

"You know what I'll do?" I said. "I'll go back to that corner landlord and rent the very same store the thief wanted to take. For three, four hundred dollars I'll fix up a laundry there for you right opposite his, and you can compete with him. Whatever he charges, I'd charge less, and in three weeks I'd have him move right out of there. If not, my name isn't Baraban."

Anyway, I threw them into such a dither that the greenhorn practically flung his arms around my neck and kissed me. His good-looking wife blushed and became prettier than ever before. That same day I rented the store for them and quickly installed a new laundry with a sign, tables, and all the accessories. My couple set to work, and fierce competition ensued between them and the old laundryman. They undercut each other's prices as much as they could. If the old man charged twenty-four cents for a dozen sheets, they charged eighteen and threw in a bedspread free. If the other guy lowered his prices for shirts to eight cents apiece, they went down to a cent and a half per collar. So the other guy had to come down to a penny and so on and so forth.

The upshot was that the greenhorn kissed his last few dollars good-bye and remained without a cent to his name. He didn't even have enough money to pay for the rent. So he closed the laundry at a great loss, and as the holy books say: "He came busted and left broke."

Now I've got him taking a little vacation in the Ludlow Street Jail. I've even found a good lawyer for his wife. She's suing her husband on three counts:

(1) for a return of the thousand dollars' dowry;
(2) for a divorce;
(3) and for support and maintenance, as prescribed by state law, until the divorce comes through.

The devil take him, that blasted greenhorn!

afikomen: The piece of matza hidden at the beginning of the Passover Seder and eaten at the end of the meal.

afternoon service: One of the three weekday services. The other two are the morning service and the evening service.

aleph-beys: The Hebrew word for alphabet; specifically, the first two letters.

Baal Shem Tov: See Hasidism.

borscht: A soup made of beets or cabbage, of Russian origin.

carob: A sweet wild pod; it is known in Yiddish as *bokser,* and it is also called St. John's bread in English.

dreydl: A four-sided top that children play with during Hanuka.

Elul: The last month of the Jewish year (August-September); the month preceding the season of High Holy Days.

esrog: The citron used (in conjunction with the *lulav*) during Sukkos.

eruv: According to Jewish law, carrying objects on the Sabbath is considered labor and hence forbidden. But since a Jew is permitted to carry objects within the confines of his home (private domain), the placing of a string or wire around the community (where a fence or a wall was lacking) converted it to one huge private domain. One of the advantages of this legal device was that it permitted a Jew to carry his prayer shawl, Siddur, and other personal articles to the synagogue on Sabbath.

Ethics of the Fathers: One of the tractates of the Mishna (the body of oral law redacted c. 200 C.E. by Rabbi Judah). The tractate deals with the ethical principles formulated, often in epigrammatic form, by the fathers of the Jewish rabbinic tradition. The Ethics of the Fathers (known in Hebrew as *Pirke Avot*) is included in the prayer book and has become the most popular book in the Mishna.

farfel: Flattened dough cut into tiny pieces and cooked.

Four Questions (Heb. *Ma Nishtana*): The Four Questions are asked
   by the youngest child in the house during the Passover Seder.
   These questions prompt the reply "Slaves were we unto Pharaoh" and the recitation of the Passover story.

Gehenna: hell.

goy (pl. *goyim*): A gentile.

gut shabbes: The traditional Sabbath greeting.

gut yohr: The response ("Have a good year!") to the above greeting.

gut yontev: The traditional holiday greeting.

Hagada (lit. the telling): The book of the Passover home service
   which through narrative and song recounts the story of Jewish
   slavery in Egypt and the liberation. The Hagada is read during
   the first two nights of Passover.

Hanuka (lit. dedication): The Festival of Lights celebrated for eight
   days, starting the twenty-fifth of Kislev (November-December).
   Hanuka marks the struggle for religious freedom and the suc-
   cessful revolt of poorly armed Jews against the forces of Anti-
   ochus Epiphanes, who proscribed the practice of Judaism. In
   165 B.C.E. the Jewish fighters, led by Judah Maccabaeus, routed
   the Hellenistic Syrians and rededicated the Temple. Hanuka is
   a time when card games and gambling with the *dreydl*—usually
   forbidden—are permitted.

Hasidism: A movement founded by Israel Baal Shem Tov, the Master of the Good Name (1700-1760). The Hasidic movement, a
   revolt against rabbinism and its accent on Talmudic accom-
   plishment, stressed good deeds and piety through joy of wor-
   ship, songs, legends, and dance. It had a wide appeal to the
   masses, and its followers were, and still are, called Hasidism.

Havdala (lit. separation or distinction): The prayer of separation is
   recited at the conclusion of the Sabbath, about one hour after
   sundown; it marks the separation between the Sabbath and a
   weekday or between the Sabbath and a festival which immediately follows. The Havdala is also said at the conclusion of a
   festival.

High Holy Days: Rosh Hashana and Yom Kippur.

Hoshana Rabba: The seventh day of Sukkos; on this day there are
   seven processions around the pulpit, and all those who have
   esrogs and *lulavs* follow the cantor.

Kabala: A body of mystical lore and scriptural interpretation developed by the Kabalists, who through study and meditative speculation sought communion with God.

Kaddish (lit. sanctification): A prayer which marks the conclusion of a unit in the service and which is also recited as a mourner's prayer. The Kaddish, which makes no reference at all to death, is actually a doxology.

khalle: The braided Sabbath or holiday loaf made of white flour.

kheder (lit. room): The room in the rebbi's house where children were taught Hebrew, the prayers, and the Pentateuch.

Kiddush (lit. sanctification): The blessing recited over wine (or *khalle*) at the beginning of the Sabbath or holiday evening meal.

Lag B'Omer: A day of festivity, especially for Jewish children, who are released from their studies and taken into the fields and woods. Tradition says that on this day the plague which beset the disciples of Rabbi Akiba, who fought and died in the last and unsuccessful Jewish revolt against Rome (132 c.e.), came to an end.

l'khayim: To life!—The traditional Hebrew toast.

lulav: The palm branch adorned with myrtle and willow branches that is used (in conjunction with the *esrog*) during Sukkos.

Maftir: The concluding section of the Torah portion read on Sabbaths and holidays; it is a distinct honor to be called up to the Torah for Maftir.

matza: The crackerlike unleavened bread eaten during Passover.

mazel tov: Congratulations, or good luck.

Megillah (lit. scroll): Often used in reference to the Book of Esther, which is written on a scroll of parchment.

mezuza (pl. *mezuzos*): A rolled piece of parchment containing the verses from Deuteronomy 6:4-9 and 11:13-17, and inserted in a wooden or metal case. It is affixed to the right-hand doorposts of Jewish homes and synagogues.

Midrash (lit. explanation or interpretation): Rabbinic commentary and explanatory notes, homilies, folklore, and stories on scriptural passages.

Purim: The festival celebrating the Jews' deliverance from Haman's plan to exterminate them, as described in the Book of Esther. It is celebrated on the fourteenth of Adar (March) and is noted for its gaiety, especially its Purim plays and festive meal. In the synagogues, where the Book of Esther is read from scrolls, children twirl the rattle-clackers each time Haman's name is mentioned. Purim, too, is a time for sending sweet platters to neighbors and alms to the poor.

ram's horn: Known in Hebrew as the *shofar,* it is blown several times during Rosh Hashana and once at the conclusion of the Yom Kippur service. The awesome sounds of the ram's horn are supposed to arouse the people to repentance. According to tradition, every Jew must hear the *shofar.*

Rashi: Rabbi Shlomo ben Itzhak (1040-1105), of Troyes, France, whose commentaries on the Bible and the Talmud almost immediately became classics. No Talmud and hardly a Pentateuch is printed without the popular commentary by Rashi.

reb: Mister.

rebbe: The spiritual leader of a group of Hasidim, not necessarily the rabbi of a community. It was common for Jews to travel great distances to visit their *rebbe.*

rebbi: A Hebrew teacher, not ordained as a rabbi.

Rosh Hashana (lit. head of the year): The Jewish New Year, celebrated the first and second days of Tishrei (September). Next to Yom Kippur, these are the most solemn days of the year.

Sabbath goy: A gentile who performed tasks otherwise forbidden to Jews on the Sabbath, such as extinguishing lights, carrying food, etc.

Sambatyon: The legendary river in Africa that constantly cast stones and was still only on the Sabbath. Since travel on the Sabbath is prohibited, the Little Redheaded Jews who lived beyond the Sambatyon were always inaccessible.

Seder: The festive home ritual of the first and second nights of Passover, at which the Hagada is recited.

Sephardic: Of Spanish-Jewish origin; the Hebrew pronunciation of Jews who lived in Spain, Italy, Turkey, etc., contrasted with the Ashkenazic pronunciation of Jews in Central and Eastern Europe. To the Ashkenazic Jews of Sholom Aleichem's world, those who pronounced Hebrew with a Sephardic accent seemed to be speaking mostly with "aahs," as in the story "The Guest."

Sephardim (sing. *Sephardi*): Jews of Spanish origin.

shalom: Hello; also, good-bye.

shamesh (pl. *shamoshim*): the beadle or sexton of a synagogue.

Shevuos (lit. weeks): The Festival of Weeks, celebrated seven weeks after Passover (May-June), and commemorating the revelation at Sinai and the presentation of the Torah to the children of Israel. Like the other two major festivals, Passover and Sukkos, Shevuos has agricultural, as well as historic and spiritual, roots.

shokhet (pl. *shokhtim*): The man ritually qualified to slaughter cattle and fowl for those who observe the Jewish dietary laws.

shul: Synagogue or prayer room.

Siddur: The prayer book.

Simkhas Torah: The festival immediately following Shemini Atzeres (the eighth day of the festival of Sukkos), on which the reading of the Torah is completed and begun anew. This joyous holiday is traditionally celebrated with singing and dancing around the synagogue with the Torah.

sukka: The booth with the thatched roof used during Sukkos.

Sukkos: The Feast of Booths celebrated for seven days (nine, including Shemini Atzeres and Simkhas Torah), starting the fifteenth of Tishrei. Sukkos commemorates the Jews' living in booths (*sukkos*) during their wandering in the desert and is, in addition, the fall harvest festival.

Talmud Torah: Same as *kheder* (see *kheder*), but usually under communal, rather than private, auspices.

tsimess: Vegetables simmered in honey or sugar; usually carrots, or potatoes and prunes.

tfillin: Known in English as phylacteries, these square leather boxes containing scriptural passages are worn on the arms and head during morning prayers daily, except on the Sabbath and holidays, by male Jews over thirteen.

tsitsis: The four-cornered, fringed garment worn underneath the shirt by male Jews who observed the Biblical commandment to wear a garment with fringes (Numbers 15:37-41). Also known as *talis-kotn,* or little prayer shawl.

Yiddish: The language of the Jews of Eastern Europe, now spoken by their descendants in various parts of the world. An outgrowth of Middle High German, Yiddish, which contains Hebrew and Slavic words, is written in Hebraic characters and, like Hebrew, is read from right to left. It has been spoken by Jews for nearly a thousand years.

yohrzeit: The anniversary of a person's death.

Yom Kippur: The Day of Atonement, the tenth day of Tishrei. This
is the most solemn day of the year; Jews pray and fast all day
long and publicly confess their sins directly to their Creator
and beg for forgiveness.